CHRIS
LYNHEART

DAUGHTER OF FORAYER
BOOK 2

DALTON REUTLINGER

authorHOUSE®

AuthorHouse™
1663 Liberty Drive
Bloomington, IN 47403
www.authorhouse.com
Phone: 1 (800) 839-8640

Published by AuthorHouse 04/27/2018

ISBN: 978-1-5462-3502-6 (sc)
ISBN: 978-1-5462-3501-9 (e)

Library of Congress Control Number: 2018903621

Print information available on the last page.

Introduction

Nearly ten years have passed since Chris left with Night Hawk to train with the pre-ranking members of the Seventeen Assassins to learn how to control the powers of the Reaper, and any blood-linked abilities he may have had with his ancient ancestor, Night Blade – who was the fifth ranking of the original Seventeen. Since then, things have taken a turn for the worse. Just as Chris said it would, a second civil war has split the U.S into two separate countries, and European economies are crumbling. Western civilization as a whole is crumbling, and Islamic Terrorism is on the rise.

What was once the United States of America has been split in two. The states of Texas, Oklahoma, Kansas, Nebraska, South Dakota, North Dakota, Montana, Wyoming, Colorado, New Mexico, Arizona, Nevada, Iowa, Missouri, Arkansas, Louisiana, Mississippi, Georgia, Florida, and Tennessee have seceded from the Union and raised a new flag to represent their new country: The United States of the Republic, which also became known as the "Rebellion".

The President of the Union states – or old country, President Lane, declared this movement an act of war, and sent what remained of the U.S military to Republic states to restore order. But in doing this, the world was introduced to the Republic's military, and it became clear to most people, the Rebels were not going anywhere. As the Republic's military grew stronger, the old military – that was already less than one-million in number – weakened. Within a year, Republic troops took several military bases, naval yards, and ports, making their economy and military strength even stronger. By the end of the second year, the advance of Republic troops seemed almost unstoppable. The old military was spread thin, and the West Coast continued to weaken.

The advance of Republic troops to the east was quick, and cities fell under Rebel control seemingly overnight. The old government in D.C was losing ground, and it was clear to almost everyone, that the Rebels would win one way or another. What remained of the crumbling military was outmatched in almost every possible way. The only advantage the military had over the Rebels were their tank battalions, but even that advantage disappeared in time.

By the third year, the United States of the Republic had officially become its own country, and was gaining allies in Asia, Europe, Australia, and a few select countries in the Middle East. Canada continued to be a strong ally, and Mexico sided with the Rebels after they took Georgia and South Carolina. During this time period, the Republic had also built manufacturing and research facilities to build and mobilize their mechanized army. Soon, the Republic introduced tanks with more fire power and heavier armor than what the old military had, and their weapon ranges became more powerful. However, most of the Republic's funding went into strengthening their border defenses. Before long, it became impossible for the U.S government to order an offensive strike in Republic controlled lands.

Now, in the fourth year, the military is on its last legs, and only a handful of states remain under Washington's control. The East is ready to fall, but the Republic has now mobilized its forces and invaded the states of Oregon and Washington State. Within two months, the Rebels have nearly surrounded both state capitols, cutting off most military supply routes, and ordering the state governors to surrender.

In the East, only the remaining half of Virginia and Maryland stand between the Rebels and Washington D.C. Their front is spearheaded by 600 prototypes of their first heavy armored tanks, and the Republic Air Force has all but devastated what little remains of the old Air Force.

CHAPTER 1

A New Beginning

Ten years after the events of book 1

Jessica woke to the sound of her alarm clock on the table next to her bed. She slowly opened her eyes, only to jam them shut again from the blinding sunlight reflecting off the walls of her apartment. After waiting for a few moments, she slowly opened her eyes again, bracing herself for the blinding light, and kept them open so they could adjust. Once she could see clearly, she rubbed her eyes, trying to remove the sleepiness from her eyes, and stared at her ceiling fan, watching it spin in endless circles for a few seconds. Somehow, it seemed to help her wake up faster and focus more on the day ahead of her. She had a lot to prepare for. Fridays were always busy days at work.

After what seemed like forever, Jessica rolled off her bed, and quickly unplugged the alarm clock, silencing the buzzing noise that was about to drive her insane, "I hate that noise!" She groaned in a half-asleep voice, "I hope whoever invented that alarm, got what was coming to them." She sighed in relief from the silence, stood from her bed, and started stretching. She stretched her arms behind her back, over her head, and touched her toes. She then held her arms out and twisted her body from side to side before moving to stretching out her legs and lower body. Once she was finished, she proceeded to the kitchen area of her apartment and decided what she was going to have for breakfast, "I guess waffles would be good enough." She said, shrugging her shoulders,

"They'd be the fastest at least." She took some Eggo Waffles out of the freezer and put them in the toaster. She then wandered around the kitchen, grabbing whatever else she wanted or needed. As she did, she grabbed the remote from the bar, turned on the TV, and changed the channel to a news station, curious about any news about the war. Jessica would never openly admit it in public, but she supported the Rebels. In her opinion, the Rebels had demonstrated the lost potential that the United States once maintained, but had lost due to political correctness. The Rebels were strong, fierce, disciplined, highly trained, and battle hardened. In fact, she had just recently learned that a recruit's final test before they can graduate is to survive an actual combat situation. She wasn't sure if she agreed with their motives at times, but she couldn't argue with the results that the average Rebel recruit maintained after his graduation. She knew a lot about the Rebels, but that wasn't saying a lot, even for someone as intelligent as her. The Rebels were large and lethal, but they were also very secretive. The Rebel leaders only told what the public needed to know about the warfronts, but nothing else. At first, Jessica didn't understand the motives behind the reasons to be so secretive, but she eventually understood it as a way for the Rebel leaders to keep the media quiet and could easily call out any lies certain channels made up on their own.

Once her waffles were done, she put them on her plate, covered them with peanut butter, poured some syrup on them, and started eating her breakfast. Jessica also had a glass of milk and some fruits to maintain a more or less healthy meal. As she ate her breakfast, she searched the news channels for some news on the warfront. As her luck would have it, all the stations were only reporting weather and traffic reports. "Another thunderstorm's coming?" Jessica asked out loud, "Sheesh! If this keeps up, I'll have to find a place to rent a boat to get anywhere." She continued to watch the weather reports until she finished her breakfast, but turned the TV off as soon as she finished eating.

After she'd finished washing off her plate and silverware, Jessica grabbed some clean clothes and proceeded to the bathroom where she turned on the shower and prepared her makeup and other things she'd have to use once she'd finished her shower. While she waited for the water to heat up, she studied herself in the mirror and tried to picture what type of hair style she'd wear for the day. She had changed a lot in the past ten years. Now at the age of twenty-four, she stood at a height of 5'11, her skin had darkened from a consistent schedule of tanning, her body had become more curvaceous from age and keeping herself in shape, her eyes had brightened to a lighter shade of brown, her hair had darkened to a very dark shade of brown, but the light brown highlights she had in her hair when she was younger had faded away over time. She had been told on numerous occasions that she had matured into a very kind and beautiful young woman. She had never been one to boast about herself, but she had to admit they were right.

Jessica now lived in an apartment not far from the main DC area of Washington DC. After her parents returned from their final tour in the Middle East, they helped her buy a suitable apartment she could live in on her own. Shortly after, they moved back to Orland California to be closer to their older friends and family. However, due to a poor economy and only a large demand for jobs that she had little to no skill in, she was forced to stay in Washington and take up a job at a small flower shop that was just a few blocks away from where she lived and work for minimum wage. She was leading a hard life, but she had managed to make a number of good friends with some of the girls she worked with, as well as some regular customers. She might not have been rich, but she did what she could to make the most out of life.

Once she finished her morning routine and gathered what she needed for the day, Jessica left her apartment and headed to work. As she descended the stairs from the apartment building onto the street, she met her biggest rival, Ashton, who was also one of her closest friends, if not her best friend. She was a little shorter than Jessica with long blonde hair, blue eyes, and an athletic body.

"Well, well, looks like someone's running a little late." Jessica teased as she walked up to Ashton.

"Me? Late? Never. I was just... my alarm clock didn't go off." Ashton said, trying to think of a quick excuse.

Jessica crossed her arms and raised an eyebrow, "Yeah, sure it didn't."

3

"Oh, shut up, Jessica!" Ashton pouted as she started walking again, "Well, I guess it's a good thing I met you, then. You always seem to somehow clock in just before you're late. Now I'll know how you do it."

Jessica laughed, "Well, I've been working there a little longer than you have. I know all the tricks to showing up on time now."

"What, is there an alley you run through? Or do you own some kind of portal device you use to magically teleport yourself there on time?" Ashton asked teasingly.

Jessica shrugged her shoulders and rolled her eyes in the opposite direction of Ashton, "Fine. Mock my portal gun. I was thinking of letting you use it, but after that little outburst, I'm starting to reconsider. That mixed with your reckless behavior is sure to be a recipe for disaster."

Ashton stopped walking and glared at Jessica, who was still walking, "*My* reckless behavior?! There hasn't been an incident where we were both involved in something! Come to think of it, you're more reckless than I am! Remember what happened with the taxi last week for example?"

Jessica stopped walking and glared back at Ashton.

Ashton smirked and crossed her arms, "That's right. I went there."

"The taxi 'incident' is all just a big misunderstanding, Ash." Jessica said, "So I did something that made the rear passenger tire go flat, it's nothing a man shouldn't be able to handle."

"Except it wasn't a male driver... was it?" Ashton grinned.

"Yes it was. He just... had really long and straight hair with... a feminine voice. That's all."

Ashton rolled her eyes, shook her head and started walking again, "You're hopeless."

"Hopeless? I've got more hope in my pinky finger than you'll have in the next twenty years!" Jessica said.

"You sure about that? Because you seem pretty hopeless throughout most of the day." Ashton said.

"It's because I'm stuck being around you all day." Jessica said, making a silly face at Ashton.

"Oh, that's *real* mature, Jess." Ashton said, rolling her eyes.

"Yeah, like you have a lot of room to talk about maturity." Jessica smirked, "I recall a certain blonde jumping in a bounce house in the fairly recent past."

"What?! You're counting *that* against me? I was baby-sitting my nephew!"

"Sure, you were."

"I was!"

"Uh-huh."

"You know what? Go skip through traffic."

"Humph! Fine, be that way." Jessica pouted, "Deny it all you want, but it still happened regardless." She pulled her cell phone out of her back pocket and looked at the time, "Speaking of skipping through traffic…"

"We're running late, aren't we?" Ashton asked.

"We're cutting it close." Jessica said, "We'd better hurry."

After a long day of work, Jessica, Ashton and some of the other girls who worked at the flower shop went out for pizza.

"Well, girls, shall we toast to another long work week?" Ashton asked as she held her glass of water in the air.

"I'll gladly toast to that." Jessica said as she and the other girls who were sitting at the table raised their glasses. They each took a swallow of their water and returned to their meals.

"So, Jess, it's your turn to host the sleepover this weekend. Got anything special planned?" A girl named Jasmine asked. Jasmine was another one of Jessica's close friends. She stood at a height of 5'8 with long black hair and blue eyes.

Jessica shook her head, "No, I'm afraid it's going to be the usual this time. But, as always, I'm open to ideas. We could go to the movie theater, I suppose."

"Blech! I think I'll pass." Another girl, Krista said with a disgusted face, "The movies these days are just a bunch of cheap re-makes with un-original ideas." Krista was a new girl at the flower shop and still getting into the groove of things with Jessica and her friends. She stood at 5'9 with shoulder length red hair and green eyes.

"I have to say I agree." Ashton said, nodding in agreement, "We'd be better off looking for something on the classic channel."

"I don't have a problem with that." Jessica said, "I like watching classics. There aren't many I don't like, come to think of it."

"Well, it depends on what you mean by classic." Jasmine said, "I like a lot of classics, but the classics these days are a lot different from the classics we watched as kids, you know."

"Hmm, true, But I'm good with anything, even if it's a horror movie." Ashton said, "It's been a while since we watched a good scary movie."

"Oh, I know a good one!" Krista said, catching the attention of the other girls, "There's a new scary movie that just got on Netflix. It's called "The Hallways." It's supposed to be really good from what I hear. It's also rated five stars. You don't see that very often with horror movies. In fact, you're lucky if you can find a three star anymore."

"The Hallways? Ohhh, I like it. Just the name gives me shivers." Jasmine said, "I don't really like scary movies, but I'll make an exception for this one. That just sounds interesting. Do you know anything about the plot of the movie, Krista?"

Krista shook her head, "No, not really. Besides, I find it a lot more enjoyable when you watch a movie blind, especially horror films."

"I can agree with that. Do you think you can have it by tomorrow, Krista?" Jessica asked.

Krista smiled and nodded, "Sure thing! I'll move it to the first movie on my queue."

"Awesome! Any particular snacks you girls want?" Jessica asked.

"Just the usual I think." Ashton said, "If this movie is real gory, I don't think I'll be eating much anyway."

"Yeah, I think just the basics would be good." Jasmine said, "You know, some chips, popcorn, some pop, maybe a little alcohol."

Jessica raised an eyebrow at Jasmine, "With you in my apartment? I don't think so."

Krista busted out laughing, "I'll assume there's some kind of 'tragic' story behind that?"

Jessica nodded at Krista and glared at Jasmine, "You might could say that."

"Or, you could say it was tragic for those two, but humorous for the rest of us." Ashton said, catching a nasty glare from Jessica.

"I think *you* especially had too much of a good laugh with the incident." Jessica said. She sighed to gather herself, and looked at Krista, "About a year or so ago, Ashton, Jasmine, and a few other girls who worked at the flower shop were invited to a party by a fairly regular customer who had a special…interest in one of the girls."

"You mean he liked her, right?" Krista asked, "I know how these stories go. Boy meets girl. Boy develops a crush, boy builds up the courage to ask the girl out, girl accepts and causes some sort of tragedy."

"Well, that's…one way of putting it." Jessica said, trying not to laugh as the memory came to mind, "The girl the guy took a liking to was actually Jasmine's sister, who was one of our more…wild…girls at the shop. She never stopped partying, even when she'd have to get up early the next day for work. She was a real character." She stopped talking as she heard Jasmine clear her throat.

"Don't talk about my sister like she's not around anymore, Jess. She still lives in her apartment, you know."

Jessica rubbed the back of her neck with an embarrassed look on her face, "Err…sorry, Jasmine." She regained her composure and looked at Krista again, "Well, while Jasmine's sister was being busy being the life of the party, she took things a little too far. To cut the long story short, the police sent a SWAT team to the party looking for Jasmine's sister, who is also her *twin* sister. Some of the guests mistook Jasmine as her sister, and I got cuffed for trying to defend her."

"Then what happened?" Krista asked curiously.

"We were taken to the police headquarters." Jasmine said, "We were interrogated and asked all kinds of questions that didn't make any sense to the situation. We were at the Police HQ for I don't know how long. Maybe six hours until they let us go."

"Why were you there for so long?" Krista asked.

"I've been wondering that myself." Jessica said, "Taking our fingerprints and looking at our ID's were some of the first things they did when we were there. Then again, that was about the time whispers of Rebel spies and Assassins being in DC had reached the city. Maybe they wanted to make sure we weren't part of the Rebellion."

"Well, nothing's impossible, I guess." Krista said, "However, I wouldn't think you're assassins or even agents working for the Rebels at first glance. Sure you two are in good shape, but I don't think you'd make the cut as military material, especially for the Rebels."

"Yeah…you have a point, actually." Jessica said. She took the final bites of her food and leaned back in her chair, sighing as she did, "Man, I'm full."

Ashton blinked and looked at Jessica, "Really? That's all you're going to eat?"

Jessica nodded and looked at Ashton, "I'm just not all that hungry I guess. It's just been one of those days, I guess."

Ashton remained silent for a moment before saying, "Well…if you say so. Usually, you're the pig of the group."

"I am not!" Jessica said loudly as she glared at Ashton, "Besides, you don't really have a lot of room to be talking, you know."

Jasmine giggled and looked at Ashton, "She has a point. To be fair, you're both pigs compared to the rest of us."

"Oh, shut it, skinny girl!" Ashton and Jessica said at the same time.

"Well, girls, it's been fun, but I better get a move on if I want to get to my apartment before the sun goes down." Krista said as she grabbed her purse and stood from the table, "I'll see you all tomorrow. Hopefully I'll be able to get the movie."

"Sure, Krista, see you tomorrow at the shopping mall." Jessica said. She glanced at the sun and saw it was indeed starting to get low and she lived the second furthest away from where they currently were. She grabbed her things and stood from the table, "I better get going, too. I'll see you two tomorrow. Have a good rest of the evening, and sleep well."

"Yeah, you, too, Jessica. See you tomorrow." Jasmine said as she and Ashton watched Jessica leave the table. They waited till she was out of sight and resumed conversations of their own.

Nearly an hour after Jessica had spoken with her friends, she made it back to her apartment with several bags of groceries. She sighed in relief as she heard the click of the lock on her door, signifying the long day was officially over. She twisted the door knob and pushed the door open with a grin on her face and walked into her apartment. She sat the bags of groceries she was carrying on the counter, sighing in relief as she did, and stretched her arms out and rotated her shoulders, "Finally! I wish there was a place closer to my apartment where I could buy food and other things. This is a little ridiculous." She stood in place for a few minutes, taking a break from the long walk and letting her hands take a break from the weight she had been carrying for the past several minutes. Once she felt she had the energy, she started putting her groceries away. She wasn't able to buy much, but she was able to buy just enough to get by. There were people out there that had it a lot worse than she did and she knew it. It saddened her, knowing there were people who weren't able to find a good enough job to sustain them. No cooling on hot summer days, and no heating during the harsh winter weather. Every now and then, when she could spare some money, she'd go out of her way to donate some cash to charity, or to a person she might have accidently run into who was in desperate need of money. Sometimes, karma, which was something Jessica had learned wasn't something to ignore with her experiences, would return the favor and something good would happen to her in return.

When Jessica finished putting her groceries away, she collapsed into her favorite recliner next to the window with a groan of relief the day was done, "I've been waiting for this moment all day! My legs feel like Jell-O." She sat in her chair for several minutes, enjoying the peace time for a while, and also browsing the book titles on her book shelf.

"Hmm...it's been a while since I last read something." She said to herself, "Perhaps it's time I pay the bookstore another visit. There's no telling what new books they might have. The newest copy of Star Explorers might be out now, too. Ashton would probably appreciate a trip there as well." She continued to look at her bookshelf, recalling all the adventures she'd taken from real life in the past. However, due to lack of interesting releases in the past year, it had been a while since Jessica last visited the book store for some new reading material.

"It kind of stinks when you're in the mood to read something and you don't have anything new." Jessica moaned. She stared out her window for a while, taking in the view from her window. This was one of the main reasons she wanted the apartment so badly. There was an intersection practically right below her window, and she could see the entire street ahead of her, which was especially pretty to look at during the holiday seasons. But, her favorite feature, was that she could just see the Washington Monument in the distance over the other buildings. For her, the Washington Monument was more than just an important structure of history and the old country, it was a memorial to her own childhood. Every now and then, when it was quiet, she would look at the monument for what seemed like hours recalling her childhood days, especially the days when Chris was around. Even though a decade had passed, she still waited anxiously for Chris to return. For some people, the years seem to get shorter. For her, it was the exact opposite. Since Chris left to train with Night Hawk and learn the actual truth behind his mysterious past, the years seemed to get longer, and longer as they went on. There wasn't a single doubt in her mind that he would come back someday, but she wished it would be sooner rather than later...or did she? No matter how badly she wanted him to return, a part of her knew that he wouldn't be the same person that she remembered.

"After all, one doesn't keep their old personality through that kind of life." She thought to herself, *"A person can't have the life Chris had, learn the actual truth about what happened to his family, spend a decade training with the most dangerous people on the planet, and still keep his old personality. But would he change for better, or for worse?"*

While Jessica continued to look at the very tip of the monument, she remembered the last words Chris had spoken to her before he left:

I will return one day, and it is on that day I
will take control of the government

She'd never really given it much thought in the past, but she was starting to realize that, *"Everything Chris said all that time ago has come true."* She turned her attention to a picture of Chris on the bookshelf, *"He said the government would become more corrupt, and that a civil war would, at some point, break out because of it. Among all kinds of other things. He warned of new terror groups rising in the Middle East, as well as something...worse... The Agroneese."* A shiver went down her spine as she thought of the name, *"No matter what we do...one thing after another leads to war. There's no stopping it."* Deep down, she had to question if the people would still be ignorant, or arrogant, or maybe even just stupid enough to deny that fact. Of course, the truth about the Agroneese hasn't been revealed to the public yet, but Jessica couldn't help but wonder how things would turn out when it came time for the people to know.

"So what happens if someone announces the arrival of the Agroneese? Would people just dismiss them as a regular terror group out of ignorance, or would they accept that they're something worse? It's scary to think that there are people out there who would just dismiss them in total." Not wanting to dwell on the thoughts going through her head any longer, Jessica shook her head and tried to dismiss the thought of another war. "Maybe I should just turn in." She said aloud, "But first, I should check and see how Mom and Dad are doing."

She stood up, and made her way to her laptop on the kitchen counter. She ran her finger over the mouse pad, turning the screen on, and logged onto her E-mail. Right away she saw she had a couple of messages from her Mom and eagerly opened them to see what was going on in her hometown.

Dear Jessica

Hello, my daughter, I hope this message finds you well. Your father and I are doing well, and have just returned from my brother's place after a week-long vacation. Your father has gotten very good at golf since you last saw him. It seems like he's never home anymore, bless his heart.

Anyway, how are things going in your world? I hope you're staying safe and not doing anything rash like your brother. There's not a day that goes by without me worrying about you. I'm always watching the news fearing that moment when the headlines say Washington D.C was invaded by the Rebels. I pray for your safety every day; hope we'll see each other again soon. Maybe the war will be over by your birthday and we can see each other then. I certainly hope so.

Anyway, I'll talk again soon. Lots of love

P.S Your father and I will be going to Alaska in the near future.

Mom

Jessica smiled softly, knowing her mother and father were safe and sound let her rest at ease for a bit. She sat in her place for a few moments, trying to think of a few things to say, and started typing:

Dear Mother

It's good to hear from you again, Mom, and I'm so happy to know you and Dad are okay. I'm like you, really. Your safety and well-being are always on my mind, and I'm always on edge knowing Dad's not in an entirely stable condition after getting wounded during his last combat tour. What if something were to happen and I couldn't make it there? What if I couldn't say my final good-bye to my own father? I'd be heart broken.

So Dad has gotten good at golf, huh? I never thought I'd live to see the day. I guess there's truth in the words "an old dog can still learn a new trick" haha. I'm so happy you two are enjoying your retirement! And don't worry, I'm always watching the news and keeping an eye on the shifting warfronts. I'll be ready when the Rebels start closing in around D.C. It's funny, though, isn't it? The Rebels are so close to Washington, but their attack still seems so far away...

Well, I hope you two have fun in Alaska! It sounds so exciting! I wish I could go with you! I could really do with slamming a snowball in Scott's face after what he did to me last time we saw each other, the jerk! That's probably the only reason he went to that meeting! Well, tell my pesky older brother his little sister says hello... and smack him on the back of his head for me, too!

Well, it's getting late now, and I'm really tired. I'll talk to you soon, Mom. Tell Dad I miss him!

Your Loving Daughter
Jessica

Jessica sent the message and closed her laptop before wobbling her way back to her bedroom and collapsed on her bed. The comfort of knowing her parents were okay let her mind rest at ease, and she faded away into dreamland.

The next day, Jessica woke to the sirens of an Ambulance speeding down the street below. She moaned and shifted her position, trying to fall back asleep. However, the buzzing of her alarm clock threw away any chance to fall asleep again. She slowly opened her eyes, bracing herself for the bright sunlight to reflect off the walls of the apartment, but it still seemed dark. She rolled over to look out her window and saw it was a very cloudy day outside, and the sun was completely blocked.

"Ah, excellent! My favorite kind of weather." Jessica said cheerfully as she threw the blankets off her. She looked at the alarm clock, which was still buzzing, and saw it wasn't even 8:00 yet, "Really? It's only 7:40? It feel more like 10:00 to me… Oh, well! It gives me some extra time to get around and get things ready for tonight."

She stood from her bed, stretched her arms and back, and proceeded out of the room, turning off the alarm clock as she left. "Let's see…what should I make for breakfast?" She asked herself as she wandered into the kitchen. She browsed through her cabinets and pantry for a few minutes, but didn't find anything she really felt like eating.

"I guess I can just eat some more Eggo Waffles." She took the waffles out of the freezer, put them in the toaster, and sat down at the bar while she waited for the waffles to finish. Out of habit, she reached for the remote, turned on the TV, and flipped the channel to FOX news to check on the warfront. She looked away from the screen for a second while the channel loaded, but her apartment suddenly filled with the sounds of gunshots and yelling. She was caught off guard by this and nearly fell backwards off the stool she was sitting on. Once she regained her balance, she looked at the TV screen and felt her body go numb. At the bottom of the screen, she read the headlines:

Fighting Intensifies On Western Warfront

A reporter who was standing on top of a hill overlooking a current battle sight near Seattle, Washington was on the right side of the screen, while another reporter at FOX headquarters was on the left side. Gunshots, explosions, and all kinds of battle sounds could be heard in the distance behind the reporter on the right. Jessica turned the volume up as he started talking.

"I'm telling you, Jane, it's getting really bad for the old military here on the west coast. Just last night, around three A.M or so, the Rebels secured the final supply line the old military had going into Seattle, and the fighting

has only gotten worse since then. As the military continues to suffer more and more casualties and be pushed farther and farther back, the size of the Rebel force here just continues to grow! Just a few hours ago, five platoons of Rebel troops, fresh from the Midwest, came to reinforce the frontlines. They brought everything with them. Heavily armored tanks, fast attack vehicles, ground transports, helicopters, jets, you name it. The Rebels want Seattle and they're not taking no for an answer."

"Why do the Rebel want Seattle so badly, Mike?" The woman on the other side of the screen asked curiously

There was a brief pause before Mike started his answer, *"Well, that's a good question, actually. The military here in Washington is dwindling, and that goes for Oregon and California as well. The military is heavily outnumbered and outgunned here. The fact is, Washington would give the Rebels complete control of the northern border for most of the country. The Rebels have a lot of allies that are helping them supply their weapons and armor, and Canada just so happens to be their biggest ally. Ever since the war first started, Canada has been allowing these other countries that support the Rebels to transport their weapons, vehicles, and other supplies across the border and into Midwestern states. The weapons and equipment are then sent off to places the Rebels need resupplied the most, and if the Rebels take control of Washington, they would not only have the entire western part of the northern border secured, they'd also have access to ports and naval yards, which would give the Rebels an overwhelming advantage over the military in the west. I'm saying 'if' as if it's possible for the Rebels to lose now, but it will take nothing short of a nuclear bomb to stop the Rebels now. They've pushed too far into the state to turn away, and they're only a short distance from entering Seattle's city limits."*

"So, what's going on behind you, there at the bottom of the hill? Is that a village currently caught in a crossfire?" Jane asked.

Jessica focused her attention on the town below, ignoring what the other reporter was saying. "If that's not the site of a battle, then I don't know what is." She said out loud. The town had been ripped apart. Houses and office buildings were completely destroyed, trees had been blown into millions of pieces, the roads had craters from artillery and mortar fire, and there were several destroyed cars scattered around the town. It was clear there was still a very large battle going on. Machine gun fire, tank blasts, and the occasional loud explosion. It was a grim sight, and it was clear Mike wasn't over exaggerating the size of the Rebel force in the state. However, there was one question Jessica wanted to know about the town, "Were any innocent civilians killed in the wake of all this?" She focused her attention on Mike as he continued talking, hoping to know the answer.

"The Rebels hit this town pretty hard last night. They've been avoiding towns and settlements as much as possible, but this was a strategic point they needed in order to resupply and set up a fallback position in case things started to go bad. Fortunately, they sent some messengers to the town to tell the people living here they were going to attack the town, giving the people who lived here a chance to get away safely. Most people left the town and headed to the closest town behind Rebel lines, but some people stayed regardless of the news they received. At the moment, we don't know of any civilian fatalities, but we do know at least five people were hurt in the attack. Three men and two women were taken to the medical tents a while ago, and we've been told the two women are in a state of shock, one of the men has a broken wrist, and another man has fragments of glass in his right leg, which Rebel medics are taking care of as we speak. The last man, however, had a run of bad luck and happened to be in the wrong place at the wrong time. He was fleeing the sight of one battle, and unknowingly ran into another warzone. A Rebel soldier mistook him for military reinforcements and shot him in the shoulder. The man has been in critical condition, but the medics say he'll live and will make a full recovery. Rebel soldiers are allowing people who might have gotten lost in the battle to return to the camp and look for their friends and family. They are offering food, water, and medical treatment if needed."

"Thank you, Mike, we'll check back later and see how things are coming along." Jane said, only receiving a nod from Mike as his half of the screen was filled in with Janes'. There was a brief pause before Jane continued, "That was a report on the West coast, but how are things going on the East coast? During the last commercial break we received word that the Rebels are pushing closer to Richmond, Virginia, the last line of defense for Washington. Military scouts have reported a large force of Rebels reinforcing the front line, putting nearly one-million Rebel Soldiers on the Eastern warfront. It seems things are going exactly the same in the east as they are in the west. While the military continues to shrink, the Rebels continue to grow. But my question is this: will D.C. surrender before the Rebels invade the city? Or will the Rebels have to attack in force in D.C. as well? Many generals in the military have said the war is practically over, and that there's little point to continue the fighting now. They've said the Rebels outnumber the military nearly six to one, and if that's the case…what's the point of continuing the war? That's my question to President Lane. You, Mr. President, are constantly saying you will turn the war in your favor, yet you haven't done a single thing to prove you're telling the truth. The Rebels take Michigan, you do nothing. The Rebels take Illinois, you do nothing. The Rebels near Richmond, Virginia, the last line of defense for Washington D.C., and you still do nothing. Do you want the Rebels to invade Washington D.C, or have your plans already been put into motion and they're just really slow to take action? President Lane, if you don't act fast, your days of being safe and secure in the White House will grind to a halt quickly. Nothing you have done thus far has worked! That's all for now, stay with FOX news, we'll keep you updated."

Jessica turned off the TV, completely unaware her waffles had popped up a long time ago, *"Things are definitely getting worse by the day."* She thought, *"I just hope mom and dad stay out of harm's way. They're saying the Rebels won't invade California, but I'm not so sure. Once Washington State and Oregon surrender to the Rebels, California will be the only state left supporting D.C."* The sudden growling of her stomach made her realize she was hungry, and she immediately reheated her waffles and prepared everything else she wanted to eat.

In the later hours of the morning, around eleven, Jessica met with her friends near the Washington Monument.

"There you are! I was wondering if you were ever going to show up." Ashton said as Jessica approached the group.

"Well, you know me." Jessica said, panting out of breath, "If I show up on time, something's wrong."

"So what's your excuse this time?" Ashton asked.

Jessica paused for a moment as she thought up her response, "A lot of black cats." She finally said, managing to laugh a little.

Ashton rolled her eyes while Jasmine and Krista giggled quietly, "It was only black cats? Are you sure there weren't any ladders or mirrors involved as well?" Ashton asked.

"Uh…there might have been one or two." Jessica said, taking a deep breath and regaining her composure. "But to tell you the truth, I was watching the news on the war. Things are starting to look bad on the West coast, and I can't help but worry about my parents."

"Oh? Well, all you had to do was say so, Jess." Ashton said, "I'm not going to hold a grudge against you for worrying about your family. Is everything okay back home?"

Jessica nodded, "Yeah, and thank you, Ashton. Anyway, what's on the agenda for today?"

Ashton turned to look at Krista, who was sitting against a tree stump in the shade, and said, "Well, we decided we'd let Krista call the shots today. She's new around here, and we only see it as fair that she gets a moment to introduce what she likes to do."

"Uh…really?" Krista asked, shocked about the news, "I really kind of planned to just shadow you guys for the day. I mean, I'm so new here that I-"

"Oh, c'mon, Krista, don't be like that!" Ashton interrupted, "We won't hold anything against you if you turn out to have a different set of hobbies than we do. Besides, it's always refreshing to be introduced to something new."

"That's exactly right, Krista." Jessica said, smiling at Krista, "You work at the flower shop now, which makes you one of us. One way or another, you're family now, and families stick together regardless of their differences."

Taken aback by the kindness that was being offered, Krista was speechless and didn't know what to say for a few moments. Taking some time to gather her thoughts, and stop grinning, she managed to come up with an idea, "Well…perhaps we…we could go to the mall? There's a shop that just recently opened, and I'd like to take a look at it."

"I don't see a reason why not." Jasmine said, "It's been a while since we were last there, anyway."

Jessica nodded in agreement, "Yeah, and I've been wanting to check out that new jewelry store again, too. Not to mention I could go for some mall food again, especially the cookies."

"Oh, right! The cookie store we always go to!" Ashton said in excitement, "I almost forgot about that place! Well, that settles it for me. I'm going to the mall with or without you guys."

Krista laughed and stood, "Well, I guess we all have our reasons of going to the mall now. Shall we take a cab or a bus?"

"Or we could walk and save a little money." Jasmine suggested, "It's not like we're all made of money here, and Jessica was saying she's getting low on money now anyway."

"Oh, yeah, that's right." Jessica said, "This hasn't exactly been a friendly month to my paycheck. I'm only living off maybe another four-hundred dollars. I should have asked my mom last night if she and dad could send some money."

"I doubt it would have gotten through, anyway, Jess." Ashton said, "I tried asking my brother for some money, but he said the Rebels aren't allowing anything through to Washington that requires UPS or FedEx transportation."

"Wait…isn't your brother a soldier in the Rebellion, Ashton?" Krista asked.

Ashton looked at Krista and nodded, "Yeah, he's a tank operator. Why?"

"I was just curious." Krista said, "I overheard you talking about him earlier this week and thought I heard you say he's part of the Rebellion. Do you mind me asking why he joined the Rebels?"

"Well, I can't really say to be honest, Krista." Ashton said, "Not because I don't want to, but because my brother was never really one to voice his opinions on matters. He let his actions speak for themselves, and I guess him joining the Rebels is his way of telling us he didn't like the way things were going."

"How long has he been with the Rebels?" Krista asked.

Ashton remained silent for a moment as she thought about the question, "Well...I'd say give or take three years. I guess another reason he might have joined is because it got him out of the East. He was having trouble finding a job that he could really cling to, and that's when he saw the Midwest as a better place to live."

"I see." Krista said, nodding, "Uh...before you guys ask, you should probably know I don't really have much of an opinion in today's politics. I think our President Lane is by no means the best, but I'm not sure if another second civil war is the answer to everything happening these days."

"There's more to this war than just taking back control of the government, Krista." Jessica said, "In fact, a very small part of the Rebel military force is fighting the military right now. You have to remember the military was only eight-hundred-thousand at most when the war started, and the Rebels have an army far larger than that."

Ashton thought for a second, then looked at Jessica, "Has it ever been said how strong in number the Rebels actually are? I remember them mentioning a number on the news once, but that was a while back."

"Hmm...I think I remember CNN saying the Rebels have an army of at least two-million, but that was a long time ago. Everyday more and more people join the Rebellion, and a lot of them are ex-military. To be able to take the fight to what's left of the U.S military, the Mexican drug cartel, patrolling the Northern border, keeping terrorist organizations out of the country, as well as maintaining enough men in reserve in their home states to keep the peace, they have to have a number larger than two-million. I'd be surprised if it was anything less than four-million at this point. The Rebels are not a force to be messed around with, and they've proven this every single time someone tried to prove them wrong."

"True. But I have to wonder why they can't just outflank the military, or start attacking Washington from long range." Ashton said, "One would think that wouldn't be a very difficult thing to do. I mean, Richmond isn't exactly that large of an obstacle to go around."

"No, but it would allow the Rebels to invade the city without having to worry about their southern flank. Plus, it'd also drive President Lane and his administration insane knowing their last line of defense was wiped out." Jessica said, "Plus, Richmond would give the Rebels a place to resupply and rearm before their final assault."

"Hmm, I guess I can see the point of that." Ashton said, carefully taking everything Jessica said into consideration, "Anyway, enough about politics. Let's do some things that are *actually* important. Such as clearing all the stores in the mall! Let's go!"

Later, the girls made their way to the mall food court.

"Jeez, Krista, you think you could slow down for a while?" Ashton asked, as she collapsed into a chair at a random table, "My feet are killing me!"

Krista rubbed the back of her head nervously and laughed nervously, "S-sorry, Ashton, I guess I got a little carried away at those last five stores."

"Oh, don't listen to her, she's just a big baby." Jessica said. She focused her attention on Ashton and rested her hands on her hips as she talked, "You know, for trying to be my so called 'rival', you haven't been doing a very good job lately."

"Oh, ha ha!" Ashton mocked back, "At least I attract more boys than you. It's only natural that they'd go after me, being the most gorgeous of the girls in the work place."

"You? Attracting boys? I guess there *is* a first time for everything." Jessica said, trying to hold in her laughter.

Ashton growled and mumbled under her breath for a moment, "Well, at least I'm the most mature of the group." She pouted, crossing her arms.

"She said, forgetting she's the one who started the food fight last week." Krista said.

Ashton looked at Krista and opened her mouth to say something, but paused as a thought ran across her mind, "You know...I don't have a comment on that matter other than it was self-defense."

"Sure it was." Jessica said sarcastically as she rolled her eyes.

"You know what, Jessica?! You just wait 'till we get to your apartment!" Ashton said.

"I've been waiting all week." Jessica said, sticking her tongue out at Ashton.

Ashton only squinted her eyes and gave Jessica a silent stare.

"No comeback?" Jessica asked.

"No comeback." Ashton said, admitting defeat.

"Uh-huh. That's what I thought." Jessica said. She claimed a seat next to Krista and watched the kids in the new arcade that had opened up a little over a year ago.

"So, anyway, Ashton, how long have you been living in D.C?" Krista asked.

Ashton remained silent as she thought about the answer, "Um...I'd say roughly eight years or so." She finally said, "Jessica and I went to high school together, and have been friends since then."

"Where are you originally from?" Krista asked, "I mean, if you don't mind me asking. I just thought I'd take some time to get to know you a little better since we're slowing things down for the moment."

"Oh, it's fine, Krista." Ashton said, "You don't need to act so nervous around us. I'm originally from Florida. Like Jessica, I'm from a military family as well, but my family wasn't made up of mostly Marines. Most of my family was either in the Army or Navy."

"Do you have any relatives in the old military?" Krista asked.

Aston shook her head, "Nope. Once the civil war started, anyone who was in the military in my family just dropped their guns, threw away their badges, and said they're not risking life and limb to defend Washington from the Rebels. That goes for both the Republicans and Democrats in my family. Most people in my family are Democrats, or were at least, up until the war started."

Krista nodded, "I see. So…your family is more Republican now?"

"I wouldn't go quite that far." Ashton said, "But we're a lot less liberal now. One could say we're Conservative Democrats now. The Rebel Leaders, who are mostly conservatives, have established a far more superior economy and working force than Washington ever could, which was ruled by far left liberals. Mostly because they have work experience outside of an office. Which is more than could be said for the politicians here in Washington."

Krista nodded and looked at Jessica, "What about you Jessica?"

"Hmm? Oh, I'm from a small town in California called Orland." Jessica said, "I moved here ten years ago with my parents before they were sent on their last combat tour in the Middle East several years ago. The war was practically over, but they were being sent to 'help keep the peace' as the note said. Yet, my dad somehow comes back with a wounded leg."

"Do you know what happened to him?" Krista asked.

Jessica shook her head, "No, my dad was either too ashamed or too embarrassed to talk about it. I don't know if it was just a freak accident, or if he actually took a bullet to the leg. He doesn't like to talk about it, and he hasn't been the same since then."

"Aw! I'm sorry. Tell your dad I thank him for his service next time you talk to him." Krista said.

Jessica smiled softly and nodded, "Will do, and thank you, Krista. That means a lot to him, as well as me."

Krista smiled back at Jessica and stood from her seat, "Well, anyway, are we ready to continue on?"

"If Ashton's done being a baby, then yeah." Jessica said, standing from her chair.

"Oh, shut up, Jessica!"

A few hours later, in the early hours of the evening, the girls left the mall and headed for Jessica's apartment, where their weekly slumber party was about to begin. A thunderstorm wasn't far in the distance, so they called a cab, and Krista volunteered to pay for the trip. Jessica took the front seat next to the driver, while Ashton, Krista, and Jasmine crowded in the back. As fortune would have it, rain started pouring from the sky as soon as the taxi driver turned on the street where Jessica's apartment building was located.

"Well, this is typical." Ashton said, looking out her window, "You couldn't wait another ten minutes, Nature? No, you just *had* to start raining *now* of all times."

Jessica laughed and looked towards the back of the car, "Well, you should know by now the woman hates us. Seems every time we plan something, Mother Nature just *has* to come along and tell us to go another time."

"Ah, but contraire, Jessica." Krista said in her best French accent, "Tzee vwoman hatez everybody. Not just us."

Jessica laughed and looked at Krista, "Truer words were never spoken. However, I stand by what I said earlier. Nature seems to hold a very big grudge against Ashton for some reason or another."

"Man, you're telling me!" Ashton said, "It's either big scary bugs finding a way into my apartment, or never ending bad weather this time of year. What did I ever do to deserve all this nonsense?"

"I have a few ideas." Jessica said.

"Hey! That's enough out of you, Jess. I've had enough of your shenanigans for one day." Ashton said, turning her head to look out the window again.

Jessica rolled her eyes and returned to her rightful position in the seat. A few moments later, her apartment building came into view.

"Are they wet?" Jessica asked.

"No, not really. Maybe a little damp." Krista said.

Jessica thought for a moment, looked at Krista's socks, and then looked back up at Krista, "I think you better give me your socks. I'll wash them for you, and give them back once they're done."

"Oh, well…if you insist." Krista said, lifting one leg up and sliding her sock off, doing the same with the other foot, "Is that all?"

"Yeah, that should be all. Make yourself at home, Krista, I'll get the food and drinks out in a bit." Jessica said. She walked past Krista and turned the corner around the kitchen counter, and disappeared into another room.

Krista, who was still in the kitchen area, took her time looking at Jessica's comforts in her apartment. The apartment was decent sized. All four of them could fit in the living room area with ease, and Ashton and Jasmine were already relaxing in recliners reading some magazines. Krista took her first step into the living room, which had white carpeting with white walls and a white ceiling. There were picture frames of people all along the main wall which she assumed were past friends and family members. Her TV was on the far side of the wall with an old gaming station and blue ray player. Next to the TV was a collection of guitars and other musical instruments next to a pile of handwritten songs.

"Hey, Ashton. Is Jessica a musician? I can't help but notice her guitar collection."

Ashton looked up at Krista from her magazine and looked in the corner Krista was pointing at, "Oh, yeah! She's always playing her musical instruments and singing. She's pretty good, and she's written a handful of songs. If you wanted my honest opinion, she should play for money. She's got the skill and voice for it."

"What does she play?" Krista asked curiously.

"Pretty much anything, really." Ashton said, "However, she tends to stick with rock and country the most. She was a big fan of Toby Keith and Nickelback back in the day."

"Oh, really? That's pretty cool. Thanks for telling me."

Ashton nodded and returned her attention to her magazine as Krista continued to look around. Along the opposite wall of the guitar collection were three book shelves full of books ranging from fiction, fantasy, non-fiction, romance, history, and a lot of really popular titles such as Harry Potter and Lord of the Rings.

"I guess she's a reader, too, huh?" Krista asked.

"And a writer." Jessica said as she entered the living area, catching Krista's attention, "I'm currently writing a novel inspired by some of my songs."

"W...wow! You're a busy woman, Jess." Krista said in amazement, "You're full of surprises I'll give you that."

Jessica grinned and looked out the window Ashton was sitting by, "Man, that storm is not letting up. I hope we don't lose power like we did last week. It was off for hours."

"Yeah, that'd be nice if the power stayed on." Jasmine said, "Anyway, Krista, did you remember to bring that movie?"

"Uh-huh! I got it right here." Krista said as she pulled the movie out of her bag.

"Great! Let's put it in before we lose power. I'd say it's dark enough, especially with that storm outside." Jasmine said.

"Yeah, that's probably a good idea." Jessica said, "Why don't you take a seat, Krista, I'll put the movie in."

"Yeah, sure. Here you go." Krista said, handing Jessica the movie.

Jessica took the movie from Krista's hand, looked at the cover, and instantly regretted wanting to watch this movie. She stared at the cover as terror started to course through her body. She held the cover up so Ashton and Jasmine could see it, "Uh...you guys still want to watch this?" She asked, fearing the answer.

Ashton and Jasmine looked at the cover, looked at each other, and then looked at the cover again. "Uh...Krista...what did you say about this movie?" Ashton asked.

"It's supposed to be the scariest movie of all time, apparently." Krista said, "I've been wanting to watch it for a while now, but I don't really want to watch it alone, either..."

Jessica looked at the cover again and shrugged her shoulders, "It's just a movie. What's the worst that could happen?" She asked as she walked over to the TV and put the movie disc in the Blue ray player.

"Famous last words right there, Jessica." Jasmine said.

"Yeah, I was just about to say that." Jessica laughed, "Anyway, let's get this over with so we can watch some cartoons or play some old Nintendo games after this is all done."

"I'll make the popcorn!" Ashton said, jumping out of the chair and rushed to the kitchen.

Krista remained silent for a moment as she watched Ashton prepare the food. "You know, Ashton...it's a little insulting how fast you volunteered that."

"Not to mention suspicious." Jessica said.

"Well, if you must know, I'm plotting to take over the world, and I'm starting by taking you three as hostages." Ashton said, sticking her tongue out at Krista and Jessica.

"Yep. Figured as much." Krista and Jessica said at the same time.

A few hours later, once the credits started playing, Jessica and the others slowly lowered the blankets from over their eyes, asking if it was over. There was a long silence before Krista started laughing.

"Ahahaha! Man, they weren't kidding when they said it was the scariest movie ever made! What a trip!" Krista said loudly.

Jessica, Jasmine and Ashton started laughing as well, and they stood up. "I have to say, I've never been so scared in my life, but I've never had *that* kind of rush before. Definitely a good horror movie. Five stars from me." Ashton said.

"Yeah, I loved the first glimpse of the actual monster." Jessica said as she made her way to the Blue ray player and pulled out the disc, "It was so well done! Krista, I think you should pick our movies from now on. I was not disappointed in this film."

"I'll second that, Jess." Ashton said, squeezing her legs together, "Whew! So...anybody want to walk me to the bathroom? Haha."

"Sure, I have to go myself, anyway." Jessica said, handing the movie back to Krista. She looked at the clock on her wall and saw it was barely past 9:00 P.M, "And look, girls. We still have plenty of time to play games and get that movie off our minds."

"How about a game of Super Smash Brothers?" Ashton asked, starting to make her way to the bathroom.

"Awe. In the mood to get your butt kicked again, I see." Jasmine said in a competitive tone.

Ashton smirked and looked back at Jasmine with a competitive glare, "You mean *you're* in a mood to get *your* butt kicked!"

"Um, I hate to be a total weirdo and ask this question but...what's Super Smash Brothers?" Krista asked.

"Oh, it's a famous Nintendo game title." Jessica said, "It's basically all of the really popular Nintendo characters fighting each other. You know, Link, Mario, Zelda, Donkey Kong, Star Fox, and so on. It's absolutely hilarious."

"It especially gets funnier when you have a full set of people." Ashton said. She glanced at Jasmine quickly, then looked at Krista again, "Jasmine and I have an all-out war with each other when we play this game. Just so you know, we'll be screaming, hitting each other, and calling each other names in the very near future."

"She speaks the truth, Krista. I'd prepare yourself for anything." Jessica said.

Krista giggled and started cleaning up the mess they had made while watching the movie, "I did that when I woke up this morning."

A few hours later, around 1:00 AM, the girls decided to call it a night. Jessica prepared some places for her friends to sleep and gave them some pillows and sheets from the closet in her bedroom. Krista and Jasmine took places on the floor in the living room area, while Ashton claimed one of the recliners.

"So, what'd you think of your first day actually hanging out with us, Krista?" Ashton asked.

"I think I know the definite answer to a question I've been wondering ever since I first met you guys." Krista said.

Ashton rolled over to look at Krista, "Oh? And what question is that?"

"Whether or not you're all insane!" Krista said, bursting out in laughter.

Ashton rolled her eyes and returned to a comfortable position, "Good night, girls. Sleep tight."

"You too, Ash."

While the others were falling asleep, Jessica stayed awake, gazing out her bedroom window at the sky. In her hand she held one of her favorite pictures from her childhood, and could remember the day it was taken like it was yesterday. She continued to look out her window for a while longer before sighing and looking down at the picture. It was one of the only pictures she and her parents had ever taken of Chris when he was living with them. In this picture, she and Chris were having a pillow fight, and she was holding a pillow over her head, getting ready to strike. It reassured her that she really did make a change in his life, and even though it was just a picture, she could tell he wasn't lost anymore by the look in his eyes. He knew he was wanted, and that he more or less had a family he could call his own.

The more Jessica looked at the picture, the more her emotions got to her. Tears started to build in her eyes as she thought back to the day she first met Chris and defended him from Mathew. The things he'd told her, and the things he didn't tell her were rushing through her mind. Before long, Jessica's tears were sliding down her cheeks, and falling to the floor,

"Where are you?" She whispered, trying to keep her emotions together, "It's been ten years now, and you still haven't come back, even though you said you would. Have you forgotten about me? Have you found someone else? Or is your training taking longer than you originally thought it would. Ten years go by, and you haven't sent me one letter letting me know how things are going. Ten years go by, and I still wait for you to come back. Do you know how inappropriate it is to keep a woman waiting?! How much longer do I have to wait for you to return? How many more men do I have to turn down believing I already have what I want? I'm trying my hardest to believe you'll come back, but I'm running out of patience. I miss you!"

With emotions of all different kinds coursing through her body, Jessica began to silently cry, praying she'd see him again sometime soon.

CHAPTER 2

Events in Motion

Dallas FT. Worth, Texas: Carswell Rebel Supply
Base, 0039 hours (12:39 A.M)

The landing gear of an R-H-E6-550 Rebel Heavy Transport Plane touched down on the tarmac of the main runway, and slowly started to taxi its way to its parking destination: a large hanger where a high ranking member of the Rebellion was scheduled to meet President Davis, the elected politician to serve as president for the United States of the Republic, and his administration, including a few generals. Rebel troops were everywhere. Snipers on the rooftops, and Rebel special elite forces, such as the Cobras, were hiding in the shadows, keeping a sharp eye out for any potential threats. On each side of the administration members, standing in perfect alignment, were full platoons of Rebel Elite Forces, equipped with new advanced weaponry, combat gear, and some new prototypes of night-vision goggles. They were geared up for a full assault on the base, and ordered to kill on sight if they spotted any potential threat.

As the Rebel Transport Plane made its final turn to the hanger, President Davis and his administration took a deep breath, readying themselves to meet face-to-face with someone who outranked even them. The plane came to a stop, and President Davis and his administration released their breath with a sigh, and prepared themselves. There was a brief pause that felt like an eternity to everyone in the building before the hydraulics of the gigantic plane started working. The entire front part of the plane lifted into the air, revealing the cargo area in the fuselage. A ramp as wide as the plane's body lowered to the ground, and several Rebel Phantoms, the second most elite fighting force in the known Rebel military, came rushing out of the plane to their positions on each side of the ramp, and stood at attention. A few short seconds later, another person appeared at the top of the ramp, emerging in an eerie fashion from the darkness of the cargo bay.

President Davis, felt a new meaning of fear and stared in awe at his superior. The man was tall, and dressed in a tattered solid black hooded cloak that hid his face in shadow. Only his mouth and nostrils could be seen, but he looked far from pleased. An aura of fear seemed to spread through the hanger, as the entire administration was now shaking, some paralyzed by fear. Upon closer inspection, one of the generals could see spikes on the knuckles of the man's gloves, and could tell he had recently used them in a fight.

As the man walked down the ramp and made his way towards the administration, President Davis stepped out of position and greeted his superior, "Ah, general, welcome to Dallas Ft. Worth. I'm pleased to finally meet you in person on this unexpe-"

"You may stop with the pleasantries, Mr. President." The man interrupted. His voice was chilling, and sent shivers down the spine of everyone within hearing range, "I hardly believe my coming here was unexpected."

"Er...of course, sir." President Davis said in a respectful tone. He pondered about what to say next and continued, "Then, if I may ask, sir, why have you come here?"

The man gave President Davis and his administration a chilling glare, and shoved them aside as he continued walking to the back of the hanger, "If you must know, I'm here to put you back on schedule. Your generals have lost their focus and are wasting too many resources on one particular battle."

President Davis, who was struggling to keep up with the man's pace, thought about his response before saying, "Sir, with all due respect, we cannot push our troops any faster than we already are! If we push the war effort any harder we'll lose more men than what is necessary."

"Then perhaps you're not using the right tactics." The man replied coldly.

"Sir, our generals are doing the best they can. What else would you have them do?" President Davis asked, not knowing what to expect.

The man suddenly stopped and turned to face President Davis, "We expect better results, Mr. President. I find it hard to believe this is the best your generals can do. The Republic outnumbers the military ten to one, and you seem to be losing more men over one city that means virtually nothing to us at this point, rather than taking what the military believes to be their final stronghold against us in Virginia."

"Then what do you expect us to do?" President Davis asked.

"As of now I am relieving your generals." The man said, "It seems you do not know what it takes to win a war. I, on the other hand do, and this war has taken up too much time as it is. You're fighting a weakened military with little organization led by an administration that has no idea how the game of war is played. Yet you seem to lack the drive to get our troops to Washington. If you fought a foe which was any weaker you'd be fighting infants!"

Completely caught by surprise from the harshness of his commander, President Davis was speechless.

"Oh, and one more thing, Mr. President." The man said, catching President Davis's attention once again, "It would be wise of you to return to your administration and tell them to prepare for the arrival of the rest of my order."

President Davis's eyes widened in fear, and he was speechless once again for a few moments. When he finally built up enough courage, he asked, "T...the other six are coming here?"

"That is correct, Mr. President, and they are most disgusted with your lack of progress."

"...Then we will do what we must." President Davis said.

"Good. But remember this, and this is a message for your entire administration." The man said in a cold voice, gaining the full undivided attention of President Davis, "The others are not as forgiving as I am."

He then turned his back to President Davis and continued on his way, leaving President Davis speechless. Getting the hint his superiors were not messing around, he went back to his administration and delivered them the news.

CHAPTER 3

The West Falls

The next morning, Jessica woke up early and snuck her way into the kitchen where she started making breakfast for everyone who were still asleep after their sleepover. She was an excellent cook, and was often sought out to make special treats for certain events such as birthdays, weddings, and sometimes even funerals. She had made a lot of friends over the years, and she was always happy to make a favored treat for her friends. Her hotcakes were especially a big hit. However, she wasn't exactly a quiet cook.

"Well, you're up a little earlier than usual." Ashton, who was still reclined in her chair, said just loud enough for Jessica to hear.

Jessica shifted her attention from her current task to Ashton, "Yeah, I couldn't sleep. Sorry if I woke you, but I needed something to do."

Ashton yawned, sat the recliner upright, stood from the chair, and walked into the kitchen, "Well, I couldn't really sleep, either. I think that movie we watched got to me a little more than I thought it did. Anyway, would you like any help?"

Jessica nodded and returned her attention to what she was doing before, "Yeah, sure. If you could make the eggs, I'll make the hotcakes."

"Oh, it's been too long since I last had one of your hotcakes, Jess!" Ashton said, "If it gets me some food a little faster, I'll do whatever you ask of me."

Jessica chuckled, shaking her head, and started multi-tasking with the hotcakes and sausage.

"So, what's on the agenda for today, Jess?" Ashton asked.

"Um...I'm not real sure yet, really." Jessica said, "I haven't looked outside yet, so I can't really say for certain. I'll probably just do some housework and do a little exercising. It's been a few days since I last went jogging. After that, I might work on my novel and practice with my musical instruments for a while."

"After our tradition of watching some old cartoons before leaving, right?" Ashton asked.

Jessica giggled and nodded, "Yes, Ashton, of course. Anyway, do you have any plans for the day?"

"Being lazy." Ashton replied simply, "Once we're done here, I plan to go back to my apartment and read a new book I got recently."

"Oh? And what book is that?" Jessica asked.

"Oh...it's just that new Galaxy Adventures book that came out a few weeks ago."

Jessica's body froze for a moment, "G...Galaxy Adventures? A new book just recently came out?"

Ashton turned to face Jessica and stuck her tongue out at her, "I told you I'd get the new book first."

"Ashton, I love that book series!" Jessica said loudly, trying not to yell, "Where'd you get your copy?!"

"I got mine off Amazon." Ashton said, "It's not a cheap book, though, and it's pretty darn long, too."

"Well, they've all been long up to this point." Jessica said. She growled and returned her attention to her hotcakes and sausage, "Great. This is just typical. I'm living off the last few dollars of my paycheck, and can't afford to buy the latest book of a book series I've been following since my senior year in high school."

"The universe is truly a cruel place, isn't it?" Ashton asked, trying to hold in her laughter.

"Yeah, and it seems to enjoy our misery a little too much." Jessica said.

"Well, I'll let you borrow it once I'm done with it." Ashton said, "It's pretty long, though."

"How many pages is it?" Jessica asked.

"Nearly a thousand." Ashton said, "The font's pretty big, as well, so that probably has something to do with the page amount."

"Yeah, that's probably true." Jessica said, "Anyway, let's get on with finishing this stuff. I'm starving!"

Ashton nodded in response and focused all her attention on her current task.

A while later, Jessica and Ashton had finished making the hotcake meal. The smell woke Krista and Jasmine from their sleep, and they immediately went to the kitchen to grab a plate.

"Come and get 'em while they're hot, girls." Jessica said, pouring orange juice into their glasses.

"Mmm…these smell so good! It's been years since I had a pancake!" Krista said, stacking two hotcakes on her plate, followed by a few eggs.

"Well, you'll never eat anyone else's after you take your first bite of Jessica's." Jasmine said, "She makes the best pancakes I've ever eaten."

Jessica giggled and shook her head, "Sorry, guys, but you're wrong. My *mom* actually makes the best pancakes."

Ashton paused for a moment, and thought about what Jessica just said, "Hmm…yeah, I suppose you have to give credit where credit is due. How is your mom, anyway? Is everything going okay back home?"

"She's fine." Jessica said, "She's a little worried for our safety over here, but she's doing okay. Last time I heard from her, she said my Dad has actually managed to get good at golf."

"Well, that's good." Jasmine said, "You're close with your family, so it's nice to know you keep in touch. Are they planning to go on any more trips?"

"I think my mom mentioned something about Alaska in her last email." Jessica said, "I'll need to see if she's sent any more messages to me over the past few days, but I do recall her specifically mentioning Alaska."

"Why Alaska?" Krista asked, "Its cold in Alaska, I'd have gone to Hawaii myself."

"Ugh…don't mention Hawaii to them." Jessica said, "They were stationed in Hawaii for two years and hated it."

"Seriously?! How can one hate Hawaii of all places?" Krista asked.

Jessica shrugged her shoulders and said, "Matter of opinion, I guess. Anyway, let's start eating before our hotcakes get cold."

The others nodded, gathered what they wanted to eat on their hotcakes, and claimed areas to sit around the TV.

"Let's see what's on the classical channel first." Ashton said, watching Jessica flip through the channels, "It hasn't been showing anything interesting lately, but you never know."

"Yeah, I know exactly what you mean, Ashton." Jessica said, nodding her head, "Nothing good has been on TV for a while. It's all news reports on the war, and re-runs of really crappy movies filmed over fifteen years ago."

"We may end up having to watch a movie again, which I'm fine with." Jasmine said, quickly eating her hotcakes.

Jessica searched through a few more channels, hoping to find something interesting, but nothing came up, "Yeah, it's starting to look that way. Anybody have any special requests on the movie?"

"Do you have any Looney Toons?" Krista asked. "When you guys said classic stuff, I kind of went on the assumption you meant old cartoons."

Jessica stopped searching through the channels and tried to recall what movies she had, "Well…hmm, I'm not sure if I have Looney Toons such as characters like Bugs Bunny, Daffy Duck, and that group, but I *do* have some older Disney movies if you'd rather watch those."

"Hey, that's even better." Krista said, "If you have Aladdin, it's settled."

"I take it you liked Aladdin?" Jasmine asked.

"Yeah…hey, wait a second…" Krista said, thinking about the coincidence of Jasmine's name, "We already have you here, might as well get Aladdin in here, too."

The others laughed, completely understanding Krista's joke, but they stopped once Jessica started putting in the numbers of a certain channel.

"I just want to check on the news first, guys." Jessica said, "You never know what might have happened overnight while we were all asleep." Jessica typed the numbers for CNN's channel, and waiting a second for the channel to load, "Ah! It's on advertisement!"

"Try FOX, Jess, their advertisements are a lot shorter than CNN's." Ashton said.

Jessica nodded in response, and changed the channel to FOX NEWS. She waited for the channel to load, and was pleased to see the channel wasn't on a commercial break. She listened to the people on the TV talking for a moment, but saw they weren't talking about anything particularly new. There was a video of Rebel troops pushing deeper into Oregon State, and a string of words at the bottom of the screen saying an Al-Qaeda camp was discovered and attacked by Rebel soldiers. Other than that, there wasn't anything particularly interesting.

"So, is it movie time now?" Jasmine asked, taking the last bite of her breakfast.

Jessica nodded her head and said, "It is indeed." She looked at Krista as she thought about her movie request, "Hey, Krista, why don't you look in the closet in the hall for Aladdin. I'm fairly sure I have a copy of it somewhere. I'll look here in my collection of old movies under the TV."

Krista nodded, and went to the closet Jessica mentioned, and started digging through the movies in the closet.

Later, after the girls had watched the movie, and went their separate ways, Jessica had changed her plans for the day by staying in her apartment and working on her novel. Writing was a hobby she had picked up in high school, though she had written music long before then, but she had never written novels. Over the years, she had become somewhat well known in the immediate area, and online from a lot of short stories she'd written. She had a small group of followers that called themselves 'fans' of her work, which made her chuckle. It simply amazed her how she had written a handful of short stories, but was fairly well known in the part of the city she lived in.

As she sat at her desk, Jessica reviewed what she had written the last time she worked on her novel, and looked at what she had planned for this round, *"Hmm…let's see… I need to finish chapter 12 today, and hopefully make some ground in chapter 13. I have 80,000 words, so if I write another ten thousand today, I should remain on schedule. Then, once I'm done writing, I need to practice my music for a while."*

She gathered her thoughts, and started typing on her computer. As she wrote, she wrote down notes in a journal on areas she thought needed more detail, but didn't stop writing until she either ran into writer's block, or reached her goal for the day. Fortunately for her, she didn't have a lot of trouble with writer's block. The novel she was writing was based off something that took place in her life a long time ago, and was making an alternative story of the events. She kept certain things in line, but changed lesser details about the event as she went on.

Though she didn't consider herself the best writer on the planet, she took pride and joy into the fact that others liked what she wrote. In her eyes, if one person liked her work, it was a success.

Once Jessica had finished writing, she saved her progress, and closed her laptop. She then walked over to her guitar collection, grabbed her favorite guitar, and started playing, and singing along with the music. Hitting every note perfectly, and remembering the rhythm of the song, she had no trouble with the lyrics. The song she was playing was a song she had written for high school graduation. It was about never giving up on one's goals, and never to abandon one's dreams. Though it was only meant to be played one time, she kept it just in case her own dream was recognized.

Once she finished the song, she continued to play another fifteen songs before officially calling it quits for the day. Her voice was dry, and she was very thirsty. She made her way to the kitchen where she drank straight from the faucet. Once her thirst had been quenched, she grabbed an apple from the fruit bowl she had on the counter, and made her way back to the living room area where she grabbed a book, sat in her favorite recliner, and read for the rest of the afternoon.

Later on, when Jessica was eating her evening meal, her cell phone started ringing.

"Huh. I wonder who's calling me at this hour." She thought. She ran over to her cell phone, and checked who was calling her, *"Ashton?"* She paused her thoughts as she looked at the clock on the wall behind her, *"She should be in bed by now..."* Without thinking another thought, Jessica, in fear something was upsetting her best friend, answered the call, "Ashton? Is everything okay? You're usually in bed by this time of night."

"Yeah, I know. Have you been watching the news?" Ashton asked, the urgency in her voice taking Jessica by surprise.

"No...why, what's going on?" Jessica asked curiously as she walked over to the kitchen counter to grab the remote control.

Ashton paused briefly before saying, "Washington State and Oregon have surrendered to the Rebels, and even more Rebel troops are converging on the eastern warfront."

Jessica's eyes widened, and she scrambled to put the numbers in for CNN, "Are you serious, Ash? This isn't some joke is it?"

"Would I be awake this late at night just to prank you, Jess?" Ashton asked, "I was already asleep when Jasmine called and told me the news. Hurry up and turn your TV on if you haven't already. Things are looking pretty bad."

"I'm way ahead of you." Jessica said, just as a reporter came on the screen. She listened to what the reporter was saying, and read the headlines at the bottom of the screen:

Washington State and Oregon Surrender to
Massive Rebel Assault in Western States.
Rebel activity Increases along Eastern Warfront.

> *Vice President Kerry, and Secretary of State Georgia*
> *Hill Captured While Fleeing Seattle.*

"Ashton, am I really seeing this?" Jessica asked, scarcely able to believe what she was seeing.

"Yeah, and one of my friends is saying Rebel Forces out of Nevada are re-enforcing the California border right now." Ashton said.

"But...how is this happening?" Jessica asked as she sat on the floor in front of the TV, "The last time I watched the news, the Rebels were just invading the outer parts of Seattle. How could they have pushed that far that fast?"

"Maybe the military was weaker in Seattle and Oregon than we thought." Ashton said.

"Either that, or the Rebels were stronger in number than we thought." Jessica said, "Anyway, I better get off before I miss an important detail."

"Yeah, and I'll bet you anything work will be cancelled tomorrow as well." Ashton said in a depressed tone.

"Well, crap." Jessica said, "I *need* another paycheck! At this rate, I won't be able to afford my apartment much longer."

"Hey, don't worry, girl. We'll help you out. We're family remember?" Ashton asked.

Jessica smiled softly for a moment before replying, "Yeah...of course. Thanks, Ash. Anyway, I hate to cut this short, but I need to hang up before I miss anything important."

"Yeah. Try and have a good night, Jess. See you tomorrow."

"Yeah...see you then." Jessica ended her call and focused her attention on the reporter on the screen.

"Welcome back to CNN, I'm Michael Black. If you're just now catching up on current events, the Rebels have officially taken Seattle and Oregon State. No less than two hours ago, the military in those two states threw down their weapons and surrendered to Rebel forces. The Rebels have taken over five-thousand military hostages, and the death toll of the battle has yet to be released. The city of Seattle was invaded in force. Rebel troops pushed into the city with a force the military just couldn't hold back. Take a look at this video."

The TV then started showing a video a civilian had taken with their cell phone camera. The civilian was trapped in a hot zone where Rebel Forces were advancing deeper into the city, and engaging military personnel. The gunshots, even on the TV, were deafening, and voices of the troops on both sides could be heard but not understood. The civilian, who was barely able to hold his phone, stuck the camera out from behind a dumpster and recorded the most intense and violent video that had ever been shown on the news since the war first started. Two military troops were kneeling behind a barricade set up on a sidewalk, firing their guns at targets that were hidden behind a building on the right. One of the soldiers ducked down and reloaded his gun while the other covered them with covering fire. Another soldier came into view from behind the building on the left with a heavy machine gun, and started to set up his weapon behind another concrete barrier. However, once he finished and stood to see over the barricade, an explosion right next to the barricade sent all three of the soldiers flying. One of the solders flew in the direction of the camera, and his screams of terror and agony could be heard as he flew by. The camera focused on the lifeless soldier for a moment, then focused on another group of U.S soldiers who were running to take up position where the last three soldiers were. But before they could reach their target, Rebel Soldiers, men dressed in solid black combat armor, and wearing face masks turned around the corner, shooting three of the soldiers, and sending the other four scrambling to some cover.

Another intense firefight resumed, but the military started to fall back after a short time.

"Holy shit, they've got a tank!" One of the soldiers yelled before a loud bang echoed through the air, followed by the sound of heavy machinegun fire.

The civilian poked the phone out again, and the video showed a heavily armored Rebel tank sitting on the street near the area where the first three military troops were. Suddenly, a voice could be heard on the video, "Hey, you! What are you doin' here?! Get your ass out of here! *Move!*"

The screen then went black, and the CNN reporter was on the screen once again,

"As you can probably tell, the Rebels invaded Seattle with a larger, and more organized force than the military originally believed was capable of attacking the city. We're awaiting the report on the condition of the city, and how many civilians may have gotten caught in the crossfire, but until then, we have two guests with us here tonight. Joining me now from FOX news is Michael Rich, and Kevin McClure from MSNBC. Now...Mr. Rich, I'd like to start by asking you a few questions first. You've interviewed members of the Rebel governmental system before, you've seen things no one else has, and before the war even started, you interviewed President Davis and a few other members of the Rebel administration. I'd like to know your exact thoughts on what's happening now. The Rebels have obviously proven they're larger in number, and far more organized than military generals originally believed. In fact, some generals are questioning if they have a new commander. What are your opinions on the matter? Do you think California could be invaded next?"

Michael Rich gathered his thoughts for a few seconds before saying, "Well, it's a bit of a tricky topic, really. The Rebel States, or "United States of the Republic", have never said more than they thought was necessary on the media before. They keep as much about their governmental system, military, and whatever else in the dark as much as possible as a way of keeping themselves as secretive from Washington as possible. It's impossible to really know what the Rebels are planning, and what their next target might be. They outnumber the military by large numbers, and there's not really a lot we know about them. We know their government has remained a very strong Republic, we know their economy if completely off the charts compared to the old country, but we don't know a lot about their military or who's commanding it. Up to now, the Rebels have always been three steps ahead of the old military."

"So, what are your thoughts on the Rebels attacking Seattle and Oregon?" Michael Black asked.

"I'm not that surprised." Michael Rich answered, "People knew this was going to happen, and the Rebels have been preparing for the better part of two months to invade the city. They cut off all military supply lines to the city, and waited for just the right moment to invade. The military had next to nothing compared to the Rebels in the city, and they just couldn't hold the city. They were too thinly spread, and the Rebels just had too many troops in the region. You have to remember the Rebels are nearly four-million strong in number now, and the military has less than half of its original strength when the civil war first started. Frankly, I'm amazed the Rebels didn't invade the city sooner than this."

"Do you think the Rebels may turn their attention to California now?" Michael Black asked.

Michael Rich shook his head and said, "I doubt it. I mean, it's possible, but I don't see the Rebels even bothering at this point. California is too weak both militarily, and economically to pose much of a threat. Taking California would give the Rebels more ports and Naval Bases, but it's more likely they'll start diverting forces to the east and start converging on Richmond. However, I also see the Rebels taking West Virginia and parts of southern parts of Pennsylvania. Doing that would allow them to hit D.C from several different directions. As the economy of the Rebel States grows, so does their military. The people in the "Republic States" are manufacturing new weapons, ammo, vehicles, gear, and other basic materials their soldiers need. They outfit their troops with weapons that have larger clips, longer range, better accuracy, and just overall more power. In fact, I have to laugh when President Lane says he has 'plans' to turn the war in his favor. The war was decided from the day it first started. He's fighting against a stronger military, stronger economy, and better trained generals."

"So, do you think a Rebel attack on D.C may be imminent?" Michael Black asked.

Michael Rich remained silent for a moment, before saying, "I don't think so. I mean, it's not impossible. The Rebels certainly have the numbers and means to just skip Richmond completely, but a relatively large military force is in Richmond right now, and could threaten the Rebel's southern flank if they don't attack the city. However, there's nothing stopping the Rebels from invading West Virginia, and southern parts of Pennsylvania. Taking those places would give the Rebels multiple directions from which to attack Washington, and would spread the military thin in these areas. There's no real way of knowing what will happen over the next few days, but I predict the Rebels will be in D.C by the end of August or early September."

Michael Black nodded, understanding Michael Rich had a very strong point, and turned his attention to Kevin McClure, "So, what are your opinions on what Mr. Rich just said?"

Kevin remained silent for a moment before saying, "Look, I don't mean to turn this into some kind of huge debate, but Michel Rich is completely wrong about the Rebels on so many different accounts that it's laughable. Michael Rich, you claim we know so little about the Rebels, but go on to say they have a stronger economy, that they have better generals, their troops are better trained than the military. If we know so little about them, how can we take your words one-hundred percent seriously? Yes, the Rebel States, or the "United States of the Republic" as they call themselves, may have some unique features about them, I highly doubt they'll be in Washington by the end of the month! The thought is just absurd! President Lane has said time, and time again that the war will soon be turned in a new direction."

"Yes, that's true. But how often have his words been true?" Michael Rich asked, "And don't try putting my own words in my mouth. I have met with many Rebel leaders numerous times for interviews and other questions. I know what I'm talking about."

"Hmm. I'm sure." Kevin smirked, "And what have these "Rebels" told you during your visits? That they have no intentions of harming the innocent? That they fight for restoring America to her former glory and enforce stronger laws for politicians? What a joke. The Rebels are terrorists. Nothing more, nothing less. They have been responsible for hundreds of innocent deaths, and that number is continuing to rise with each passing day. Need I remind you of what happened to those five people on the news the other day?"

Michael Rich rolled his eyes and sighed quietly, "More of this stuff? I thought you guys would have moved past this by now, but apparently you need a lesson concerning reality. Those people you're talking about chose to stay in the town, even after the Rebels sent messengers saying they were going to attack in a few days. Also, those people were not attacked by soldiers on purpose. They were simply in the wrong place at the wrong time. Using those people as a 'point' to make your argument seem more legit is in very poor taste. What you're arguing about is just the nature of war, something people like you will never understand."

Kevin growled and stood from his chair, "The Rebels will *not* attack D.C! They do not have the men, and they do *not* have the firepower to do so."

"Washington State and Oregon were well defended, and possibly better defended than Virginia." Michael Rich said calmly, "They seemed to take those states with little trouble."

Kevin narrowed his eyes at Michael and said in an aggressive tone, "The Rebels will *not* attack D.C, and that's *final!*" He then grabbed his papers and disappeared off the screen.

The TV was silent for a few moments before Michael Black turned to the camera and said, "Well…I guess that's all the time we have for right now. Mr. Rich, thanks for coming in." The screen then proceeded to show the title of a fiction series Jessica had been reading for several years as Michael continued, "Anyway, moving onward to our next topic for the night. Could this author be writing the next big title series? Samantha Frost, the author of the "Galactical Insurgency" meets with us right after the break."

Jessica turned the volume down once the commercials started running. She had to chuckle about Kevin losing his temper and storming out of the room, "That poor guy. He's so caught up in his virtual reality that he'll believe anything his news sources tell him. It was actually kind of silly for him to challenge Michael Rich to a debate over this topic. He's in for a heck of a surprise once the Rebels actually invade D.C."

She took a deep breath to regain her composure, and looked at the clock on the wall to check the time, and saw it was way beyond her bed time, "Drats! I want to see this interview with my favorite author! But…if I don't go to bed now I'll basically be a walking corpse tomorrow at work." She stood indecisively, "Well, assuming I have enough money to pay the bills this month, I'll surely be able to find the interview on the web somewhere." She turned the TV off, and made her way to her bedroom, gathering her pajamas along the way. Once she washed her makeup off, and put her pajamas on, she climbed into bed, and called it a night.

CHAPTER 4

Two Targets

*Dallas FT. Worth, Texas. Carswell Rebel Supply Base
Observation Control Center. 22:30 (10:30) P.M*

Escorted by two generals and four Rebel Cobras, President Davis made his way to the observation room where one of his superiors was awaiting his arrival.

"Do you have any idea what this is about, general?" President Davis asked one of the generals following him.

"Not a clue, sir. All I was told is that our superiors want to see us immediately." The general said.

President Davis then looked over his other shoulder at the second general, "What about you?"

"I'm afraid I only know what you know, sir." The general said, shrugging his shoulders.

"Hmm.... I see." President Davis turned around and continued down the corridor, taking a right at the first turn. Ahead of him was the entrance to the observation center, an enormous room filled with computer and TV screens that was designed to allow generals and other high ranking members of the Rebellion to see what's happening in battle zones, and keep in contact with deployed units. However, it was only to be used until the Rebels finished building their own control center, which was a second pentagon.

As President Davis entered the room, he saw his superior standing in the center of the room watching a replay of an earlier news broadcast. President Davis and the generals took deep breaths before approaching him, "You wanted to see us, sir?"

The man didn't reply, and stood as still as a statue as he watched the news replay.

"S-sir?"

"Where is the rest of your administration?" The man asked.

President Davis looked around the room and saw that he and the two generals that followed him were the only high ranking members of the government of the room. Dreading the outcome of what could happen, President Davis tried to come up with a reasonable excuse, "I-I'm sure they're on their way, sir. I mean...this was such a sudden turn of events, and I'm sure their work delayed them."

The man still didn't turn to face President Davis or his generals, but still continued talking, "It's always one excuse after another with you people, isn't it? Regardless, they've likely already seen this, and I'm going to go on the assumption that you've seen this man on the news before." The man pointed up at the screen.

President Davis and the generals looked up at the screen, and listened to the conversation. It was the same interview that was on CNN a few hours before. He looked at the man again, who was still staring at the screen, and said, "Uh, yes, sir, that is Kevin McClure from MSNBC, one of President Lane's most loyal reporters. He hates the Rebellion and everything we stand for."

"I see...another waste of breathable oxygen." The man said.

"I suppose you have a course of action you'd like us to take, sir?" President Davis asked.

"I'm sure he does." Another voice said from the back of the room.

President Davis and the generals turned to face the source of the voice and saw another man clothed in dark colored hooded robes. This one, however, looked even more dangerous than the original, "It would be wise of you not to forget who you're talking to, President Davis!" The man said in a chilling tone. His face was hidden in shadow, but President Davis could still feel his intensifying stare.

Startled, President Davis stood at attention, "Ye-ye-yes, sir!"

"Now then, I assume you've already devised a plan to deal with that lowlife?" The second man asked the original.

The original turned to face the second man, and nodded, "Yes. The next dawn will not have risen before these fools who still support President Lane are introduced to a little thing I like to call 'reality'. This fantasy world those idiots are living in is about to come to an end starting *now*! Starting tomorrow, the media will have their hands full covering three things at once, and that will put my plan into effect."

"I suppose this is why you dispatched those battle groups into the Gulf, then?" The second man asked.

"One of the reasons, anyway." The original man said as he turned to face the screen again, "This is the type of opening I've been waiting for." The screen turned to a sea chart that showed the locations of five Rebel fleets in the Gulf of Mexico.

Confused about what was going on, President Davis looked at the original superior and asked, "W-what exactly are you planning to do?"

"Just watch. You might learn something in the process." The man said, "Those fools are so loyal to President Lane that they'll make up any excuse to support him. I think it's time we damage their reputation... for good." The man pointed to a communications officer, "You there! Contact the captain of the Rogue Wave and tell him his destroyers have two targets: The Washington Monument, and the street just outside the Capital Building!"

"What?!" President Davis nearly screamed, "You can't be serious!"

The man turned to look at President Davis, "Do I look like I'm joking to you?"

"But what about civilian casualties?!" President Davis exclaimed.

The man narrowed his eyes at President Davis, "That is the exact reason why we haven't invaded D.C yet. You worry more about civilian casualties than advancing the war or taking out important members of the opposing side. Three months ago you could have executed one of the opposing generals, but you didn't because you were afraid of 'civilian casualties'. And because you were afraid of 'civilian casualties' this general was able to launch a missile strike at our frontline killing almost one-hundred of our troops on the front line. You people are too soft to have any kind military duty."

"But, sir! Those are innocent people you're talking about!" President Davis said.

"And those were innocent soldiers!" The man said back, "In wartime there is no such thing as 'innocence'. Now, collect the rest of your generals, and tell them to prepare for a briefing."

Unable to argue with his superior, President Davis nodded, and left the room with his generals. As they passed by, the new superior watched them, and once they left the room, he faced the original man, "Humph! Politicians. They never understand."

"Sometimes I wonder why I'm even bothering to do what I'm doing." The original replied.

The second man nodded, "You told me these people were weak minded, but I never thought it would be this bad. Anyway, I leave things to you."

The other man only nodded, and listened to the fading footsteps of the second man. He noticed a person standing at attention to his left, and turned to face the person, "What is it?"

"Sir! The captain of the Rogue Wave wants confirmation of your orders, sir." The communications officer said.

"They're confirmed." The man said.

"Yes, sir!" The communications officer returned to his station.

The man turned his attention to a map of current plans written by the generals, studied it for a few moments, then ordered them to be shredded.

CHAPTER 5

A Message With A New Threat

BANG!

A sudden terrifying explosion in the distance woke Jessica from sleep, making her jump for the ceiling. The building shook as if a strong wind had hit, which made her even more uneasy.

"What in the world was that?" Jessica asked as she threw the covers off her, then made her way into the main room of her apartment where she looked out the main window in the direction the explosion seemed to come from. She scanned the horizon for a few moments, and saw what looked like a tall building in the distance had caught fire and blown some kind of gas line. However, upon further observation, she knew it wasn't just any building, "What happened to the monument?!" She yelled out loud.

Outside her door she could hear people making their way into the hall, probably trying to find out what the terrifying noise was, which made her start to worry, "*Oh, no. If they see what's going on, and start to panic…. this could be bad.*" She looked at the monument again and started debating with herself, "*Is this a Rebel attack? No…it can't be. They're barely into Virginia, and they've never done anything like this in the past. This is too bold a move for them. A terrorist attack, maybe?*

Security in D.C is thinly spread, and there's little to no military presence in the city other than the Secret Service, Pentagon, and a small contingency on the base. The Monument would be a prime target for a terror attack, but it's under remodeling, and closed off to the public. Nothing is making any sense here!"

Just then, her cell phone started ringing, and she could tell by the ring tone that it was Ashton. She ran over to her phone, and answered, "Hey, Ashton, are you okay?"

"Are you kidding? My heart hasn't pumped like this in years!"

"I guess you heard it too, huh?" Jessica asked.

"Yeah, it sounded really close, too. Do you know what happened?"

"I think so." Jessica said as she rolled her eyes to the window, "I think the Washington Monument was attacked."

There was a long silent pause.

"Are...are you serious?" Ashton asked, her voice shaking in fear, "Is it the Rebels?"

"I have no idea." Jessica said, walking back to the window, "But I doubt it's them. They've never been this bold to attack like this before, and there's no way they're invading the city yet."

"Then what's going on?" Ashton asked,

"A terrorist attack is my best guess." Jessica said, "Security is thin in Washington. Troops are spread far and wide, trying to hold back the Rebels. Most of the security forces are more focused on finding Rebel spies, and keeping an eye out for assassins, and who knows what else? This would be the perfect opportunity for a terror group to strike."

"But why the monument? It's been closed off to the public for months for remodeling, and it'd be closed at this time of night, anyway." Ashton said.

"Maybe it was meant as a warning or something." Jessica said, "But still...I'm adding two and two together here and getting ten. Something's not right."

"Well, it'll be a while before the media actually starts reporting with any credible sources. I'll bet they immediately blame the Rebels, though." Ashton said.

Jessica giggled, "That's a guarantee. Anyway, in the event the Rebels actually *are* somehow invading the city. Don't leave your apartment unless the authorities come and get you." Jessica said, "You'd be more likely to run into Rebel troops, and have them mistake you for military reinforcements."

"Yeah, I'd rather not go through that. Anyway, I'm going to get off here, and keep an eye out for any news on what's going on." Ashton said, "Stay safe, Jess."

"You, too, Ash." Jessica ended the call and turned on the TV, turning the channel to CNN, hoping they'd start reporting soon. The sirens of emergency vehicles started to echo throughout the city, as well as war sirens, telling the people to take cover. Outside her door, Jessica could hear all kinds of chatter, and silently hoped a panic didn't start.

Just then, an unexpected knock at the door caught Jessica's attention, and she raced to answer it. She opened the door to find a short elderly man standing at her door.

"Mr. Howard? Can I help you?" Jessica asked, trying to be as polite as possible. Mr. Howard was a man Jessica, Ashton, and Jasmine had made food for in the past when they heard both his grandsons had been killed in the war, leaving him with only one granddaughter.

"I'm sorry to disturb you, ma'am, but do you know what's going on?" Mr. Howard asked, "I've tried asking a few people here, but no one will tell me."

Jessica, feeling sorry for Mr. Howard, looked in his eyes, and saw he was desperately wanting to know what was going on. She pondered for a moment, but decided to tell the truth. She leaned down to Mr. Howard's ear, and whispered, "Look, I don't want to start a panic, but it looks like the Washington Monument was hit by something."

Mr. Howard's eyes widened, looking shocked,

"Are…are you sure about that?" He asked.

Jessica nodded, "I am. However, I don't know if it's the Rebels or some kind of terror group. It's too early for the media to start reporting, and emergency vehicles are just now leaving their stations."

"Do you think it's an actual invasion?" Mr. Howard asked.

Jessica shook her head, "I doubt it. The Rebels haven't penetrated deep enough into military territory to post that kind of threat yet. But in the event it is some kind of invasion, stay in your room until the authorities tell us we need to leave. Just in case, though, pack some things you'd need in the event we have to leave. Money, insurance claims, clothing, and anything you hold dear to you. If it's necessary for us to leave, I'll help you out of the building. Okay?"

Mr. Howard nodded, and started walking as fast as he could back to his apartment down the hall. Jessica went back into her apartment, closing the door behind her, and sat in front of the TV, anxiously waiting for a news program to come on. After what seemed like forever, CNN came on, and the reporter started talking.

"We interrupt this program to bring you an immediate update from D.C! Just a while ago, the Washington Monument was hit by an unidentified object, which the military believes to have been a missile. It is still unknown how many people were hurt or killed in the event, but we have crews heading to the scene as of this very moment. What we do know is that the military has already started investigating what the object was, and where it came from. Right now, the city is a mess, and it's going to take time for our reporters to get to the scene, but stay with us, we'll keep you advised once we get some more information."

"What? You can't be serious! A commercial?!" Jessica yelled. She rested her head in her hand, angry, but understanding of the break, "I guess they can only report so much right now." She looked out the window, and saw flames were rising high above the buildings, and the sky was turning into a hellish red color because of the flames. Not knowing what else to do, she calmed her nerves as best she could, and waited patiently for an update from the media.

Twenty minutes passed, and the media finally had something to report. Just outside a police barricade, a CNN reporter stood with her back turned to the monument. Jessica couldn't believe her eyes. The upper part of the monument had completely been blown off from the impact, and debris was scattered all over the ground. She turned up the volume as the reporter started talking.

"This is totally insane. Around thirty minutes ago, the Washington monument was struck by what the military believes to be a missile launched from the south somewhere. They haven't traced it back to its source yet, but it shouldn't be too much longer before we know what's going on. However, for those of you who don't know, there was a second missile that hit D.C. That one landed just outside the capital building. We don't know the statistics of that part of town yet because the military and police have that entire area completely sealed off. We're not sure how many people were harmed in that attack, but there were only three people injured from the attack on the monument."

The TV cut to the reporter who was at the news HQ as she asked, "You know, there were some people who were afraid this is a Rebel invasion on the city. Has anything of that nature been confirmed?"

"This is not a Rebel invasion." The reporter on the street said, "We still don't know what the motives are behind the attack, but we'll let you know when we find something out."

"Hmm…. so it's not a Rebel invasion? I didn't think so." Jessica said to herself, "But why did they launch two missiles at D.C? They haven't been bold enough to do stuff like this in the past. Well, at least there weren't many casualties. Only a few people injured, and they're more than likely security guards working night shift at the monument." She turned the channel to FOX news and listened to a conversation that was already taking place,

"Look, I'm done playing nice and holding myself back. That MSNBC idiot, Kevin McClure, brought this on himself, as well as every other fool that works for MSNBC. They've gone on and on about how the Rebels will never be able to attack DC for whatever reason, and what happens next? BAM! The Washington Monument's destroyed, and the capital building is nearly hit as well. If that's not an attack, then I don't know what is." One man out of a group of eight people said.

"You know.…. I do kind of have to agree." One of the three women said, "I think the Rebels just wanted to put people like Kevin in his place. But they've never attacked this aggressively in the past, though. I mean, the monument was a good target because it was under remodeling, and no one would be working on it after two in the morning. But the capital building is what concerns me. No other news station has been able to get close enough to see the damage because the military and police have the area completely sealed off. That area is usually crawling with tourists and law enforcement. A lot of people might have gotten hurt…or worse."

"That's very true, Kathrine." One of the men said, "This isn't like the Rebels at all. Usually they either try to avoid settlements before sending messengers to warn the populace they'll be attacking soon, giving the people of the town a chance to flee. But they didn't do it this time, and it has me curious about something."

"And what would that be?" Kathrine asked.

"Well, recently there have been rumors that the Rebels are under new management." The main said, "This is only a rumor, so take it for what you will, but for a while now people have been saying the Rebellion has someone new in control, and it kind of makes sense when you think about it. They've been more aggressive lately, and their numbers are growing larger and larger by the day. Not to mention their mechanical war machines are getting stronger and stronger, too. I think there's a bigger picture we're all overlooking."

"Hmm…come to think of it, I do remember those rumors being something of a big concern in the not too distant past." Another reporter said, "But we can't be sure about anything because the Rebels are just too secretive. They don't want the government to learn any of their weaknesses or find out the locations of some of their most important positions in the Midwest and other states. That alone is one of the main reasons the Rebels are winning the war. How do you win against an enemy you know so little about?"

"That's very true." The second woman said, "Even the military is telling President Lane to surrender, but he refuses to listen. The Rebels are leading the way not only militarily, but economically as well. Gas is only $1.05 a gallon in Oklahoma, and only slightly more expensive in Texas and the rest of the Midwest. Shopping prices are down, businesses are booming, and the economy has recovered at a rapid rate. What I want to know is how the Rebels transformed an economic hell hole into the strongest economy on the planet in such a short amount of time. Things like that don't happen unless you have exactly the right people in exactly the right places."

"Those are questions we may never know the answer to, but we're getting a little off track here." Another reporter said, "It's a shock the Rebels attacked DC, yes, but I think there's more to it than just an attack. The military believes the missiles that struck the monument came from the south, and the Rebels control every state in the south... but what if it didn't come from a state?"

"What do you mean by that?" Kathrine asked.

"It's actually fairly simple now that I think about it." The reporter continued, "What else do the Rebels completely control in the south, and have restricted to all outside forces?"

"The Gulf of Mexico!" The first reporter said.

The reporter nodded and continued, "Exactly. The Rebels have already shown Washington and the rest of the world the strength of their ground and air units, but their Navy still remains a mystery. Navy ships aren't exactly cheap or quick to design and build, but if they were able to put the right economic people in the right places... who's to say they don't have people who excel at designing and building ships?"

"What are you getting at, exactly?" The third reporter asked.

"My point is that this wasn't just an attack, but something far more meaningful and intimidating." The reporter said, "This was a message. I believe the Rebels have assembled their first naval fleet and have deployed it in the Gulf for protection at the moment." He paused as he saw everyone's eyes widen, and continued, "If my prediction is correct, and the Rebels first fleet has actually been assembled..."

"They can completely skip over the military strongholds in Richmond and other towns, and attack from the Atlantic." Jessica said. She turned the TV off, believing she had enough info on what was going on. She stood up, and wandered around her apartment thinking to herself, *"This is both a good thing and a bad thing at the same time. If the United States of the Republic have assembled their first war fleet, chances are their ships are far more powerful than anything the military can throw at them. A fleet in the Gulf of Mexico can mean several things, and none of them good for D.C. Idea number one is they keep a bunch of destroyers loaded with medium and long range missiles off the coast, and bombard key military installations from afar, move the fleet so the missile can't be traced, and attack again. Idea two, and the most likely of the things to happen, the fleet moves into the Atlantic, just off the coast of Maryland and Delaware, and send air strikes on the city from aircraft carriers, assuming the fleet has them. Idea number three...they fill the ships with infantry and ground vehicles, and completely invade from the Atlantic. None of those things are good from D.C., but more importantly its people."* She stopped and looked out the window at the street below, *"I have to wonder how much of this area will have changed after the attack on DC. If the Rebels are bold enough to strike Washington with a missile now, there's no reason to think they won't do it again. This area is far enough from the DC area that it wouldn't pose much tactical importance, but they have to get their troops here somehow, and this area is only a few miles away from* a major highway." She started to chuckle as another thought crossed her mind, "*I guess I took more out of those strategy lessons dad taught me in my youth than I thought. I never really cared for strategy much, but it's quite fascinating when one starts working their imagination a bit. I can see now why Chris loved playing my dad in chess so much all those years ago.*" Her eyes narrowed as she got serious again, "*However, that reporter is definitely onto something.*" She looked out the window as she continued, "*If those missiles were just meant to serve as a message, the Rebels, or whoever are responsible for the attack, have definitely succeeded. Nothing makes a clearer message than a column of thick black smoke rising two miles into the air. This tactic, though… I feel like…*"

The sound of her phone ringing distracted her from her thoughts, and she scrambled to answer it

"Hey, Ashton. How are things going?" She asked.

"I was just wondering if you'd seen the report on FOX." Ashton said, "CNN is still trying to get reporters close enough to the capital building to see the damage, but the police refuse to let anyone near."

"Well, can you blame them?" Jessica asked, "And, yes, Ashton, I just finished watching FOX a few minutes ago."

"What do you make of it, then? Do you think the Rebels could actually have a fleet now?" Ashton asked.

Jessica released a sigh, and said, "Admittedly, it's a bit of a shock to me, too, but it's definitely not in the realms of impossible. What that reporter said is true. The Rebels have the strongest economy on the planet, or at least one of the strongest, and things like that don't appear in such a short amount of time unless the right people are involved in exactly the right places. I can't wait to see how President Lane tries to wiggle his way out of this one. If the Rebels do have a strong fleet, they're bound to have ships with stronger hulls and weaponry than what the old Navy has now. And with the kind of technology they have… let's just say it's not good for the military."

"Yeah, I figured that one out on my own. You should be so proud of me." Ashton said, cracking a laugh on the other end of the phone, "Oh, and before I forget, Shelby called and said work is cancelled tomorrow. She's in shock big time."

"Well, that's not much of a surprise." Jessica said, "However, it's still annoying because I still need money in order to pay this month's bills. And unless I find a money tree in the park somewhere, I'm sunk. My land lord isn't exactly a patient man."

"You'll find a way, Jess." Ashton said, "If all else fails, there's a thing called feminine wiles, you know?"

Shivers went down Jessica's spine once she realized what Ashton meant, "You are such a pervert, you know that?"

"Not as bad as Jasmine." Ashton countered.

"Uh…well…yeah, that's sadly true. Anyway, thanks for letting me know about work, Ash. I'll talk to you later."

"See ya."

Jessica ended the conversation, and rested her phone on the table next to her. She had completely forgotten about her previous thoughts, but her mind was as focused on the idea of a Rebel fleet in the Gulf of Mexico somewhere. It wasn't any secret a lot of Rebel vehicles were undetectable by radar, and some were even EMP resistant, making such tactics completely useless to the military.

"Needless to say, whoever this new general for the Rebels is, he knows how to fight a war." Jessica thought to herself, *"Based on what just happened, it'll take more than a few plans to stop the Rebels now."* She shook her head clear of any other thought and tried to block any more from coming into her head.

"I've had enough for now. If work is cancelled tomorrow, I need to figure out a way to make some extra cash before the month ends. Maybe I can convince my land lord to give me a few extra days before I have to pay my rent…that's not going to be easy, though." She shuddered at the thought of what could happen, or the favor he could ask. Looking for a quick escape from the thought, she looked outside as an ambulance and two firetrucks sped past the building on the street below.

"Well…I guess there's nothing else to do now other than to go back to sleep." She closed the curtains, and returned to her bed.

The following day, Jessica woke to the sound of her alarm clock going off.

"Oh, great. I forgot to turn that stupid thing off," She thought. Annoyed at herself, she reached over to the clock's chord and pulled it out of the wall. She then turned over and tried to fall asleep again, but the sound of her phone going off caught her attention. She rolled back to the table she had her phone on, checked the number, and saw it was the main office. Curious about what was going on, she answered, "Hello? Jessica Holland speaking."

"Hello, Ms. Holland, I'm sorry to bother you this early, but we have a situation." The person on the other end of the phone said.

"Why? What's going on?" Jessica asked, rubbing her eyes.

"There was a man here who wanted to see you a moment ago, but he left when I told him I'd give you a call. He left a package here and said it would be in your best interest to get it." The person said.

Jessica stood from her bed and slipped on her slippers, "Uh.... what did the man look like?" She asked, very skeptical of the situation.

"He looked pretty normal, really." The person said, "He was Caucasian, wearing a red T-shirt, jeans, and a baseball cap, and looked friendly enough. Could he be an old friend perhaps?"

Jessica shook her head, "No. I doubt it. Hold the package for a few minutes. I'll be down to collect it in a bit."

"Very good, ma'am."

Jessica ended the call, but she was more than puzzled about what was going on, *"Why would someone ask for me, but leave the second the people at the desk say they'll call me? It doesn't make any sense. Or...I guess it could be an old high school friend or someone like that and they were just nervous or...no. That's nonsense."* She put some clothes on, and made her way down to the person who had called her.

"Good morning, Kristine. I'm here to pick up the package." Jessica said as she walked up to the desk.

"Ah, of course, Jessica. It's right here." Kristina rested the package on the counter, allowing Jessica to see it. She observed the package for a few moments and noticed there was no name or return address.

"Um…is this even a legal package?" Jessica asked, pointing at the box, "There's no name or return address."

"Yeah, I noticed that, too." Kristine said, "However, he brought it here himself, so I guess it's not really illegal."

"But still. You'd think he would have at least put an address of some kind on there so I could send him a thank you letter or something." Jessica said.

"He said to take it as a gift." Kristine said, "Anyway, why don't you take it back up to your apartment and see what it is? It feels really light for such a big box."

"Yeah, now that you mention it, that is rather.… odd." Jessica said, "Anyway, thanks for letting me know, Kristine. I'll let you get back to work now."

"Alright. Have a good day, Jessica."

"You too."

Back in her apartment, Jessica sat the package on the kitchen counter, and sliced a steak knife through the tape that held the cardboard box together. Once she was able, she opened the box and reached inside to grab a small yellow envelope that felt like it contained nothing at all. Puzzled by this, Jessica pressed her thumbs against the envelope, looking for something that she figured was very small. At the bottom right corner of the envelope, she found something hard, but also somehow hollow. She pinched the item through the envelope, cut the top open, and held it upside-down above her hand. The item fell in her hand, and she finally took her first look at it. What she saw amazed her. She was holding a pure golden ring with rubies on exact opposite sides of the bend. But even more astonishing to her were the markings going around the ring.

"Hello. What's this?" She asked herself. Upon further study, she saw the markings on the ring were identical to one another, but not quite the same, which lead her to conclude one thing, "These markings… they're a language of some kind." She ran over to her writing desk and pulled a magnifying glass from the top drawer and looked closer. She had completely forgotten the fact that there was no name or return address on the package the ring came in, but that was the least of her worries at the moment.

"Hmm...interesting. This language is like nothing I've ever seen before. Arabic, Chinese, Japanese, Korean...it's certainly not an origin of Asia or the Middle East. Definitely not Europe, and it's certainly not an older form of English. Maybe an ancient African or South American language? Hmm...."

She continued to stare at the ring, completely entranced with its beauty and mystery. The language on the ring was written in a ruby red, and an ocean blue somehow reflected from the inside, despite the ring's golden color. Jessica was completely lost looking at it, and could barely tear herself away from the ring. "It's so...beautiful. I wonder if it fits me."

She started to put the ring on, but a call on her cell interrupted her thoughts. She sighed in annoyance, and picked up her phone, "Hello?"

"Hey, Jessica, it's Krista. I was just calling to check and see if you were okay after the events of last night."

"Oh, hey, Krista. I didn't know it was you. I don't have your number saved in my phone yet." Jessica said, standing from the desk, "I'm doing okay, despite the monument being wiped off the face of the earth. How are you doing?"

"I'm shocked, really." Krista said, "I must have been passed out or in a deep trance because I didn't hear anything. I woke up this morning, turned on the news...boy, was I surprised. I got a text from Ashton saying work was canceled today due to what happened. I guess it scared the living daylights out of Shelby, then."

"Well, it'd only make sense if it did." Jessica said with a giggle, "She lives pretty close to where the monument was."

Krista laughed, "Yeah, that missile must have given her more than a midnight scare."

"I'd imagine so." Jessica laughed, "Anyway, thanks for giving me a call, Krista. I'll see you later."

"Okay. Bye, Jess."

Jessica ended the call, gave the ring a quick glance, and started to search for Ashton's number on her phone, *"I bet she'll want to see this."* She thought as she put the phone up to her ear. The phone rang several times, and it seemed like an eternity before Ashton finally answered the phone.

"Mmm…hello, Jessica. You know I don't like it when you call me this early." Ashton said in a half asleep tone, which made Jessica laugh a little.

"Hey, Ash, sorry to call you so early, but I just got a package I think you'd be interested in." Jessica said.

There was a loud yawn on the other end, which made Jessica yawn too.

"Will you cut that out?!" Jessica yelled, "It doesn't matter if you're half way into another galaxy or in the same room, yawns are still contagious."

Ashton laughed, "Sorry, Jessica. So what's this big package I'm supposedly going to be interested in?"

"It's a ring." Jessica said, turning her attention to the ring lying on the desk, "But it's not just any normal piece of jewelry. This one's…. different."

"How so?" Ashton asked curiously.

"I think there's a language written on the bend, but it's not anything I've ever seen before." Jessica walked over to the desk and picked up the ring, "The only language that I can think of that's still in use that comes slightly close to what's written on the ring is Arabic, but I can tell you for a fact that it's not."

"How can you tell?" Ashton asked.

"Have you ever seen Arabic writing? It wouldn't be terribly out of place to say it looks sloppy compared to some other languages. The markings on the ring are somewhat similar, but they're still nothing alike."

"Hmm…that is interesting. Who gave it to you?" Ashton asked.

"No idea." Jessica said, shaking her head, "The person left before I was able to meet him, and there's no name or return address on the box it came in."

"Yet you opened the package anyway?" Ashton asked in a slightly displeased voice.

"Well…I couldn't help it." Jessica said, "You know how my curiosity is a killer at times."

"Yeah…I know firsthand." Ashton said, "And you wonder why I never feed ducks with you anymore."

"That was a one-time incident, okay? Anyway, I thought you'd like to come over and take a look at the ring and see if you could make any sense out of it. You specialized in foreign languages in high school after all."

"Mmmm…. yeah, you talked me into it." Ashton said, "I'll be over in a couple of hours or so. See you then."

"Sounds good."

Jessica ended the call, put the ring in the top drawer of the desk, pulled out her laptop, and started working on her novel.

Hours later, Ashton arrived at Jessica's apartment.

"So where's this big mystery ring?" Ashton asked as she walked through the door.

"It's in my desk right now." Jessica said, leading Ashton to the ring's location. She opened the drawer, grabbed the ring, and showed it to Ashton, "Take a look at it."

Ashton took the ring from Jessica's hand and looked at it for several seconds. "This is…beautiful, You still don't know who brought it to you?"

Jessica shook her head, "Not a clue. Look at the markings on the ring. Do they look anything like what you've seen before?"

Ashton studied the ring's markings for a few moments, but was unable to recognize them. "You've got me, Jess. These markings are beyond anything I've ever seen before. We never studied anything like this in school."

Jessica nodded, "Exactly. I'd like to say it's an extinct language, but that doesn't make any sense. How would it still be around now? Its origins are clearly old…thousands of years old, if not older."

"Well, there's only so much we can do if we're going to find out what the language is." Ashton said, resting the ring on the desk, "Google would probably be our best bet. Let's see if we can find anything similar to these markings on the internet. There's bound to be something that reveals their origins."

Jessica nodded in agreement, "Right. I'll search on my laptop. Why don't you make yourself at home? We could be here for a while."

"Will do, Jess."

"Just take it easy on the food for now, okay?"

"You obviously don't know what "make yourself at home" really means."

Hours passed, but neither of the girls were able to find anything that even remotely resembled the markings on the ring, and they eventually gave up.

"Okay…either you're wrong about this being a language, or it's part of a civilization so old and forgotten about that there's no trace of it." Ashton said.

"Either that, or the people who made this ring decided they wanted to get really fancy with it." Jessica said, "Anyway, I think that's all I can handle for one day. My eyes are hurting from sitting in front of the screen for so long."

"Yeah, so are mine." Ashton said, squeezing the bridge of her nose, "I wasn't made for office work. That's for sure." She went around the apartment collecting the stuff she brought with her, "Well, I better get back home, Jess. Let me know if you find anything later."

"Okay, Ash. Be careful on your way home. I'll see you tomorrow."

Ashton nodded and walked out the door, leaving Jessica alone in her apartment.

"Well, that was a colossal waste of time." Jessica said, sighing as she collapsed onto her favorite reading chair. She sat in the chair for several minutes, staring up at the ceiling, trying to decide what she could do for the rest of the day. She looked at the clock on the wall, and saw it was only a little past five in the evening, giving her plenty of time to do something.

"Hmm.... I can't afford to waste any money. I'm stocked on food and drinks for right now, so food isn't much of a concern. If only work wasn't cancelled today." She hung her head down, and thought about what would happen if she didn't make enough money for the month. "Maybe I should give mom and dad a call, and see if they can loan some money. I'm going to need nothing short of a miracle as things stand now." She pondered for a while, but decided against it, "No. I'm an adult now. It's my responsibility to look after myself. Although, it wouldn't be a bad idea to contact them."

She stood from the chair, walked over to her laptop, opened her email, and checked to see if her mother had replied. To her relief, she had. She immediately opened the email, and started reading.

Dear Jessica

Hello, Jessica, I hope you're doing okay. I read your email a while ago, but I was never able to reply to it. I did as you requested to your brother, Scott, and he's not too pleased with you. He told me to tell you you'd better watch yourself next time he sees you. You two always crack me up with your constant pranks and other shenanigans you pull on each other. Your father also says hello, and we're going to try and send you some money in the future. Your friend, Ashton, contacted us and told us you were having money issues, but were too stubborn to call for help. You don't need to be ashamed to ask for help, Jessica, especially in the economic situations we're living in now. So don't try and make it on your own if you know you can't. But I applaud you for trying to remain independent, and be a grown up girl.

Well, California is preparing to surrender to the Rebels. There's talk that the Rebels will invade Cali in the near future, but California is just too weak to continue fighting, regardless of what the state governor and President Lane say. Rural areas aren't putting up with the nonsense anymore, and are threatening to stop producing food for the state if they don't surrender. But by the way things are sounding, the war will be over soon. The Rebels have a new person in command, and it's said this guy isn't messing around.

My battery is running low, so I'll have to end the email here.

Love Mom

Jessica smiled, and started typing her response.

5/13/2030

Dear Mother

It's good to hear from you again. I'm sorry I've been so stubborn, but I just hate to ask you and dad for help after you've done so much for me already. I have to admit I'm a little annoyed at Ashton, but I can see she was concerned about me and, only wanted to help. She's a true friend, and has always had my back. She re-enforced dad's lessons by telling me that when you feel like you've hit bottom, the only place to go is up. I wish I could tell you to keep your money, but who am I kidding? I'm desperate now. So thank you in advance for the money. I only need eight-hundred dollars, and that will cover it. I don't want you to send more than what's necessary. You've worked hard to be where you are now, and I want to work hard for my living, too.

So California is going to surrender to the Rebels? I can't say I'm surprised. California joining the United States of the Republic would be the smartest thing the people of that state have ever done. But will the Rebels keep California? That's the real question."

Anyway, you won't believe what happened today. I received a strange package from a stranger that turned out to be the most beautiful ring I've ever seen. It's gold with rubies, and what Ashton and I believed to be a language written on the bend. However, we weren't able to find out what the language is. We think it may just be a fancy design the people who made it came up with, and doesn't really mean anything. It's such a beautiful ring, though. In fact, I think I'll just send you a picture.

I assume you know what's happened in D.C by now. The Washington Monument was hit by a missile, and maybe also the Capital building. Last I knew, the police and military had the place completely sealed off, and keeping people away. There might actually be something reported now, but I've had my mind in other places today.

I hope you, Dad, and Scott remain safe.

Your loving daughter
Jessica

Jessica took a picture of the ring, copied it to her computer, attached its file to the message, sent the message, closed out of the internet, and started writing in her diary, listing the events of what happened during the day and past night.

CHAPTER 6

Overseers of Death

Dallas FT. Worth, Texas: Carswell Rebel
Supply Base, 60 hours (1:00 A.M)

Escorted by six Rebel Cobras, President Davis and two generals made their way to a meeting room where they were to meet with their superiors about a new tactic for taking Washington D.C. Though the attack had certainly made a few things clear to the media and President Lane's administration, President Davis and a number of generals within the Rebellion were uncomfortable about attacking the United States former capital city. Few people near the Washington Monument were hurt, but there were several casualties outside the Capitol Building, leaving many in the Rebellion feeling uneasy about the superior's methods. For that reason, President Davis drastically wanted to bluntly speak his mind to his superior. However, he also knew doing this would likely be the end of him.

The Cobras took a sharp turn to the left down another corridor, and all the way to the end where they opened the door to the meeting room, a large dark room with an enormous table in the middle. The far right wall was actually an enormous television screen that was already showing some of the things President Davis and the generals were about to discuss. There were already several other generals in the room from the different factions that made up the Rebel military, including a large number of Rebel Cobras and Phantoms, dressed in full body armor, and heavily armed.

The Cobras escorting President Davis parted from formation, and took their assigned places to stand guard along the walls. President Davis and the generals took their seats and studied the plans being shown on the large TV. President Davis couldn't make much sense of it, but looking at the numerous generals in the room, he could tell they were, to say the least, very impressed with what they saw. Just as he was about to open his mouth and say something, the main double doors to the room slammed open, and three men dressed in hooded cloaks entered the room and made their way to the TV screen. The Cobras and Phantoms stood at attention as they passed by, and President Lane and the generals stood up.

A darker aura than usual seemed to enter the room, making everyone feel uncomfortable. President Davis started to sweat, and he couldn't help but feel he was in some serious trouble as he watched the men make their way to the front of the room. Once the men were in position, there was a long pause that seemed like an eternity, and President Davis started to hold his breath.

The main commander, the man dressed in a tattered solid black cloak, looked around the room for a few moments, making sure everyone was in place. After a very long time, he finally motioned for everyone to sit down. Everyone in the room started breathing again.

"As most of you know by now, we're not ones for making long speeches, so I'm going to make this quick and to the point." The main commander said in a chilling a voice, "As you can see on the screen behind me, I've put my plans for attacking Washington into play. Our forces we dispatched from the West to the East will be arriving soon, and with them will be some new prototypes of vehicles which are nearing the end of their final tests as we speak. From there, our forces will split into four main armies. The first will consist of forty-thousand men, and will take the bulk of our older weapons and vehicles to attack Richmond, Virginia to the south while the other two go around and attack from the East and North. These armies will be smaller in number, but will only serve to keep the military from moving north and attacking the fourth army. This will also serve as a distraction to keep the media from reporting our fourth army. This army is going to take a straight shot at Washington, and will consist of only our most elite factions in the Rebellion. These units will have the privilege of testing our new weapons and vehicles, which are EMP resistant and undetectable by radar. We have three new jet designs, five new helicopter designs, ten new fast attack vehicle designs, and one new heavy armored tank. The tanks will not roll into the city until the jets complete their third objective, and our infantry storm into the streets. The Washington Police Department and a small number of military personnel are all that stand between us and victory. The one and only job the generals will have is coordinating the attack on Richmond. You have several Battalions of artillery and heavy armor at your disposal. Messages have already been sent to the city saying our forces will be there soon, and many people have already started leaving, and the military is preparing fortifications of the city. Whether you actually invade the city or just siege it, is up to you. But once you start your bombardments, no one is allowed in or out of the city. Is that clear?"

All of the generals nodded slowly.

"Good. Now prepare your plans. You're in for a few sleepless nights." The commander said. He turned to face one of the other men and started talking to him.

President Davis stood up and called out to one of the generals. The general turned to face him, "Yes, sir?"

"Just to let you know, the ones you requested arrived on the base shortly before this meeting started. They should be making their way here in just a few short minutes." Said President Davis.

"Really? Very well, then. I'll inform the commander."

President Davis nodded, and continued out the door.

The general waited a few moments, thinking about how he would approach the subject. Once he thought it through, he turned towards the commander, took a few steps toward him, and spoke, "Commander?"

The commander turned to face the general with such a cold stare it made his blood run cold, "What is it, General?"

"Um...I just wanted to let you know that the ones you requested have arrived on base and should be here shortly." The general said.

"Good. Bring them in immediately." The commander said.

"No need sir. They're already here."

Just then, four men dressed in some of the Rebellion's finest body armor, face masks, and heavily armed with sniper rifles, pistols, and knives walked into the room, "Overseers of Death, reporting in, sir." The presumed leader of the group said.

The commander observed the men for a few moments, "So these are the ones I requested?"

"Yes, sir, these men are what make up the Overseers of Death." The general said, turning his attention to the group of men, "The most elite sniper unit in the Rebellion. Over six-hundred confirmed kills as a unit, five accomplished assassinations, and are responsible for the bombing of the military's largest supply base."

"I'm aware of who they are, general." The commander said. He motioned for the men to come to him.

The men consisting of the Overseers looked at each other, then made their way down to the commander, "You have a mission for us, sir?"

"I do." The commander said, reaching into his cloak for something, then pulling it out, "I want you to go to Washington D.C where you will safeguard this woman." He handed the group leader a picture.

The leader of the group took the picture from the commander's hand and studied it, "What's her purpose?"

"The details aren't important, and are on a need to know profile." The commander said, "All you need to do is protect this woman while staying out of sight. You will not interact with her directly, nor will you let her know you're following her. Is that clear? You will follow this woman, learn her daily schedule, and keep watch over her as she goes about her daily life. She has certain...interest to our order, and we do not want her harmed in any way."

"We're not running an assassination mission?" The squad leader asked, "We're trained to kill, sir, not babysit."

"You'll have plenty of killing to do later on." The commander said, "Now gather any gear or provisions you deem necessary. You'll be leaving in a few hours."

"Understood, sir." The squad leader said. He saluted, stepped back from the commander, and led his squad out the door.

In the corner of his eye, he could see the General still standing in his spot, "Do you have anything else to bring to my attention, General?" He asked.

"No sir."

"Then what are you doing standing around? You've got work to do." The commander said in a cold tone.

"Er...yes, sir!" The general saluted, and quickly left the room.

Once there was no one else in the room, one of the other members of the Unknown Order stepped up to the commander's side, "Are you sure sending the Overseers of Death to D.C is really such a good idea? They're better suited on the field and taking lives than they are for recon."

"The Overseers of Death will work just fine." The commander said, "Besides, she's something we can't afford to lose. I assume you've sensed it, too."

The other man nodded, "Yes. Our enemies are preparing to move. They must be looking for her as well. Which can mean only one thing..."

"We're running out of time." The commander said, "Every day we waste on this pathetic civil war brings us one day closer to them mobilizing their army and beginning their attacks. As things stand now, we have a huge disadvantage. By the beginning of next week, Washington will have fallen. But then there's the issue of the newer generations. These younger generations are not exactly what I would call a perfect fighting force. Most of them have never had to face any kind of discipline in their lives. We saw what happened when Trump won the presidency a few years back. However, once the draft is called, their "opinions" on certain matters won't matter any longer."

"Rebel relations with countries around the world only continue to strengthen. Once we declare what the real danger is, there won't be many who question what we say." The other man said.

"Speaking of which…it's about time we announce ourselves to the public. We don't need to be seen yet, but it's time the world knows who's really in control of the Rebellion."

"Agreed. It's time we announce ourselves."

"Very well. I'll have President Davis meet with another reporter soon and have him announce the name of our order to the public."

CHAPTER 7

Ring of Nightmares

After closing hours, Jessica stayed several hours in the flower shop trying to earn a little overtime. She took stock of the plants in the store room, and watered every plant in the store, which took more time than she expected. Even though she was supposed to receive some money from her parents, she wanted to play it safe and earn as much money as possible before the end of the month, which was the end of next week. Once she was finished, and had done everything she could do, she clocked out, and closed the shop.

"Whew! I never would have thought it, but the flower shop is actually kind of creepy when you're there alone," she thought to herself as she locked the door. She put the keys in her jean pocket, and started walking in the direction of her apartment. She held her hand over her stomach as it growled, just noticing how much time had passed, "Dang, it's already getting close to night time." She said out loud while looking at the sky, "I better hurry home. This isn't exactly the safest place after dark." She set her watch, and started running down the sidewalk to her apartment, racing both her time, and what little light the sun was still putting out.

Once she arrived at her apartment, Jessica ended her time, and compared it to her best time.

"Darn it! If I'd gotten here two seconds faster I'd have a new best time. But that's what I get for over shooting a corner." She said, disappointed with herself. She took the keys to the shop out of her pocket, and sat them on the counter next to the door, and started preparing something to eat. She gathered some fruit, crackers, and poured herself a glass of apple juice. Her stomach started to growl more intensely, demanding she start eating immediately. She put everything on a plate, and carried it over to her writing desk, where she watched a few YouTube videos on her laptop as she ate, and worked a little on her novel. However, the mysterious ring that was lying next to the computer caught her eye, and she started to focus all her attention on it.

"Just where did you come from, anyway?" She said out loud as she picked up the ring and looked at the weird markings on the bend, "You're certainly unique, but at the same time…you don't feel quite right." Curiosity getting the best of her, she slid the ring on her ring finger, and was shocked to find out it was a perfect fit. "Well…I guess it's not too out of the ordinary for a random ring to be a perfect fit, but the fact this was brought to me by a stranger whose identity I have no idea of…this is more creepy than anything else."

She started to slide the ring off, but a feeling she had was telling her to leave it on. She stared at the ring for a few seconds, conflicting with the feeling, and eventually shrugged her shoulders, "Well, it's just a ring. What's the worst that could happen? …she says, forgetting about the entire Lord of the Rings plot." She shook her head, clearing her thoughts, and returned her attention to her novel.

Having reached a good stopping point, Jessica saved the progress she had made on her book, and closed her laptop. She stood from the desk, stretched her arms above her head, and tried thinking of something else to do. After pondering for a while, she looked at the time, decided to call it a day, and prepared to take a shower.

After finishing her shower, and preparing herself for bed, Jessica stood next to her bed, staring at the ring that was still on her finger.

She couldn't quite explain why to herself, but there was something that just didn't feel right about the ring.

"I'm probably just being superstitious." She told herself. She stopped looking at the ring, went around her apartment turning off the lights, and got into bed.

What sounded like heavy breathing woke Jessica from her slumber. She rolled over to look in the direction the breathing was coming from, and saw a terrifying sight. Standing in front of her door was the outline of a figure. Fear overcame her, and she went numb. The figure started to slowly walk towards her, bringing tears to her eyes. The breathing was a low pitched other worldly demonic sound, and it only intensified as the figure started to draw closer. Slowly, the figure crept towards her, taking slow, small steps, making it all the more terrifying.

Just as the figure approached her bed, Jessica managed to gather the courage she needed, reached under her pillow where she hid a steak knife, and leaped at the figure. But before impact, the figure disbursed into a cloud of black smoke, and she suddenly found herself falling into a black void. She screamed as loud as she could as she fell, and eventually landed on the side of a hill, and started rolling for the bottom. Part of her wanted to stop, but another part of her wanted to keep going, fearing the dark figure she saw was still following her.

Once she reached the bottom of the hill, Jessica kept her momentum, and used gravity to her advantage as she did several summersaults, followed by three back flips, dropping into a fighting stance as she slid backwards on her feet. But to her relief, the figure was gone, which eased her a bit. She laughed nervously, and looked around trying to figure out where she was.

"Um…how did I get here?" She asked herself as she looked around, "This definitely isn't D.C." She turned around and looked up the hill she had just rolled down, "Maybe I can get a better sense of where I am if I climb the hill." She nodded to herself, and started running up the hill as fast as she could.

Once she reached the top, she was able to confirm she wasn't in D.C anymore...not even the United States.

"W-what is this?!"

In the distance was the Iranian capital city, Tehran. The city was the center of a major conflict between two massive armies. Even though she was miles away, the sounds of battle could still be heard. One after another, black columns of smoke rose to the sky, and the thunder of explosions could be heard farther away.

Taking her by surprise, several fighter jets flying at low altitude flew over her, the roar of their engines nearly deafening her, but they were fighter jets she recognized.

"Those are fighter jets that belong to the Rebellion!" She said in awe as she watched them disappear into the distance.

Another wave of fighter jets roared overhead, but this time they were followed by carpet bombers. Jessica watched as the fighter jets broke off from formation, and the three carpet bombers emptied their payload on the ground outside the city where she assumed a large number of troops on the opposing side were hunkered down and causing some problems. However, after that, the unthinkable happened. There was a blinding flash of white light, followed by a loud bang and a mushroom cloud rising to the sky. The city was leveled, and both armies were wiped out. Jessica's eyes widened, and she started racing down the hill, but a strong gust of wind hit her back, sending her flying through the air like a ragdoll. She slammed hard on the ground, badly hurting her arm. She winced at the pain, and lay on the ground for several minutes, trying to gather her confusion into logical thought but millions of questions being asked at once.

After several minutes, Jessica was able to stand up, but her arm felt like it was broken, after the fall. She growled at the pain, but curiosity was more important to her than an injured arm. She slowly made her way back up the hill to see was going on. Once she reached the top, she witnessed total devastation. The city skyline was gone, and the night sky looked like a river of molten lava in the deepest reaches of Hell. She stood speechless, overlooking the destruction and wreckage of the past battle.

Wanting a closer look, Jessica started down the hill, but something caught her eye. Thick columns of black smoke started to rise to the sky, but started to take an unnatural shape. The smoke made several patterns, drawing something, and after several seconds, the smoke had created what looked like giant closed eyes. Just as she started to open her mouth to say something, the eyes opened, and looked directly at her,

I SEE YOUUUU

Terrified beyond what she thought was possible, Jessica screamed as loud as she could, and started running as fast as she could in the opposite direction. She stopped and slid on the ground once she saw the eyes were behind her too. She backed away slowly, but backed against a tree that wasn't there before, "What the?!"

Before she could finish, the branches of the tree wrapped around her mouth, arms, legs, stomach, and neck, trapping her.

Lightning struck the ground in front of her, and the dark figure she saw before appeared. Standing in front of her was a tall hooded skeletal being. She tried to break from the tree, screaming as she struggled, but stopped once she noticed the figure was standing inches in front of her. She breathed heavily, terrified, not knowing what the being's intentions were.

Without warning, the skeletal being grabbed her cheeks, and inspected her face. It brought its face closer to hers, and licked her right cheek with a long tongue that was split at the end like a lizard. Jessica closed her eyes as it happened, holding her breath, but a bright flash made her open her eyes again to see the figure was gone, but a wicked and terrifying evil laugh echoed through the sky.

I'VE FOUND YOU, DAUGHTER OF FORAYER!

The tree released its hold on Jessica, causing her to fall to the ground. She scampered away from the tree as quickly as she could, but was blocked by someone standing in front of her. She looked up only to see another terrifying sight. In front of her was a tall man, nearly twice her height, with pale white skin, extremely long black hair that went halfway down his back, and hid the right half of his face. He had a sinister smile with fanglike teeth and glowing yellow eyes.

Jessica yelped and crawled backwards as fast as she could to get away from the man, but he followed her. She backed herself against the tree again, trapping herself with no escape.

The man approached Jessica, grabbed her by her hair, and pulled her up to his level. Her feet were hanging several inches off the ground, but she couldn't do anything but scream from the pain. He pulled her close and whispered something in her ear in a language she didn't recognize, and then threw her to the side where she slid several meters on the ground, hitting her injured arm against a large rock, forcing her to scream in pain again.

The man laughed, stared at her in a way that more than creeped her out, and disappeared with a flash of lightning.

Too injured to move, and terrified by what just happened, Jessica stayed on the ground, and slipped into unconsciousness after several minutes.

Jessica shot up in her bed, screaming as loud as her lungs would allow with tears rolling down her cheeks. She nervously looked around her apartment for anything out of the ordinary. She turned on the lamp next to her bed, and lay on her back trying to catch her breath over the experience she just had.

"It was just a dream." She told herself, resting her right hand on her forehead, wiping away some sweat. She took a deep breath, held it for a few seconds, and released it, trying to calm her nerves. She held her hands out, and saw they were shaking like crazy.

"What was that? That was the worst dream I'd ever had!" She said out loud. She took another deep breath to calm her nerves, stood from her bed, and walked to the kitchen where she poured some water into a glass. With just a few swallows, the water was gone, and she walked back to her bedroom where she crawled into bed and tried to fall asleep again, leaving her lamp on.

The following day, Jessica ran the cash register at the flower shop.

"What a perfect time to have had the worst nightmare of my life" She thought. She yawned and leaned against the counter, waiting for the next customer. She watched the man take his time selecting what she presumed were his wife's or girlfriend's favorite flowers, and eventually making his way to her.

"Good afternoon, sir. Did you find everything okay?" Jessica asked as she brought up his price.

"Yeah, I think that's it." The man said, reaching into his pocket for his wallet, "You seem to be having a good time today."

"I don't think that's the word I would use." Jessica said, yawning shortly after, "let's just say last night wasn't particularly fun for me."

"Nightmares?" The man asked, handing his money to Jessica.

Jessica nodded, and gave the man his change, "Like nothing I've ever experienced in my life. It felt so...real. Like I was actually there. I don't really remember what it was about, but I remember that...thing standing over me." She shivered as the memory of the man in her dream came back to her.

"Well, it's over now." The man said with a kind smile. He tipped his hat to her, "You take care now."

Jessica smiled kindly, "Yeah, you, too." She watched him leave the shop, and turned her attention to Ashton who was walking her way.

"So what's wrong with you, Jess? Did you see what you look like without any makeup on this morning?" Ashton asked.

"Oh, ha ha, Ashton, very funny." Jessica mocked back, "You should see what you look like without makeup on sometime."

"I have, and I have to say I don't look a lot different." Ashton said.

"Maybe from your perspective." Jessica said between coughs.

"Hey! You watch it, Jessica!" Ashton said, "Anyway, what's wrong? You don't seem like yourself today. The day's halfway over, and you haven't tried to insult me nearly as much as you do regularly."

"Well, where do I start?" Jessica asked as she stopped leaning on the counter, "All I can say is that last night I had the absolute worst nightmare in my entire life. I don't remember most of it, but I remember being beaten by some kind of...demon or some other terrifying creature."

"Really? Do you remember what it looked like? Was it any kind of connection to that horror movie we watched a while back?" Ashton asked curiously.

Jessica shook her head and crossed her arms, "No. This was worse. He...or...it...had pale white skin, glowing yellow eyes, and long black hair. It stood at nearly twice my height, and was extremely strong. I remember it picked me up by the hair and whispered something in my ear in a language I didn't recognize, and I swear I could feel the pain from my hair being pulled when I woke up."

Ashton's eyes widened in interest, "Did... did he say anything else to you?" She asked.

Jessica thought for few moments as she recalled her dream, "I think he did, actually. Right at the end he called me something. He called me....a...'daughter of Forayer'. I have no idea what that means."

"Neither do I." Ashton said, "I don't even know the name of Forayer from any of the fantasy novels, games, or movies I know."

"It was more than terrifying." Jessica said as she lowered her head, "I can't get his face out of my head. I can still see that sick smile he gave me before I opened my eyes."

Ashton rested her hand on Jessica's shoulders, "Cheer up, Jess. I've known you for a long time now, and I know a dream isn't something that'll bring you down. Once we're off work, the girls and I will take you a few places to clear your mind, and we'll all have a great time." Jessica smiled, and put her hand on Ashton's hand, "Thanks, Ash. I must sound pretty silly."

"Not at all. If that…thing was that scary to you, I'll take your word for it." Ashton said, "Anyway, I'm going to head to the back and take stock again. We should be getting another truck here soon."

"Okay. Talk to you later, Ash."

Later on, Jessica and her friends spent the better part of their evening window shopping, and hanging out at their favorite restaurant.

"So how'd the overtime go last night, Jess?" Jasmine asked, taking a sip of her drink. The girls were sitting at an outside table, using the shade to keep the sun out of their eyes.

"Oh, it went okay." Jessica said, "The shop's kind of creepy when you're there by yourself, but other than that it went fine."

"That's good. How is your family doing?" Jasmine asked.

"They're doing fine, but my mom told me some news I found a little…disturbing." Jessica said, gaining everyone's attention, "Supposedly, they're saying the Rebels will be invading California soon. Once they get more men stationed along the border, another army is going to run through Cali."

"Do you believe it?" Ashton asked in a skeptical tone with a raised eyebrow.

"Well…not really." Jessica said as she exhaled loudly, "I don't really see why they would other than just gaining some new land. California is too weak to stand on its own. Not only that, the Rebels are pushing closer and closer to Richmond every day. Why would they waste the resources taking Cali? It doesn't make any sense to me."

"It's probably just rumors being spread by the fearful." Krista said, "I mean, I don't pay a lot of attention to politics, but even I know there's little point for the Rebels to invade California at this point. When they're literally just weeks from reaching D.C? I'd be surprised if they did it, but I'm not a Rebel general or political leader."

"Well, they'd have plenty to gain by taking California, and the Rebels have a lot of support from rural areas and smaller towns. But…I don't know. Like Krista said, I'm not a general in the Rebellion, so whatever happens, I guess."

"Well, anyway, have either of you two seen Jessica's new ring?" Ashton asked, "It's a beauty."

"Oh, let's not get started on that thing." Jessica said, "It's just a ring."

"But it's a very beautiful ring." Ashton said, "Seriously, you guys have to see it. It's very intriguing."

Krista made a funny face as she thought about something, then looked at Ashton, "Um...how can a ring be 'intriguing'? That's a word I've never heard describe a ring before."

"Well, long story short, it has these weird markings going along the bend." Ashton said, "At first, Jessica and I thought it was some kind of language, but we weren't able to find anything that even came remotely close to the markings on the ring."

"Hmm...that is interesting." Krista said, "I wonder if it's a part of some kind of collection. Who gave it to you, Jess?"

"No idea." Jessica said, shaking her head. She took a drink of her water before she continued, "I got a call from the lobby saying there was a man who wanted to see me, but when I got down there he'd already left. He left me a package with no name or return address, I opened the package, and it turned out to be the ring."

"No note or anything?" Jasmine asked.

Jessica shook her head, "Nothing of the sort."

"That's.... not creepy at all." Krista said sarcastically, "Personally, I wouldn't have taken the darn thing. For all I know, it could have been a bomb of some kind."

"Well...that's true. But what's done is done. You can't change the past...even though we'd love to more often than not." Jessica said.

The girls laughed at the joke and focused on eating their meals for a while.

"So who's hosting the party this weekend?" Jasmine asked, looking around the table.

"I believe it's my turn now." Krista said, "I hope so anyway. I already have everything set up. I have the food, drinks, movies and games all ready."

"Already? Looks like we finally have an over achiever in the group." Ashton said. She looked at Jessica and continued, "It's about time we had one to counter this lazy bum's habits."

"Oh, har har, Ashton." Jessica said, "You're always so funny that I forget how to laugh at your jokes."

"Hey, at least I can joke!" Ashton replied, "You guys should see my parents. They can't joke to save their lives...especially my mom. She couldn't make a decent joke at all."

"She made you." Jessica said, trying not to burst out into laughter, despite her face turning bright red. However, Jasmine and Krista laughed long and hard.

Ashton's mouth hung wide open, and she seemed to be completely frozen, which forced Jessica to start laughing as well. After several seconds, Krista managed to pull herself together, looked at Ashton and said, "Would you like some ice for that burn, Ashton?"

"Yeah, let's see you top that one!" Jasmine managed to say, even though she was still laughing.

"I....I....I'll think of something...eventually." Ashton said.

"You take your sweet time, Ashton. I'll be waiting for a better comeback." Jessica said, giggling a bit.

"Damn, that's going to be a tough one." Ashton said, "I suppose I'll look back and laugh at it one day, though."

"Well, we're laughing at it right now." Krista said, erupting into a fit of laughter again.

"Oh, yeah, sure, ha ha, we'll see who has the last laugh!" Ashton said, pointing at Jessica.

"Well, I can already see one flaw with your plans, Ashton." Jessica said, calmly taking another bite out of her meal.

"And what would that be?" Ashton asked.

Jessica took a sip of her drink, and rubbed her napkin on her lips, "You're a blonde." She finally said in a calm voice.

"...Jessica... I hate you sometimes."

Back in her apartment, Jessica closed her laptop after finishing another chapter in her novel, and started to prepare for bed. Once she was ready, she turned off all the lights in her apartment, and dimmed the lamp next to her bed. She rolled over, facing the opposite direction of the lamp, closed her eyes, and fell into a heavy slumber.

"Hey, Jessica…JESSICA!"

Jessica opened her eyes to find she was lying on her back in the National Mall with her friends under a tree. She sat up and looked around, confused by how she got there.

"Hey, Jess, welcome back to the world of the living." Ashton said, handing her a drink, "You've been out for the past ten minutes."

Jessica took the drink from Ashton's hand, still confused on what was going on, "Is this another dream?" She asked herself quietly, "It feels so…real." She watched as Ashton tossed an apple to Krista.

"Hey, Krista, excellent party last night. I love your apartment, and the food you served."

Krista smiled and took a bite out of the apple, "Hey, thanks, Ashton. I'm glad you liked what I did for you guys. What did you think of the movie?"

"It was pretty good. But not as good as the one you picked for Jessica's party." Ashton said.

Krista laughed, "Well…yeah, I kind of have to agree with that. So any idea on why Shelby canceled work today?"

"I can answer that one for you, Krista." Jasmine said, "Shelby's parents live in Richmond."

"Oh…ohhh! I get it now." Krista said.

Too confused to say anything, Jessica just let things play out without opening her mouth.

"So…have the Rebels invaded the city yet?" Jasmine asked.

Ashton shook her head, "No. The battle is taking place on the outskirts of the city now, but the Rebels holding Richmond under siege. Nothing is allowed in or out of the city."

"Well, that's not good. I guess it's only a matter of days now before The Rebels are here." Krista said.

"Wait…do you guys see that?" Jasmine said, pointing at the horizon in the sky.

The girls looked where Jasmine was pointing, but couldn't see anything.

"See what, Jasmine? I can't see anything." Ashton said.

Jasmine stood up, and held her hand up to block the sun, "There's a small speck on the horizon. It looks like a….a plane."

"Well…the airport is just over there, Jasmine." Krista said, pointing in the direction of the airport.

"Yeah, but why would it be approaching the airport at this angle?" Jasmine asked, "There's no runway facing this way."

Suddenly, Jessica could see what Jasmine was pointing to, "I see it." She said as she stood up, "Um…that plane is approaching fast, and from the direction of the Rebellion's front line."

"What?!" Ashton stood up and looked in the same direction

"It's getting closer." Jessica said. She and her friends watched as the plane flew overhead. Moments later several missiles were shot at the Capitol Building, making their jaws drop. The missiles exploded, and suddenly the world went completely dark around her.

She looked around, completely confused about the situation, and readied herself for the unexpected. She stood in place for several minutes waiting for something to happen, dreading the thought of seeing the man in her previous dream. She took a few steps forward, but was then held in place by fear, and couldn't move.

"Wha…what's going on?" She said, struggling to get free from whatever was holding her. As she struggled, she saw the outline of a figure slowly making its way towards her. Fearing it was the man from her previous dream, her eyes widened in fear, and she started to struggle harder, trying to free herself. She looked at the figure again, and saw that there were now three figures approaching her. She watched as another four emerged from the darkness all around her, and circled around her. Terrified, she closed her eyes and waited for something to happen.

The seven figures stopped circling her, and each placed their hands on her shoulders, making her open her eyes. She looked at the figure on her right and saw a familiar face.

"…Chris?" Jessica's eyes filled with tears, and she tried grabbing his hand, but he vanished just before their hands made contact, leaving her alone in a void of darkness.

Trembling, Jessica fell to her knees, and started to cry, "Why? Why is this happening? What have I done to deserve this?!"

A strong gust of wind caught Jessica's attention, just before it sent her flying in the opposite direction. She flew several feet from where she was previously, and hovered a couple of meters above the ground. Her back slammed against the wall of a building, forcing her to scream painfully. She was dazed, but managed to finally clear her head by shaking it a few times. She looked up and saw she was now in the middle of a city that had been torn apart by a serious battle. She looked around for several minutes before hearing the most blood chilling sound she'd ever heard.

A terrifying screech echoed in the distance, making Jessica instantly freeze in place shaking. She stared in the direction the screech came from, and not long after, a figure came flying out of a building, slamming through the wall of another building several meters down the street. Another figure soon followed, and clanging sounds echoed through the sky. An evil presence made the atmosphere uncomfortable, and the sky was a hellish red color.

Another screech, far louder than the previous one, echoed through the city. Jessica looked in the direction it came from, just in time to see the body of a man flying towards her at incredible speed. She ducked just in time but felt his body slide across her back. She watched as he went flying through the building behind her. Struck by awe of the power being demonstrated in front of her, she blinked in amazement, then looked in the direction the man came from to see a tall black figure with wings walking towards her. She looked down at a leaf that was lying on the ground in front of her and saw it slowly curl and die. Her eyes widened as she looked around and noticed everything was dying. Trees were withered and leafless, the grass along the sidewalks was turning brown, and even the air seemed to die around her. She looked at the figure again and saw it was holding something in its right hand.

"What's that? It's...it's a scythe. That can mean only one thing. This thing is..." She looked up as the figure released an even more terrifying screech, held out its hand, and released a giant ball of fire at her. She closed her eyes and finished her thought,

"This is Death. This...is the way the world ends."

The fire ball made impact around her, spreading fire several blocks throughout the city.

Jessica woke up screaming loudly, with her hands covering her face. She waited several seconds, waiting for fire to surround her, but lowered them when she realized nothing was happening. She looked around her room nervously, looking for anything that was out of place. She laughed nervously, sighing in relief before falling on her back, and closing her eyes again, telling herself it was just another dream.

CHAPTER 8

Proposition

Joining Ashton and Krista after work at their favorite hangout place, Jessica claimed her seat at an outdoor table under a large umbrella, and listened as Krista and Ashton finished their conversation.

"And what's the name of the book again?" Krista asked.

"Mages of the North." Ashton said, handing Krista a torn piece of paper with the name written on it, "Easily one of the best books I've ever read." She looked at Jessica as she continued, "She'd agree, too."

Jessica nodded at Krista, "Very good series if you're into fantasies. It's a long book series, and the books are nearly a thousand pages each, but you'll fly through them pretty quickly."

"How long is the series?" Krista asked.

Jessica paused for a moment as she thought, "Hmm…well, right now there's only three books out, but the writer publishes two books at a time. If I recall correctly the next two books will be released fairly soon. Not fast enough, though."

"Yeah, that's the cold hard truth." Ashton said, leaning back in her chair, "That was an evil cliff hanger the writer left us with in the last book. Good grief!"

Jessica threw her head back laughing, "Yeah, it was! I still remember how ticked you were when you finished it, too! Hahaha!"

"Hey, now. You don't have a lot of room to be talking either, you know." Ashton said, glaring at Jessica, trying not to laugh, even though her face was turning red.

Still laughing, Jessica could only nod at Ashton's response. She wiped the tears from her eyes and tried regaining her composure, "So what did you two order?"

"The usual." Ashton said, "A meat and veggie mixed pizza with some cinnamon sticks. What do you plan on ordering?"

Jessica picked up the menu and skimmed through the list of meals, "Well…hmm…I'm not really hungry. But I suppose I'll order some spaghetti."

"Um…I thought you said you weren't hungry." Ashton said with a confused look on her face, "I mean…you know how big the meals are here, right?"

"Yeah, but maybe I'll want some later on." Jessica said, laying the menu down, and taking a drink of water.

"Hmm…true. Anyway, have you discovered anything new about the ring?" Ashton asked.

Jessica shook her head, "No. I've actually given up on it. I can't find a single thing that comes even close to talking about its origins or the culture it came from. Not only is that strange, but I'm also starting to think the thing is cursed, too."

Ashton stared at Jessica blankly for a moment before saying, "You know there's no such thing as curses, right? I thought you got over that after watching the remake of the Grudge movies."

"Well, look, I'll tell you what's going on." Jessica said as she leaned in closer to Ashton and Krista, "Every time I put the ring on while I'm sleeping, I have these terrible nightmares. Ashton, I told you about the tall slender man with the pale skin, and the warzone, right? Well, there was another one where the Grim Reaper appeared in my dream, and attacked me."

"And why does that make the ring cursed?" Ashton asked curiously.

"Because these feel like they're more than dreams." Jessica said, "I can't describe why, but these nightmares don't feel like dreams at all. I swear I can feel what I'm touching, I can feel the heat of the flames, and I can feel the air coming into my lungs as I breathe." She paused as she thought back to one of the dreams, "That dream with the skeletal figure and the tall man...he grabbed me by the throat and lifted me into the air...when I woke up, I could feel where his hands were on my neck, and my arm hurt after being thrown at a rock."

"How bad did your arm hurt?" Krista asked in a shaky voice.

Jessica rolled her eyes to Krista, and could tell she was scared from her story. She thought about Krista's question and answered. "Like it had been slammed into a rock. Not quite broken, but it still hurt really badly."

"Wow...that's...actually kind of scary." Krista said, "Are you sure you weren't just imagining it?"

Jessica stared at Krista and said, "Feeling that kind of pain? I doubt that was my imagination."

"But why wouldn't it hurt now?" Ashton asked.

Jessica looked at Ashton, and then looked at her arm, "Hmm... that's a good question. It didn't hurt for very long after I woke up from the dream, but..."

Krista remained silent for a moment, then said, "Is it possible you just hit your arm against the end table next to your bed?"

Jessica shook her head, "No. My arm wouldn't have hurt nearly as bad as it did from hitting my end table."

"Hmm... Well, you must've done something, Jess." Ashton said, "It's not that I don' believe your story, but...it's not exactly within the realms of reality..."

"No, it's fine. I perfectly understand why you'd be skeptical, but I know what I felt." Jessica said, still looking at her arm, "I mean...I don't know how else to describe what happened."

"It'd probably be best if you didn't to be honest." Krista said, "I'm a strong believer in the supernatural, and I'd very much like to be able to go to sleep tonight."

Jessica looked at Krista for a moment, then looked at her arm again and nodded, "Yeah...that's probably enough of this discussion, anyway."

Ashton nodded in agreement and turned to face Krista, "So I see on your blog you've maybe found a boy?"

Krista turned to Ashton and said, "Well…not really. More than anything, I was actually saying he was kind enough to help me with a few things. However, I guess I did say he was fairly attractive."

"What was his name?" Jessica asked.

"Ivis…something. I don't remember his last name, but it was kind of an odd one." Krista said.

"What did he look like?" Ashton aske.

"Like he was out of your league." Krista smirked.

Ashton's jaw dropped, and Jessica almost busted out laughing, but managed to cover her mouth in time. Slowly, Ashton started to smile, and she looked off in a random direction, "Well…that was harsh."

"Oh, man. That was a good one, Krista." Jessica managed to say, even though she was still laughing.

"I…I can't top that one. Geeze, that was ten times worse than any insult Jessica has given me." Ashton said.

"I'm sorry, but I couldn't resist." Krista giggled, "You just left yourself open for that, and I couldn't let it slip by."

"Apparently not!" Ashton said, "That one left a mark. Ouch!"

Jessica managed to control herself, and stopped laughing, "And there goes whatever dignity Ashton had left." She said, cracking another laugh.

Ashton released a sarcastic laugh and looked at Jessica, "Ha-ha-ah! The joke's on you, Ms. Holland, I lost my dignity and pride the moment I met you."

Jessica rolled her eyes and rested her face in her palm as she leaned on the table, "Oh, come now. We both know that's not true. It was gone way before I came into your life."

"Well….yeah, I suppose that's true to a certain extent." Ashton said.

The girls laughed at each other's jokes for a while, and continued talking about random things throughout the evening.

After parting ways with her friends, Jessica started making her way back to her apartment. Along the way, she stopped at a local corner grocery store where she hunted down some things she needed. She grabbed a shopping cart, went to the back, and zigzagged her way through aisles back up to the front. Once she'd gotten everything she needed, she made her way to the checkout area where there was a line of three people ahead of her.

"Great. I was hoping I could just pop in here, and get back out." She thought annoyingly.

She shrugged her shoulders, dismissing her thoughts, and grabbed a magazine off the shelf next to her. She skimmed the pages, keeping an eye on the people ahead of her while she read, and put the magazine back on the shelf once it was almost her turn.

However, some audio coming from the TV above her caught her attention, and she took a few steps forward so she could see the screen clearly. Her eyes widened, once she read the headlines:

President Davis Says Rebellion Is Not To Blame For Attack On D.C

On the TV screen, President Davis was in an interview with a CNN reporter who was in the process of asking him some questions.

"So, you're saying there's another group in command of the Rebellion?" The Reporter asked.

President Davis nodded, "Yes, that's correct. I'm only at liberty to tell a very limited amount of detail about them, though."

"So...you claim this new organization are the supreme commanders of the Rebellion, and are the ones who ordered the attacks on the Washington Monument and Capitol Building. Does this organization have a name? How much can you tell us about them?"

President Davis remained silent for a moment as he thought about his answer, then returned his attention to the reporter, "The organization is run by seven men who call themselves the Seven Shadows. They run the Rebellion from behind the scenes. Their names and identities remain a mystery to us, and only superior rankings of the Rebellion may converse with them. I guess you could say they're overseers."

The reporter nodded, understanding what President Davis means, "So, with these "Shadows" getting involved now, what would be the one thing you would say to President Lane now?"

President Davis remained silent as he thought about the answer, then turned to face the camera before saying, "Surrender. With the Seven Shadows involved now, there's no chance of victory for the military. You'll only be causing more death and suffering. You and your administration are about to get involved in something that goes beyond our civil war. Surrender while you have the chance. You have no idea what you're about to be up against."

The reporter stared at President Davis with a blank, yet awestruck face.

President Davis then turned to look at the reporter again, remained silent for a moment, then stood up, "I think I've said enough already." He then left the camera view, but the reporter stayed put, and slowly turned to face the camera with a confused but concerned expression.

Jessica, and a small crowd that had grown around her, stared at the TV in awe. She looked down at the floor as she started thinking to herself, "*So the Rebels are actually controlled by a group of men called the Seven Shadows? That doesn't sound good. Why would they be so secretive? If they're so powerful, why not just go ahead and attack D.C now and get it out of the way?*" Her eyes widened as another thought came to her, "*The Seven Shadows... They act in a way that's almost...*" A funny feeling started to grow in her gut, and she couldn't decide whether to be happy or worried about the situation. She looked up at the TV again with a smirk, and crooked smile, "*These tactics...it has to be them. No doubt about it. I knew there was something familiar about what's going on now. One way or another, you got what you predicted to come true...haven't you?"* She smiled at the television for a moment, then realized it was her turn and started unloading her cart on the checkout conveyer.

Back at her apartment, Jessica started putting her groceries away, but her mind was still a mess, and for every question she found an answer to, another five took its place.

When she'd finished putting everything away, she started pacing back and forth in the living room of her apartment, trying to collect her scattered mind. She was sure she knew something, but she didn't know if she could actually believe it.

"But how can this be? The tactics used in the attacks, and the way the Rebellion has been acting lately...how could it not be them? His own tactics were similar to this, and they were basically unstoppable." Her lips curled into a small smile, and she smirked a she continued, "Well, if nothing else, you've definitely proven one thing to all those who doubted you...haven't you? I wonder if...well, he's smart enough. He would have noticed a pattern by now. After all, they were Chess buddies." She shook her head to clear her thoughts, and tried bringing herself back to the present. She continued to pace around the living room, but eventually released a sigh, "You know what? It's out of my control. He did say he would do *something*, and I guess this is it. Now that I think of it, it's not like he had much of any other choice, anyway."

Deciding to just put the thought to rest, she shrugged her shoulders, sat down in her favorite recliner, and pulled out something to read.

After spending a few hours reading her books, working on her own novel, singing and playing some songs, Jessica sat at her desk, just finishing a new song she'd written. She went over it a few times, rewriting lyrics if she needed to, and eventually felt content enough with the song to put it in the pile of other songs she'd written in the past.

"I guess I'll play this tomorrow, and see how it turns out." She thought as she put the song with the others. She checked the time on her computer, and saw it was already almost 10:30 in the evening, *"Are you*

serious? It's already that late? There just aren't enough hours in the day. Especially when you're having fun." She sighed heavily, quickly finished a few loose ends, and made her way to bed.

The sound of someone sobbing in the distance woke Jessica from her sleep. She opened her eyes to find she was in another void, which forced her to sit up. She looked around in confusion, and tried to identify the source of the sobbing. From the voice, she could tell it was a woman, but the sound was coming from all around her, making it impossible to pinpoint the direction it was coming from.

As she looked around, trying to figure out what was going on, a light shining through the darkness caught her attention, and something seemed to beckon for her to move towards it. She reached down to where the ground would be, and felt there was some kind of force that stopped her from reaching further into the darkened pit. She brought her hand back up, and rested it on her thighs as she thought about the situation. She pondered hesitantly, but the light continued to shine, almost seeming to beg her to come to it.

She rested her feet over the side, checking to see if the mysterious force was still there. Her feet met contact with the mysterious force, and she slowly rose from her bed, expecting the force to suddenly disappear, and send her falling into nothingness. She stood in place next to her bed for a few moments, and eventually started to slowly make her way to the light that was just a few meters away.

When she reached the light it started to dim, but another light started to shine in the distance. Hesitant to continue, but not seeing another option, Jessica continued to follow the light. The sobbing seemed to get louder as she continued on, which led her to assume the lights were leading her to the source.

Although she was surrounded by darkness, she didn't feel fear, but rather warmth and a sense that she was wanted. Almost as if something desperately wanted to see her, and she started to feel the same. She continued to follow the lights for what felt like several minutes, but as she came to one light, it didn't dim, and the sobbing sounded closer than ever.

The light suddenly brightened, and Jessica felt herself being lifted off the ground. She was forced to look into the light, making her close her eyes, and wait to see what happened.

Hardly a split second later, she felt something beneath her feet, and the light had dimmed. She opened her eyes again to find that she was now in the orphanage where Chris lived before her family took him in. She looked around, recalling all the pain and torture Chris endured here, and turned her attention up the stairs once she heard the sobbing again.

The orphanage was completely empty, which left Jessica with an eerie yet somehow pleasurable feeling. When she reached the top of the staircase, she turned her attention to the left where the sobs were coming from, and her eyes widened when she recognized the direction. Without another thought, she started running to the room Chris used to live in, and busted through the door when she got there. What she saw brought tears to her eyes.

Sitting on the bed in front of her was Chris, curled in a ball and crying. Not wasting another second, Jessica rushed over to him, and tried to wrap him in her arms, but she went right through him, which resulted in her ramming headfirst into the wall behind him.

"Owwwwch…"

Realizing it was just an illusion, Jessica took a few steps away from Chris, her heart ripping in two when she realized he wasn't really there. She sat down on the bed next to him, and noticed he was holding something in his hand. Upon further inspection, she noticed it was a picture of a woman. Her eyes widened as she noticed something, and she reached for the picture. Her eyes widened even more when she realized she could actually take the picture.

She gently looked the picture from Chris' hand, and studied the woman. She stared at the picture in disbelief, and she felt her heart beating against her chest, *"Is…is this?!"*

Jessica noticed Chris acting a bit strange in the corner of her eye. He was looking around for something, as if he'd dropped it, but his movements were desperate. Almost without warning, he flew into a screaming tantrum as he threw things off his bed, and searched through his desk, crying out something that Jessica wasn't able to understand. Tears were pouring from his eyes, and he dove back onto his bed, crying in fear. He passed right through Jessica's body and continued searching.

Minutes, that felt like hours to Jessica, seeing Chris in this state passed, and Chris had ripped his room apart looking for something. Jessica watched in sorrow as Chris slowly stumbled his way over to his bed and checked underneath it, which was the only place he hadn't checked yet. His eyes were red from crying for so long, which forced tears to form in Jessica's eyes as well. He suddenly collapsed back on his bed, passing through Jessica's body again, and closed his eyes as he tried to sleep and not confront whatever he was feeling. However, he murmured something under his breath that Jessica was just barely able to catch.

"Mom..."

Jessica's eyes widened in horror, and she returned her attention to the picture again, only to see the woman was gone, leaving her completely confused. She sighed angrily and threw the blank picture away. She then turned her attention to Chris, who was lying on his bed with his eyes closed, and attempted to brush his face, but her hand went right through his body.

Tears were pouring from her eyes, from seeing her friend and the one man she held any romantic feelings towards, in this state. Words couldn't describe how desperately she wanted to wrap him in her arms and give him the comfort he needed.

Jessica continued to sit with Chris until he had fallen asleep, and she tried to kiss his forehead, but her lips faded through him. She stared at him in sorrow for a few moments, then stood up to leave the room. But once she turned her attention to the door, she saw the same woman who was in the picture standing in front of her.

Jessica could hardly believe her eyes. The woman was almost an exact replica of herself, but with green eyes and black hair.

"Who...who are you?" Jessica asked.

The woman looked at Jessica with a friendly smile, "Don't be afraid. My name is Rachel. What may I call you?"

Jessica stared at the woman with her mind racing a million different directions, but managed to wrap her mind around her question, "My name is Jessica. Jessica Holland."

Rachel smiled kindly, and made her way to Chris, passing through Jessica as she did, and gently rubbed her fingers across his cheek. She then looked at Jessica again, "So, tell me, Jessica...what do you think of this boy? I noticed you felt some sympathy for him earlier, and I'd like to know how you know him."

Jessica looked towards Chris, then looked at Rachel again, "He was a friend once. A close friend. I saved his life and convinced my parents to take him in from the orphanage. Our story is...well, simply put, it's a long one."

Rachel smiled kindly at Jessica, "Did you love him?"

Surprised by Rachel's words, Jessica's cheeks turned pink and she looked away from her as she scratched her cheek, "Err...well, yeah. It wouldn't be a lie for you to say that."

Rachel rubbed Chris' forehead, then smiled at Jessica again, "I see. If you don't mind me asking...what attracted you to him?"

Jessica looked at Rachel, and stepped towards her as she started talking, "I met him when my family first moved to D.C from a small town in California called Orland. I saw him being treated poorly in the hallways at school, so I stepped in and told the other kids to back off. Everything just kind of...happened from there."

"I see...so, what's the part you're not telling me?" Rachel asked, seeming to be able to read Jessica's mind.

Jessica looked at the woman blankly, "The part I'm not telling you? What are you ta-" Her eyes widened as she realized what the woman must have meant, "You...do you know about...but how is that even possible?"

Rachel only continued to look at Jessica with a friendly smile, not saying anything.

Jessica pondered for a few moments, then looked at her again, "Forayer's Sight. You know about it, don't you?"

"Mmm...not really, but I've heard of it." Rachel said as she sat down in Chris' desk chair, "Do you mind telling me about it?"

Jessica crossed her arms, and glared at the woman, "Why would I do that? I don't even know who you are or where you came from."

The woman chuckled and stood from the chair, "You'll know who I am when the time is right. As for now, tell me about this Forayer's Sight."

Jessica growled and gritted her teeth at the woman for avoiding her question. She pondered about telling the woman about her gift, but saw no harm in it since she was in just another dream world, "Forayer's Sight is a gift I was born with. Whether I was blessed with it by a divine, or if it's something that runs in my bloodline is up to you to decide. Basically, I can see a persons' past by looking into their eyes. It's something I promised myself long ago I'd only use in certain situations because I have yet to learn about the side-effects it has on me. Chris was a special case that I couldn't pass up. Only he, my family, and now you know about it."

Rachel nodded, understanding what Jessica said, "I see. So, not even your closest friends know about it?"

Jessica shook her head, "They never had a reason to know."

"I see. Would you be willing to learn more about it?" Rachel asked.

Jessica nodded, "I'd be willing to read an entire library full of information about my 'power' if it meant I could help more people, I'd gladly take the offer of that situation."

"Well, it seems you're in luck, then." Rachel said.

Jessica stared at Rachel in confusion for a moment, but got the idea of what she meant, "You're telling me you can see my future? I don't buy it."

Rachel chuckled and stood from the chair before making her way over to Jessica, "Child, in this world there's more beneath the surface than you ever thought was possible. Whether you believe what I tell you is true or false, I would ask that you listen to it."

Jessica waved her hand, signaling Rachel to continue.

"The civil war is coming to an end, and when the Republic declares its victory, you will meet with those who call themselves the "Seven Shadows". Within their ranks is a man who could give you more information about Forayer's Sight than you could hope to gain by reading through *two* libraries."

Jessica continued to stare at Rachel, a little curious about what she said, but still not buying what she said, "And how could you possibly know this? I get I'm in some kind of…dream realm or something, but until I see some proof you know this is going to happen, I won't believe it."

Rachel smirked and passed through Jessica, then turned to face her again as she stood in front of the doorway, "As I said before, whether you believe what I tell you or not is up to you, but this *will* happen. Of that I can promise you."

Jessica continued to face the far wall, keeping her back to Rachel. She thought about what to say next, then turned to face her, "You still haven't told me who you are, and why you're practically my twin. I want answers."

Rachel smiled kindly, "I'm not your enemy, dear, nor should you try and make me one."

Jessica started to say something, but stopped herself. She paused for a moment as she looked at the ground, then looked at Rachel again, "I-I'm sorry. I didn't mean to sound the way I did. It's just…" She looked back at Chris for a moment, then looked at Rachel again, "I've had some other experiences with these…dream realm…things in the past, but this is by far the strangest I've been in thus far. I have no idea what to expect from them, but seeing Chris for the first time in over a decade, seeing him like this, and not being able to be there for him when he needs me…It's hard for me to take this in. I'm sorry for being so hostile. It's not like me to do that to someone."

Rachel smiled softly, and placed her hand on Jessica's shoulder, but this time she was real, and Jessica could feel her hand on her shoulder, catching her completely off guard, "All is forgiven. I can see why this would be hard for you, but…it's even harder for me."

Jessica watched in awe as tears started to fill Rachel's eyes as she looked over her shoulder at Chris. Rachel looked down at the floor for a moment, crying, then looked at Jessica again, "Listen…I know this may sound kind of odd…but can I ask just one request of you, Ms. Holland?"

Jessica grabbed Rachel's hands, and held them tightly as she gave her a friendly smile, "Sure. I'd be glad to help."

Rachel smiled softly, and wiped tears from her eyes. She looked at Chris for a long while, then looked at Jessica again, "I ask you as a mother…please, take care of my son." Once she'd finished her sentence, Rachel and the world around her disappeared, leaving Jessica in a black void again.

Jessica's entire body went numb, and her recently collected mind had exploded into a billion pieces. She started to tremble, losing feeling in her legs, making her fall on her back where she stared at the void of nothingness above her. Part of her refused to believe it was true, but she still felt where Rachel had laid her hands on her shoulder. Tears started to form in her eyes, and she started to quietly cry as she thought about what had just happened, "*Why come to me? Why not visit your own son in his own dreams? He spent so many years trying to find you, only to find out he'd been chasing after a lie. When he found out the truth, and learned you were…oh, Chris…I'm so sorry. I wish things didn't have to be this way, I wish you didn't have the life you have…I wish…I wish you'd just come back.*" She sat up, wiping away her tears as she continued her thoughts, "*Should I tell him about this if I ever see him again? What kind of effect would it have on him? Would it hurt him even more than he already is, or would he be thrilled and ask me a lot of curious questions? This isn't an easy decision to make. I don't want to cause him more pain than he's already had to endure, but what's worse? Telling him or not telling him…*" She sighed, and laid on her back again, folding her arms behind her head as she did, "*Maybe there will come a time when it's actually appropriate to tell him about it. If he is what I think he is now, it shouldn't be long…*" She sighed, closed her eyes, and fell asleep.

Jessica woke to her alarm clock, and quickly pulled the plug out of the wall. *"I've already got enough to think about, I don't need you giving me an even worse headache,"* She thought.

She rolled on her back, and folded her arms behind her head as she stared at the ceiling and watched the blades on her ceiling fan spin around in circles, *"So…Chris' mother was this Rachel woman? But how is this even possible? Why would she come to me instead of him?"* She closed her eyes as she thought back to what Rachel told her,

"The civil war is coming to an end, and when the Republic declares its victory, you will meet with those who call themselves the "Seven Shadows". Within their ranks is a man who can give you more information about Forayer's Sight than you could hope to gain by reading through two libraries."

"Do these dreams have something to do with Forayer's Sight?" Jessica continued to wonder, *"If they do, Forayer's Sight may have more power than I originally believed. If what she says about the member of the Seven Shadows is true, he should be able to give me more information about it…and that might lead me to…"* She smiled at the thought, but shook her head, "Now's not the time for that. I still have a job to put before anything else."

She climbed out of bed and prepared herself for work.

"Alright, sir, your total is $26.57." Jessica said after summing up a customer's price.

The customer reached for his wallet, handed Jessica the money, and headed out the door.

"Come again!" Jessica called out before the man went through the door. She sighed, and rested her cheek in her palm as she leaned on the counter, "Sheesh, you'd think his puppy died or something. He didn't speak a single word while he was here."

Ashton chuckled as she made her way behind the counter to water some of the plants in the window next to Jessica, "He probably didn't want to be seen in a flower shop. You know…flowers aren't manly enough to be around."

Jessica turned to look at Ashton, laughed, and turned to face the door as a new customer came in, "Well, we shouldn't judge too harshly. With the Rebels getting closer to the city, it's possible he lost a family member or something and wasn't in the mood for talking."

"True. That's the thing about war. No matter your political or religious views, it's hard not to feel a little sympathy for parents who have to bury their kids."

Jessica nodded, "I couldn't agree more. The sooner this civil war is over the better." She watched as the new customer came in, and looked around as if he were looking for someone. He spoke to Jasmine for a moment, and she pointed at Jessica, which caught her eye. The man thanked Jasmine, and made his way to Jessica, "Excuse me, but are you by chance Jessica Holland?"

Jessica looked at the man with a little confusion, "Uh…yes. Can I help you?"

The man reached his hand halfway over the counter, "Hi, my name is Joshua Day. I work with my dad who owns the Silver Tab. Have you by chance heard of it?"

Jessica nodded, "Of course. It's the most popular bar in this part of the city."

Josh smiled and nodded, "That's right. Well, believe it or not, both of us have heard you're quite the musician, and we may have an opening for you if you're interested."

Jessica's eyes widened in curiosity, and she looked at Ashton who seemed just as curious about the situation as she was. "Ashton, would you mind watching the register for a moment?"

Ashton nodded and took over the register as Jessica made her way to Josh, asked him to follow her, and lead him to another part of the store so they could talk in private.

"So, you're looking for an entertainer?" Jessica asked, claiming a seat in the breakroom, and inviting Josh to sit across from her, which he did.

Josh nodded, "That's correct. Our last entertainer went off the deep end, and we had to let him go."

"What happened to him?" Jessica asked.

"The guy became an alcoholic, and it wasn't long before he started getting into drugs as well." Josh said, "We've been looking for a new entertainer around here for a while, but your name seems to pop up everywhere we look or ask."

Jessica stared at Josh in awe and amazement, "R-really? I wasn't aware I'd become so popular. I...I really don't know what to say."

Josh smirked a laugh, "You mean you didn't know you were this popular? From what I understand, you've gone out of your way to help all kinds of people. Making them food, helping out at big events, the list goes on. Actions like that don't go unrewarded."

Jessica smiled, and nodded in agreement, "Yeah, I guess that's true judging by what you told me. So, say I accept your offer. What happens?"

"I'd ask you to come to the bar and perform this coming weekend if you're able." Josh said, "I can tell you that entertainers at our bar are paid very well, and we attract a pretty decent sized crowd on Thursdays, Fridays and Saturdays. All three days combined, you're looking at around two-thousand people."

Jessica's jaw dropped, and her eyes started to sparkle with excitement, "R-really? I've always wanted to perform in front of a large crowd. You think it could help my name get out there, too?"

Josh nodded, "Absolutely. And the money you make will depend on your performance. You'll get tips, but you'll also get a percentage of what the bar makes those three nights,"

"What kind of percentage are we talking about?" Jessica asked, getting more and more interested as the conversation went on.

"How does five percent sound?" Josh asked.

Jessica thought for a moment, then looked at Josh again, "How about an even ten? If I can form an actual band, I can make some of my own work really come to life, and my work is very inspired by a number of artists, as well as things that have happened over the course of my life."

Josh remained silent as he looked at the table for a few moments as he thought about Jessica's words. He turned his head to look at her again, "What artists are you most inspired by? What genre would you say you belong to the most?"

Jessica tapped her finger against her chin as she thought about the answer to both questions, "Hmm…well, if I had to pick a specific genre, I'd have to say Rock. I was a big fan of bands like Nickelback, Three Days Grace, Shinedown, and a bunch of others that were big back in their time. However, I was also a big fan of Carrie Underwood, and the rhythm of her music often finds its way into my songs as well."

"Interesting. So you kind of have a bit of everything in your songs, then?" Josh asked, amused by Jessica's words.

Jessica nodded, "Pretty much. The only thing I won't do is rap."

"Which is fair enough." Josh said. He handed Jessica a card that had the address of the bar and his phone number before standing up, "Well, I'd better be going. If you decide to come and perform, you should come to the bar around 8:00 P.M Thursday Night. I'll talk to my Dad about your request of ten percent, and see if we can't form an actual band for you."

Jessica smiled and rose from her chair, then shook Josh's hand, "I'd appreciate it. I'll definitely be coming this weekend."

Josh nodded in approval, "Glad to hear it. I guess we'll see you then."

Jessica, yelling in excitement in her mind, led Josh back to the entrance of the store, and took her position back at the cash register where Ashton was still waiting.

"So, what'd he have to say?" Ashton asked curiously once she saw Jessica coming back to the cash register.

Jessica grinned at Ashton with excitement and squeezed her tightly with a hug as she squealed, taking Ashton by surprise and deafening her right ear, "He wants me to sing and perform at his bar for a percentage of what the bar makes!"

Ashton's eyes widened, and she separated from Jessica, "That's wonderful news, Jess! When do they want you to start?"

"This coming weekend! He even said they might form a band for me!"

Ashton's jaw dropped, and she patted Jessica's shoulder, "That's awesome! I'm so happy for you, Jess! Your dream may finally be coming true!"

Jessica laughed and blushed slightly, "You really think so?"

Ashton nodded in a reassuring manner, "Of course! Sure, you're just singing in a bar for now – but this bar is one of the most popular hot spots in this part of the city! Not only does it attract locals, but it attracts a lot of tourists as well! If you make a strong first impression this weekend, your name may become more known to the public, and maybe, just *maybe* that'll get to an agent of some kind, and you can go on tours and release some CD's"

"And set up a lot of book signings." Jessica said, making both of them giggle.

"Maybe, but let's stick to what's important now." Ashton said, "Ohhh! This is so exciting! We'll have to find you something to wear, which of course, means another trip to the mall."

Jessica thought for a moment, then shook her head at Ashton, "Actually...I already have something for the occasion."

Ashton raised a curious eyebrow and crossed her arms, "Oh? And what would that be, hmm?"

"That dress you got me a while ago... assuming it still fits." Jessica said.

Ashton thought back, and pictured the dress Jessica was talking about, "You're planning on wearing *that* thing? Are you sure that's such a good idea? It was kind of a tight fit from the beginning. Now that your curves have become a little more...curvy, it might not fit at all. On top of that, you're pretty mobile when you're singing and playing. I don't think that dress would be appropriate for the occasion."

"Well, what would you suggest, then?" Jessica asked.

Ashton pondered for a moment, trying to decide on what Jessica would look best in, "Hmm...how about some actual club attire? Maybe some shorts, a short top, dye your hair a little darker...I think you could pull off that look. Easily. You've got the body for it."

Jessica smirked and rolled her eyes, "You really are a pervert aren't you?"

Ashton chuckled, and started walking away, "Only when it matters, Jess. Only when it matters."

CHAPTER 9

A Dream Come True Turns to a Nightmare Unleashed

Jessica, joined her friends after work at their favorite hangout place, collapsed into a chair at the table her friends were sitting at, and released a groan of relief, "Ohhhh, it feels so good to sit down for once."

"Yeah, running the cash register three days in a row is kind of a tough break, Jess." Ashton said, "But, hey, it could be worse. At least we're not required to wear high heels or something."

"Don't even think about that, Ashton. I don't want to hear it." Jessica said, trying to shush Ashton as she spoke, "If high heels become mandatory for us to wear, I will quit and find a different job."

"Oh? And where would you go?" Ashton asked.

"I...I would um..." Jessica froze for a minute as she tried to think, but couldn't come up with an answer, "Okay, maybe quitting wouldn't be such a great idea after all. Jeez, Ashton, you *always* have to bring reality to my world. Why?!"

"Well, somebody has to." Ashton mocked, winking at Jessica. "Anyway, getting off the topic of that Hell Hole we call a flower shop, have you managed to find that dress you wanted to wear for your performance tomorrow?"

"I did, but you were right. It was too small." Jessica said, smiling and thanking the waitress that brought her a glass of water. She turned her attention to Ashton again and continued, "I must have been a lot smaller than I realized when you gave me that thing because I could not for the life of me get in it."

"So, what are you planning to do now?" Krista asked from the other side of the table, "You want to put on a good show, and make a good first impression, but a new dress isn't exactly something cheap. At least not one that's fit for this occasion."

Jessica nodded at Krista, "Yeah, I know. I was a bit bummed out, but I got over it. I just decided I'd wear a black tank top and some shorts. Besides, you three were right when you said I'm too mobile on stage to wear a dress, anyway. I practiced for a while in my new clothes yesterday, and I much prefer the feeling of freedom those clothes allow me than the restrictions a dress would force on me."

"So, do you have any kind of plan for your performance?" Krista asked curiously, "I mean, do you know what kind of music Josh wants you to sing or play? I know he said he'd look into finding band members for you, but you'd need some practice before you could play your own work on stage."

"Mmm…that's a very good point, Krista. I hadn't thought of the amount of time the other band members would need to really know my songs." Jessica said, "But to answer your question, I talked with him over the phone a bit, and he said he's planning on playing a lot of Carrie Underwood music with a mix of some rock bands from the twenty-teen years."

"And how do you think you'll manage? You must be nervous." Jasmine said.

"Oh, you don't even know the half of it." Jessica said with a nervous laugh, "I've always wanted to sing and perform in front of a large crowd, but now I'm so nervous that I'm having second thoughts."

"Oh, don't say that, Jess." Ashton said in a comforting tone, "You've been singing and playing musical instruments practically from the time you were born. You'll do fine. Besides, we'll be in the front watching you. If you get nervous, just look down at us, and pretend you're singing to us. You've done it before without hesitation."

Jessica smiled and opened her mouth to say something, but was cut off by Jasmine's voice, "You have a beautiful voice, Jessica. One that few ever dream of having. If you back out now, how will you face the crowds at concerts and other big events? If you can overcome your fear here, you won't even think about the people watching you the next time you perform."

"Besides, I'd be more concerned about the boys flocking to you in record numbers just to get your phone number." Krista butted in, making everyone laugh.

Jessica smiled softly at her friends and thought about what to say for a moment, then started talking, "Thank you, guys. I feel a lot better knowing you'll be there for me in the end, even if this whole thing goes south. I couldn't ask for any better friends."

Ashton watched Jessica for a moment, and noticed her eyes were starting to tear up. She scooted her chair over to Jessica, and wrapped her arm around her, "You said it before. We're a family. Even if you perform terribly, we'll still be here for you."

"Well, hopefully it doesn't come to me putting on a bad show." Jessica said, "Anyway, I know I'm not a big drinker, but I'm thinking if my performance goes well…I might actually celebrate by having a glass of wine or something."

"Ohhhh, well look at Ms. Confident now." Ashton playfully mocked, "Celebrating with a glass of wine? Preposterous! I've never heard of such a thing."

Jessica laughed, and pushed Ashton's chair away, "Oh, shut up. If I get drunk I'm blaming it on you."

Ashton glared at Jessica, giving her 'the eye' as she crossed her arms, "If you get drunk and pass out, I am not responsible for the position you wake up in."

Jessica grinned at Ashton, and returned her glare, "Oh? And what exactly would you do with me if given that chance?"

Ashton remained silent for a moment as she thought, then shrugged her shoulders, "I dunno. Maybe tie you to a chair and make you watch a bunch of really bad movies."

Jessica smirked, "Is that the best you can do? Ha! I had a friend a long time ago who'd put you to shame."

Ashton smirked, and intensified her stare at Jessica, "Well, that doesn't surprise me. You hung out with all kinds of weird people in high school."

"Yeah, but somehow I ended up meeting and becoming best friends with the weirdest." Jessica mocked back.

Ashton laughed, "I try my best. However, it took a great mentor to teach me all I know."

"Oh, leave your mother out of this."

Ashton's jaw fell open, and she stared at Jessica in disbelief, "Really? We're pulling *that* joke out again are we?"

"Well, unless you're hard of hearing, I'd say the answer to that is a yes."

Krista and Jasmine both hunched over the table, resting their chins in their palms as they listened to Jessica and Ashton argue. *"Oh boy, here we go again."* Krista thought.

After parting with her friends, Jessica returned to her apartment, locking the door behind her. She started putting away some groceries she'd bought on the way home. She felt a little more at ease about her coming performance after talking with her friends about it. However, she was still nervous, no matter how much she tried to put it in the back of her mind.

When she'd finished putting away her groceries, Jessica proceeded to the living room and collapsed into her favorite recliner, and stared out the window for a few moments. She watched the traffic stop and go as the street lights changed colors, and observed the random people walking along the sidewalks going about their daily business. A small grin started to creep its way onto her face as she watched a woman with two little girls pass by. The two girls skipped alongside their mother happily, not having a single care in the world. One of the girls stopped to talk to her mother about something, then started skipping ahead with her sister close behind.

"Huh! You'd almost think there wasn't a war going on." Jessica said with a growing smile as she continued watching the girls. She sighed as she continued her thoughts, "The mind of a child is simply a wonderful thing. Even in the darkest hours, they still manage to find the joy in life, no matter how scary it is."

She continued watching the family until they were out of sight, then turned her attention to the traffic again. "And people still continue on about their daily lives. Even with the Republic getting closer and closer, people still go on."

She sat up in her chair as she continued to watch people go by on the street below for a few minutes, then turned her attention to her guitar collection on the wall. "Hmm...I really should practice at least one more time. I know Carrie Underwood's music practically by heart now, but it's always a good idea to keep in rhythm."

She stood from her chair, walked over to her guitars, tuned them, and started playing a number of songs, keeping the beat to the rest of the music in her head as she started singing. *Good Girl, Little Toy Guns, All American Girl,* and *Something in the Water* were among some of her all-time favorite hits, and she hit every note perfectly as she played and danced to the beat of the music. Her body moved in perfect rhythm as she danced, and her voice matched the mood of her music.

Nearly three hours passed. Jessica played a number of Carrie Underwood music, as well as several songs from other artists. Though she was a little out of breath, and her mouth tasted like cotton, her adrenaline had sky rocketed and she was more pumped up than ever before.

"Phew! Now *that's* what I call a performance!" Jessica said in an excited tone as she put her guitar back in its place. "Now...if I can pull that off tomorrow night, I shouldn't have a single problem."

She made her way back to her favorite recliner and collapsed in it. She stared at the ceiling for a few moments. She started to picture herself on stage with a large crowd watching her. Her lips started to curl into a smile as her thoughts continued.

"Ohhh! Maybe practicing was a bad idea. Suddenly, I can't wait to get up on stage!" She thought, covering her mouth as she squealed. She continued to think about the possibilities of what the next day could bring, and folded her arms behind her head as she sat back in her chair. "My life is finally looking up…if only mom, dad, and Scott could see me play." Her eyes narrowed sadly as she continued, *"Oh…and Chris, too. He always loved listening to me sing and play my musical instruments. I wonder what he'd do if he were here now. What he'd be like if he'd stayed…"* She released a depressed sigh, and turned to look out her window, "Well…wherever you are, Chris…just know I'll play a song for you, too. Besides, if my suspicions are correct…I may be seeing you soon."

Jessica clinched her shirt over her heart as tears started to form in her eyes. *"At least I hope so…"* She thought. She continued thinking for a while, but eventually stood from her chair. "Well, I'd better give mom a call, and tell her about this. I can't believe I hadn't thought of doing this before." She pulled her cell phone out of her pocket, and contacted her mom's phone, but was sent to the voicemail.

Jessica waited for the beep before she started talking, "Hey, Mom, it's Jessica. I hope you and Dad are doing okay. I'm calling to see how things are going, and give you a bit of good news. I've been asked to sing and perform at the most popular bar in my part of the city. The owner's son met with me in person and said he was directed to me by a bunch of different people. I'll be starting tomorrow and playing throughout the weekend. I'm sorry for not calling you sooner, but between practice, work, and trying to find a good outfit to wear, I haven't had any time to contact you. I'm really sorry about that because I know you'd love to be here for me. But with the Rebels getting closer and closer to the city, it's probably best you stay away. I know you're probably scared and worried about me, but please don't be. I'll be ready when the Rebels get here.

Don't worry. Anyway, other than my big announcement, everything's going great over here on my end. I hope you guys stay safe wherever you go. Love you."

She ended the call, and rested her phone on the table next to her. She sighed, and looked out the window for a moment. She watched the people and traffic continue to go about their business for a while, then turned around and walked to her computer desk. "Right, this book isn't going to write itself, Jess."

Jessica closed the top of her laptop, and folded her arms behind her head as she stretched. "Aw, man! I haven't made that much progress in quite a long time." She looked at the clock on the wall over the desk, and smiled when she realized what time it was. *"I wrote for two straight hours? Good grief, girl! You're on a roll today!"* She thought happily to herself. She patted herself on the back in congratulation.

"Well, I think that pretty much raps it up for the day." She said to herself out loud. She looked around her apartment for anything else she needed to touch up on, but didn't see anything that required immediate attention. "Well, anything that needs cleaned up or put away can wait until the weekend." She folded her hair behind her right ear, and realized her hair felt a little nasty after sweating from practicing her music earlier. "Hmm...a shower wouldn't hurt, though."

She proceeded to her room where she grabbed some fresh sleepwear, and started for her bathroom. However, she stopped as she heard her phone vibrating on her computer desk. She put her clothes on the arm of a nearby recliner, and went to pick up her phone. *"Who's calling me at this hour? Everyone should be asleep by now."* She thought.

When she reached her phone, and picked it up to see the number, she saw it was her boss, Shelby. Surprised, she answered the call.

"Hi, Shelby. I'm...a little surprised to hear from you at this time of night."

Shelby laughed, "Yeah, I thought you might be. I'm usually dead at this time of night. Anyway, I wanted to see how you're doing since tomorrow's a big day for you."

"Oh! Haha! Well, I'm pretty excited about it. A little nervous, maybe, but I'm looking forward to it." Jessica says, taking a seat at her computer desk.

"Well, good. I'm glad you finally have this chance to do what you've always wanted. Anyway, I was calling to let you know that you have vacation days for tomorrow and Friday. I don't want to see you at the shop unless you desperately need something." Shelby said.

Jessica's eyes widened, and she stood from her seat, "W-what do you mean vacation days? Shelby, I need all the money I can get. I can't afford a day off right now!"

Shelby laughed, and tried to calm Jessica down. "They're paid vacation days, silly. We *do* have those if you recall correctly, you workaholic."

Jessica remained silent for a moment, and she covered her mouth as she tried not to laugh, "Uh...er...yeah! Of course I knew that! I just...uh..."

"Forgot?" Shelby asked.

"Well...for lack of a better term, I guess that'll do." Jessica said, giggling in embarrassment.

"Well, tomorrow's a big day for you, Jess, and I don't want you wearing yourself out here at the shop. I've already spoken to Ashton, Jasmine and Krista about it, and they all agree that you should not come into work tomorrow." Shelby said.

Jessica blinked in amazement, and a few tears started to form in her eyes, "Oh...well, thank you, Shelby. Thank you for everything."

Shelby laughed loudly, forcing Jessica to hold the phone away from her ear, "Oh, don't worry about it, Jess. After all, I should be thanking *you*. You've made employee of the month, and you have the potential for a promising future. Don't let us down."

Jessica's tears started to slide down her cheeks, and she covered her mouth from the shocking news. "E-employee of the month? Really?!"

Shelby smirked, "Congratulations, Jessica. You earned it. Now, after you're finished with your performance, maybe you should find yourself a nice man. You do know most of our customers come in here for you, right? I've lost track of how many times a guy has asked me if you were single."

Though she was softly crying, Jessica still managed to laugh a bit, "Well…we'll see. No promises on that last one, though. But I promise I'll put on a good show for you and the girls. If you come. You have my word."

Shelby laughed again, "Oh, Jessica. You're too kind for your own good sometimes. Well, even if you do poorly, you're still a winner to us. Have a good night."

Jessica wiped some of the tears away with the sleeve of her shirt, and sniffed, "Yeah, you too, Shelby. Sleep well. Good night."

"Good night, Jess. Don't let the bed bugs bite."

Jessica laughed, and ended the call. She started to cry happy tears sliding down her cheeks. She sat down on the nearest chair. *"I can't believe it! I'm employee of the month and having my own concert in one week? This must be a dream!"* She pinched her arm, but stopped once she felt the pain. She chuckled a bit and stood up, "Nope. I'd say I'm wide awake right now." She smiled proudly as she continued thinking for a few moments, but shook her head to clear her mind and focus on what was important. *"Remember, Jess, you still have to put on a good show. You can't let your emotions get the better of you."* She thought.

Needing a way to keep her mind from drifting off, she grabbed her clothes, and headed to the bathroom to take a shower.

The following morning, Jessica woke up early to get a good start. She skipped her regular routine, not turning on the TV to watch the news, and eating a very quick breakfast. As soon she'd finished her breakfast, she grabbed her guitar, and started practicing more songs, including her own work. Her adrenaline was off the charts, and she performed perfectly. Her body seemed to move on its own as she danced to the rhythm of the music, and her voice intensified when she reached critical moments in the songs. She practiced for several hours, imagining she was at the bar with a large crowd of people watching her, hoping it would be enough that she wouldn't freeze up when she was doing the real thing. She played numerous songs from the bands Josh told her they'd play. She practiced several hours straight until she was forced to take a break.

Lunch time came too quickly it seemed as she was still full of energy, and didn't want to stop. She continued playing until her stomach told her to stop, and ate a quick lunch. Her voice was doing well, but her mouth had a cotton taste from singing so much. During her lunch, she drank three glasses of water, but continued practicing once she'd finished eating.

A few more hours passed, putting the day at nearly four in the afternoon. Jessica put the guitar she'd been using away, and released a sigh of accomplishment. "Okay, I think I've practiced enough for now." She said.

She turned from the guitar and walked to her room to prepare her outfit for the event. She stepped into her closet, and pulled out a black sleeveless tank top and a pair of shorts, and laid them on her bed. She took a quick glance at the time, and saw she still had a few hours before she was supposed to go to the bar.

"Hmm...well, what do I do now? It's not nearly as late in the day as I thought it was." She sat down on her bed as she thought about what to do, and looked at the clothes next to her. An idea came to her, and she grabbed the shirt and looked at it. She continued thinking and started to like where the idea was going.

"*You know what...maybe Ashton was right.*" She thought. She continued to think, and shrugged her shoulders when she'd reached a decision. "*I may as well do a little dress up game.*" She thought.

She stood up from the bed, grabbed her shorts, and walked into her bathroom where she changed clothes. Once she'd put her new clothes on, she looked at herself in the mirror, and judged how she looked.

Everything fit perfectly and made her look more athletic than she really was.

"Huh! I should wear this next time I'm with mom just to rub these in her face. She's been so jealous of me ever since I matured." She thought. She chuckled at the thought of her mother's reaction, and continued examining herself.

"Hmm...maybe Ashton's right." She whispered softly. She folded the shirt up above her bellybutton, and thought about the look. She looked herself over in the mirror from a number of different directions, holding the shirt at different heights.

"Mmmm....admittedly, I'm actually having to put some thought into this." She said, laughing at herself, "I'm usually not one for showing off more skin than what's necessary, but at the same time...this look kind of fits the attire for a bar or club. Especially the one I'm going to." She spun around, looked at her back side, and smirked at herself. She turned around to face the mirror, and debated on the outfit for a few moments. "Oh, what the hell. I'll turn this into a crop top. Why not?"

She took the shirt off and laid it on the counter, reached into a drawer of the sink counter, pulled out a pair of scissors, and cut the lower part of the shirt off. She then put the shirt back on, and looked at herself in the mirror.

"Hmm...not bad, Jess. Not bad." She said, impressed with what she saw. Because of the way she cut the shirt, it looked as if it had been ripped at one point, giving her a "street club" look. The shirt ended just above her bellybutton, and its solid black color really brought out the complexion of her skin.

She continued to look herself over for a while, and eventually concluded she liked what she saw. Satisfied with her new look, Jessica prepared herself for a shower, and spent the rest of her time preparing her makeup and hair.

When it was time to leave, Jessica did one last swoop of her apartment, making sure she hadn't forgotten anything. She was carrying her favorite guitar she had tuned earlier in one hand, and had her purse strapped over her free shoulder. She was wearing a new perfume Ashton and Krista had gotten her for the event. Its scent was something she really liked.

She had also painted her finger and toenails black to match her shirt, and had darkened her hair a bit, too. She was wearing a bit more eyeliner and eye shadow than she normally did, but it gave her a "rock and roll" look that wouldn't be terribly out of place for when she started singing songs from rock bands.

She wouldn't admit it, but her nerves were a little unsettled. She refused to believe she was too nervous to play, and continued to tell herself she was just overly excited. Her hands were shaking, and she felt the longer she took, the more nervous she'd become.

Not seeing anything she skipped over or missed, Jessica grabbed the keys to her apartment, and started for the door. She stepped into the hallway outside, locked the door behind her, and made her way to the stairs.

As she started going down the stairs, she felt her phone going off in her back pocket. She checked to see who was calling her. She grinned when she saw it was her mother, and answered the call.

"Hey, Mom. I take it you got my message?"

"I did! I listened to the message a bit earlier, but I didn't get a chance to call you back. I'm so happy for you!" Laura said in an excited tone.

Jessica smiled, and continued descending the stairs, "Did you tell dad? What did he think?"

"I told both your father and Scott, too. As well as some of our friends here in California. We're all excited for you, and can't wait to hear how it goes. Are you nervous?"

"Well…a little, I guess. But I'm trying to keep that in the back of my mind. I'm just so excited I finally have this chance! Although… I wonder what-"

"Chris would think?" Laura interrupted, catching Jessica a little off guard.

Jessica's cheeks turned pink, and she stopped descending down the stairs for a moment, "Well…er…yeah."

"Oh, Jess, I think it's so cute how you still have feelings for him. Even after ten years."

"Well, how can I not?" Jessica asked as she started descending the stairs again, "I know we didn't know each other all that long, but...still. I gave him a home when he really needed one, and for the short time he was with us...he felt like he was actually part of a family. Which is what he always wanted more than anything. I...I really miss him."

"I know, Jess. We all do. However, your father told me he has a sneaking suspicion that he may actually be with the Rebels." Laura said.

Jessica's eyes widened, and she stopped descending the stars again. "And why does he say that?" She asked curiously.

"He's not real sure. But he's almost positive he recognizes some of the recent strategies the Republic has been using." There was a long silent pause before Laura continued, "You...you don't think he's..."

Jessica nodded, and leaned her back against the wall when she reached the top of a new stair case, "I know what he's talking about. I've had my suspicions, too."

"Hmm...well, maybe he'll pop up again seemingly out of the clear blue sky." Laura said.

Jessica looked down at the floor as she laughed, and shook her head to get some hair out of her face, "I honestly wouldn't be surprised if he did, Mom. He was full of all kinds of surprises when he was around."

"Indeed he was. So, what are you doing right now?" Laura asked.

"Oh, I'm actually on my way to the bar as we speak." Jessica said as she started descending the stairs again.

"Oh, really? Did I call at a bad time or...?"

"No, I haven't even left the building yet. I'm going down the stairs right now." Jessica said.

"Oh, okay. Well, I don't want to interrupt your focus. Call me when you get back home, okay? I want to hear all about it."

Jessica smiled, and landed her right foot on the first floor, "Will do, Mom. Love you."

"Love you, too."

Jessica ended the call and headed to the bar.

As she approached the bar, Jessica saw Ashton, Krista, Jasmine, and a few of her other friends outside the main door waiting for her. She smiled and waved at them once they noticed her, and ran over to them.

"Hey, guys. Thanks for coming. I was hoping you'd already be here when I arrived." Jessica said, relieved to see a few friendly places in a strange place.

"What, you think we'd miss *this* opportunity, Jess?" Ashton asked as she stepped forward, "We're looking at what could be the first day of your future. I don't know about these girls, but I wouldn't miss this for the world."

Jessica smiled softly, and pulled Ashton into a friendly hug, "Thanks, Ash. That means a lot."

Ashton smiled, and separated from Jessica, "So, I take it you spent your off day practicing?"

Jessica nodded, "Indeed I did, actually. I *was* a little nervous earlier, but I'm so excited now that I don't have time to be nervous. I'm more fired up than ever before."

"That's good, Jess. I'm sure you'll do fine." Krista said. She reached into her pocket as she approached Jessica, and pulled out a rabbit's foot. "But on a night like tonight...you need all the help you can get."

"A rabbit's foot?" Jessica asked curiously as she took the leg from Krista, "Well, they're commonly believed to bring good luck, so wearing it couldn't hurt." She strapped the foot to one of her belt loops, and looked at Krista again. "Thank you, Krista. You may be new in my life, but you've proven to be a true and loyal friend."

Krista grinned, and rested her hand on Jessica's shoulder, "I'm here for ya, girl. Just keep any negative thoughts out of your head, and I'm sure you'll do fine."

Jessica nodded at Krista in approval with a friendly smile, "Thanks, Krista. Every little bit helps."

Jasmine stepped up to Jessica, blocking her path into the building, and crossed her arms as she gave her a snooty look. "Jessica, I hate to break it to you, but I don't think you're going to do good at all."

Jessica's attitude took a sudden change, and she gave Jasmine a look of disbelief. "Uh...excuse me?"

Jasmine started laughing, and pulled Jessica into a hug, "I'm kidding, Jess. I don't think you're going to do good because I know you're going to be great."

Jessica's rising anger suddenly vanished, and she wrapped her arms around Jasmine, "Well, geez! You played that pretty well. I thought you were serious!"

Jasmine laughed, stepping back, "No, I wouldn't do that to you. You're too nice for me to say something like that, and you've been a good friend for far too long for me to hurt you like that."

Jessica giggled, and smiled at Jasmine, "Well...I'll forgive you *this* time."

"Oh, I feel so relieved." Jasmine joked, resting her hand above her heart rolling her eyes.

"Okay, okay, that's enough you love birds." Ashton said, playfully pushing Jasmine and Jessica away from each other. She turned to face Jessica, looked her over, and smirked, "So, I see you decided to go with the look I recommended after all, huh?"

Jessica looked down at herself for a moment, then looked up and smiled at Ashton, "Yeah...well, I really prefer not to show off too much skin with crop tops, but I figured a special night like tonight called for something a little new."

Ashton giggled, and gave Jessica a reassuring smile, "You look great, Jess. You really do. The whole street club thing really suits you. Maybe you should show skin more often."

Jessica laughed, and started to walk into the bar, "I think I'll pass, Ash, but thanks for the compliment. Anyway, do any of you know where Josh is?"

The three girls shook their heads, "No, I'm afraid I haven't seen him since we got here. One of the bartenders might know, though." Krista said.

Jessica nodded, and turned to the doors again, "Well, I'll ask around when we get inside."

As the girls walked inside the bar for the first time, they were met with a blast of cold air, and saw the bar was about what they were expecting. It was a huge place that had a dance floor at the far end with the stage against the wall where Jessica assumed she'd be performing. On the left side of the building was the bar with several stools and tables lined up against the railing. On the right side of the building were the restrooms and the manager's office.

The atmosphere was energizing with club music beating from the stereos, and the darkened room that was lit only by a few disco balls, and ambient lighting along the rails and bar.

Jessica and her friends stared at the place in awe, and all four of their bodies seemed to automatically move to the beat of the music.

"So...somebody want to explain to me why we've never been here before? I love this place already!" Ashton said as she started to freely dance to the music.

"Well, you're the one who said we should never come here. Remember?" Jessica asked, giving Ashton a playful but dirty look.

Ashton glared back at Jessica as she countered, "I haven't said that anytime recently, though. How old where we when I said that? Twenty-one? They've remodeled since then. I mean, look at this place! It's awesome!"

Jessica rolled her eyes. She looked at the place a bit more, and nodded in agreement with Ashton, "I'll agree that it looks nice. I would like to see how the people here are before I make any kind of judgment, however."

"So...do you see Josh anywhere?" Krista asked as she looked around the room.

Jessica shook her head, "No. I don't see any trace of him. He might be in the manager's office, though." She turned to face her friends as she continued, "I should probably check in, anyway, and let whoever's in charge know I'm here, and see what they have planned. Krista, you and Jasmine enjoy yourselves. And Ashton...at least *try* not to make a scene this time."

"Mmmm...no promises." Ashton said, winking at Jessica in a teasing manner.

Jessica rolled her eyes and shook her head, "Fine. But I won't be helping you if the police show up...again."

"Hey! That was *not* my fault, okay?"

"Sure it wasn't."

"It wasn't!"

"Uh-huh."

"You're asking for a basket of tomatoes falling from the ceiling, Jess." Ashton said.

Jessica laughed, and made her way to the manager's office. When she reached the door, she knocked three times, and was told to enter from the other side. She opened the door, and saw who she assumed to be Josh's father, and started to introduce herself.

"Good evening, sir. My name is Jessica Holland. Are you by chance Josh's father, or the owner of the club?"

"Ah, Jessica. Welcome. Please, take a seat so we can talk about a few things." The man said, pointing to one of the two chairs in front of his desk.

Jessica nodded, and proceeded to the chair the man was pointing at, and made herself comfortable, but tried to remain respectful at the same time.

The man looked Jessica over a bit, studying her outfit, and person. He smiled and gave Jessica his full undivided attention, placing his elbows on his desk, and resting his chin in his palms. "You know... Josh told me you were very attractive, but I never expected you to be as attractive as you are" His eyes widened as he realized what he just said, and he started trying to take back what he said, "Now...wait, I didn't mean it like that. I'm a married man after all."

Jessica laughed, and gave the man a reassuring and kind smile, "Don't worry about it. I'm flattered you think I'm pretty, and I respect you for remaining loyal to your wife. There aren't many men who are still like that."

The man smiled, and regained his calmness, regaining his previous position "You can say that again. A bunch of sex crazed little brats is what they are. Anyway, my name is Marvin, and I'm Josh's father." He reached his hand over his desk to Jessica.

Jessica shook Marvin's hand, and sat back in her chair, "Nice to meet you, Marvin. So...I'll assume Josh told you the kind of music I play and sing?"

Marvin nodded, "Yes, ma'am. He said Carrie Underwood is a major inspiration to you, as well as a few rock bands."

Jessica nodded, "Yes, sir, that's correct. Carrie Underwood has been a favorite of mine for a long time, and the rhythm of her music often finds its way into my own work as well."

"What do you like most about her music?" Marvin asked curiously, "If you don't mind, I'd kind of like to get to know you a bit."

Jessica smiled kindly, and shook her head, "No, it's no trouble. Anyway, to answer your question, I think what I like most about Underwood's music is that it doesn't feel like it's one genre. It's country, mostly, but it also has a bit of a rock and pop feel to it...if that makes any sense."

"Oh, I completely agree." Marvin said, leaning back in his chair, "My wife listens to her music all the time, and I've never really disliked it, either. The club I run isn't necessarily a country club, but we often play a few country songs throughout the night. Carrie Underwood's music being some of the more common songs."

"So, you're saying I shouldn't feel terribly out of place by singing a few country songs here, right?" Jessica asked, laughing at her own joke.

Marvin chuckled, and leaned on his desk again, "No, you shouldn't have any trouble here. As attractive as you are, I have to warn you that some of the men here can become a little...much. They get the rules of "look but don't touch" turned around, and we've had a few...incidents in the past that drove a few female customers away. But I assure you that you will be safe. We've recently hired more bouncers, and these boys are tough. No harm will come to you. I promise."

Jessica smirked, and gave Marvin a confident stare, "Sir, with all due respect, I'm the daughter of two former highly trained U.S Marines, and the younger sister of a brother who was in the Navy SEALS as well as an Army Ranger. I can handle myself against a cocky drunk."

Marvin's eyes widened in surprise, and he smiled, "Well, hot damn! I might have to warn my *bouncers* to keep away from you. Not only beautiful, but dangerous too!"

Jessica laughed and continued the conversation, "So, I trust you have a list of songs you plan to play tonight?"

Marvin nodded, "Yes, ma'am, I do." He pulled out the main drawer of his desk, and handed Jessica a sticky note. "For your first night, I thought we'd go a little easy on you. We're only expecting a few songs tonight, but depending on how you do, we'll put more on the list for tomorrow."

Jessica looked at the songs on the list, and she smiled softly when she realized they were all the same songs she'd been practicing. She looked up at Marvin, and nodded in agreement, "That sounds fair enough. However, I've found it strange Josh hasn't contacted me all day today, and he was asking me questions fairly often all week. Did he take a vacation somewhere, or…?"

Marvin shook his head, and leaned back in his chair, "Your guess is as good as mine. Last I heard from him was last night. I have no idea where he is."

Jessica remained silent for a moment, then looked at Marvin again, "Um…I don't want to sound greedy here, but what if he doesn't show up? He said he'd handle my payment, and I need the money he offered."

"Oh, I'll take care of that. You held your part of the deal, after all." Marvin said, giving a kind smile to Jessica, "If he doesn't show up, I'll not only pay you, I'll let you be the one who skins him alive."

Jessica laughed out loud for a moment, then looked at Marvin, "I think we have a deal. I hope he's okay, though. He seems like a nice young man."

"Oh? He's single if you're *that* interested in him." Marvin said.

Jessica giggled, and stood from her chair, "Sorry, but…I already have someone."

Marvin nodded, "Mmm…I see. Well, your man is a lucky man. Josh seemed to like you, but I guess it's too late for that."

Jessica smiled softly, and looked at Marvin with honest caring eyes, "We can still be friends. When I said he seems like a nice man, I meant it. I'm not heartless, you know."

Marvin chuckled, and stood from his chair. He and Jessica shook hands, and he grinned honestly, "Well, I'll see you on stage, later."

Jessica nodded, "Sounds good. I hope we can continue to do business after tonight."

"Well, put on a good show, and we'll see."

Jessica nodded, grabbed her purse, and headed out the door.

Returning to her friends who were sitting on stools at the bar, Jessica sat next to Krista and ordered a glass of water. The bartender nodded, and went to fill her glass.

"So, how'd it go?" Ashton asked curiously.

Jessica smiled, and thanked the bartender with a nod before she responded, "It actually went well. A lot better than I expected. I have no idea why, but I kind of pictured Josh's dad to be a bit more…hostile since he runs this place, and has to keep things in order with the current economy."

"Well, that's good to hear. Did he say anything about Josh? What's going on with him?" Krista asked.

Jessica shook her head, and took the first sip of her drink, "He doesn't know, either. Last Marvin heard from Josh was last night, and I haven't heard from him since Tuesday. I wonder what he's doing. It's very strange."

"Not to mention disrespectful." Ashton intervened, "*He* was the one who contacted you and tried to hire you, and now he's nowhere to be seen? It's a little fishy to me."

Jessica nodded in agreement, "I know. If he doesn't show up by the time I go on stage, I'll be having a few words with him. I just hope he's okay and hasn't gotten into trouble."

"That does remain a bit of a problem, actually." Krista said, "With the Republic getting closer and closer to the city, it's likely some places have become more dangerous than others. Luckily, we all live in some fairly reasonable neighborhoods."

"True. But I doubt the peace in our neighborhoods will last long once the Rebels take the city." Jessica said, taking another sip of her drink. "Too many people are still under the impression President Lane has the upper hand, and when the truth finally comes to them it'll hit them hard. I expect riots will break out all across the city once the Republic retakes the capitol."

"Mmm…well, call me a little sentimental, but wouldn't rioting be the same as asking for a death wish?" Krista asked, "I mean, we all know about the Shadows now. President Davis was very clear when he said they're not to be messed around with. Somehow, I think we'll be seeing them taking control over D.C in the future."

Jessica nodded, and finished her glass of water. She sat the glass aside, and turned to face Krista, "It's a guarantee these 'shadows' will be in control once the war is over. What I'm curious about, however, is how they actually work. It occurs to me that they're not interested in making themselves rich, and they're certainly not power hungry. If they were, the economy of the Republic wouldn't be as strong as it is, and they wouldn't have the military might they possess."

Ashton leaned over the bar to look at Jessica, "So…what are you saying, exactly?" She asked curiously.

Jessica looked at Ashton for a moment, and shook her head, "I'm not sure. I think there's a much, much larger picture to this whole civil war than what we've been allowed to see. These 'shadows' have remained secret for the better part of five years now, so why do they choose *now* of all times to reveal themselves?"

Krista remained silent for a minute, then looked at Jessica, "Maybe it's a scare tactic? A battle for President Davis to scare President Lane into surrendering and shortening the war?"

Jessica thought for a moment, then shook her head, "No. President Davis knows Lane is too full of himself to ever surrender. And besides, didn't you see how terrified he was during that interview? He said only what he was allowed to say, and he made sure to not say any more when he started to give too much information."

"True. So…what do you expect these 'shadows' to do once they take control?" Ashton asked.

"I have no idea." Jessica said, turning her back to her friends so she could look at the stage, "But I think we'll find out soon enough." She lowered her head as she thought to herself, *"If there's anything I remember about you…it's how quick and precise your moves were in strategy games. Are you trying to send a message to me, too? How am I supposed to respond?"*

Not wanting to bury her mind in thoughts on the war, Jessica cleared her mind, and turned to her friends again, and asked them if there were any songs she'd like to play specifically for them.

Just before it was time to go on stage, Jessica made a quick trip to the ladies restroom where she made some last minute preparations, and checked herself over one last time. Her heart was pounding against her chest, and her adrenaline was higher than ever. As she looked herself in the mirror, she combed aside any loose strands of hair, and made a quick touch on her lipstick and eyeliner. She brushed her clothes off, and took several deep breaths to help calm her nerves. She then peeked outside the door, and saw people were flocking to the dance floor. Her eyes widened, and her heart nearly skipped a beat when she saw just how many people there were.

"Holy cow...how many people are here? This is *not* what I was expecting. There must be at least...two-hundred people here!" She whispered in awe.

She quickly closed the door and retreated back into the restroom to collect her thoughts. She meditated for a moment, collecting her mind, and calming her nerves. *"Okay, okay, I can do this. This is what I've been waiting my whole life for. If I can't sing in front of a few hundred people, how can I make an actual name for myself?"*

She took several more deep breaths, "Well...five minutes until it's time. I better get down there." She went through the door, and snuck her way down to the stage where Marvin was about to introduce her. He noticed her, and signaled her to stay in the shadows while he made his announcement. He tapped the microphone as he tested, catching the attention of most people on the dance floor.

"Uh, hello? Testing, testing...it seems to be working fine." He cleared his throat before continuing, "Ladies and gentlemen, good evening, and welcome to the Silver Tab. We have a very special guest with us tonight. Some of you who are returning customers would know that we ran into some...issues with our last entertainer. For some of you, the club just hasn't been the same since he left, and many of you have told me personally that we need a new entertainer. Well, believe it or not, we have a very talented singer and musician here with us tonight. This woman I'm about to introduce has made a bit of a name for herself in this part of the city. She's donated to charity, helped start charity programs for the poor, the needy, and the elderly. She's offered friendship to those who seek it, and has been there for people who just need someone to talk to. If you're from the neighborhood, or any of the surrounding places, I'm sure you've at least heard this woman's name at one time or another. Ladies and gentlemen, let us welcome our new entertainer: Miss Jessica Holland!"

The crowd only clapped at first, but as Jessica ascended the stairs onto the stage, and stood in the light where people could recognize her face, nearly half the audience erupted into thunderous applause as people cheered, screamed, and whistled.

Jessica's cheeks turned pink, and she couldn't help but smile as she took the microphone from Marvin's hand. She nodded at Marvin in thanks, and turned to face the audience as Marvin walked off the stage behind her. She waited for the crowd to calm down, and grinned proudly as she started talking.

"Wow…there is a *lot* more people here than I expected." She paused as some of the people laughed, "So, forgive me if I seem a little nervous. Anyway, I'm not the greatest at giving speeches, so how about we skip right to the music, yeah?"

The lights suddenly changed color, and the dance floor lit up, which caught Jessica slightly off guard, but she soon recovered. The stereos started blasting music, and Jessica listened closely. She smiled once she recognized the song, and started singing on cue. As her lips started moving, and her voice echoed throughout the room, Jessica's nervousness disappeared, and she seemed to be an entirely different person. Her energy went off the charts, and her body seemed to automatically move to the beat of the music. Her voice hit every note perfectly, and she was right in time with the rhythm.

Ashton, Krista, Jasmine, and Jessica's other friends were astounded by her talent.

"Are…are you guys seeing this?" Ashton asked in total disbelief.

"Good lord in heaven and the heaven after that, she's like a completely different person!" Krista shouted in amazement, "W-wow… just…damn. Someone want to remind me why she works at a flower shop?"

Jasmine shook her head, "Oh, who cares? C'mon! We promised her we'd be up in front supporting her!"

The other girls nodded, and rushed to the front of the dance floor where they either danced on their own, with each other, or managed to find a dance partner.

As the night went on, Jessica's energy dwindled slightly, but she easily made it to the end of every song. The crowd erupted in applause and cheer at the end of each song, and the cheering seemed to get louder after every song. However, as the night drew to a close, Jessica's attitude changed, and she approached the microphone one last time after letting her voice have a rest.

"Alright, everybody, are you having a good time so far?" Jessica shouted excitedly, raising her right fist in the air.

The crowd roared as the majority of the people raised their glasses, and watched as Jessica continued to talk.

"Good. I'm glad to hear it. I've been singing a lot of Carrie Underwood and other country music since I started…but for my last song…I want to do something a little different." She lowered her head for a moment as she thought, but looked up at the crowd again once she was ready. "This last song goes out to a friend I had a long time ago. Who suffered from depression, who's only dream was to be accepted and loved by a family. I dedicate this next song to anyone who, too, may be suffering with depression, or struggling with a hard time right now. Ladies and gentlemen, my next song is Lullaby by Nickelback" She lowered her head again, and closed her eyes as she thought, *"Chris… this is for you."*

Once the song was over, Jessica bowed as the crowd cheered and clapped for her, and descended the stairs on the side of the stage where Marvin and her friends were waiting for her. She smiled as she descended the stairs, but was taken by surprise when her friends ambushed her and hugged her.

"Jess, that was *amazing*! I cannot believe what I saw with my own eyes!" Krista said, separating from Jessica.

Ashton nodded in agreement, and backed away as well. "You know, for all your talk of being a little nervous, you certainly did a good job of hiding it. It seemed like the second you started singing you were too focused to be nervous, and acted as if you'd done that a million times already. You're too skilled for your own good."

Jessica laughed, and returned Ashton's hug, "Well...I have my friends to thank for inspiring me." She released Ashton, and turned to face Marvin. "So...what do you think?" She asked, folding her hair behind her ear.

Marvin smiled, and shook her hand, "Welcome to the Silver Tab, Jessica. You promised a good show, and you definitely delivered...with interest. Speak with me when the bar closes, and we'll discuss your payment."

Jessica's eyes sparkled, and her excitement got the better of her. She jumped back to her friends, and screamed in excitement. Her friends all hugged her one more time, and squealed in excitement with her.

Once they'd calmed down, Jessica and her friends went back to the bar where they sat on the stools, and engaged in random conversation.

What remained of the night flew by quickly. The crowd that once took up the entire dance floor slowly disappeared, and eventually left only the bar's employees to clean up the mess, and prepare things for the next day. The night didn't go by without incident, however. Jessica had been forced to defend herself more than once from drunk men who couldn't keep their hands to themselves. One man had tried to grope her from behind, but his 'fun' was brought to a quick end when Jessica spun around and roundhouse kicked the side of his head, forcing him to slam his nose on the bar. The second situation was an incident that the bouncers protecting Jessica took care of, forcing the attacker to be banned from the bar. Despite these incidents, however, Jessica had thoroughly enjoyed the night, and was eager for the next day.

As closing time came closer, Marvin met Jessica in private, and discussed her payment.

"Well, Josh never showed up throughout the entire thing, despite my constant calling and calling. I'm starting to get a little worried about him, but before I call out a search party, we have business to discuss. I believe Josh said he agreed to a ten percent cut, but I think you deserve better now that I've seen what you can do." He pulled out a box, and started collecting some dollar bills from it, then closed the case and slid it under his desk again. He then started counting out the money, and handed the cash to Jessica, "How does eight-hundred dollars sound?"

Jessica's eyes widened, and her jaw dropped open, "Uhh...e-eight-hundred...dollars? R-really?!"

Marvin nodded, "That's right. And this is just the beginning. I've decided I'm going to give you a fair cut. 20% of what the bar makes every night. This is one of the more popular hot spots in the city, so there will be nights where you may even earn up to a thousand dollars after the night is over. I'm glad Josh found you. I don't think we could have found a better singer had we searched for another four years."

Jessica took the money from Marvin's hand, and quickly brushed through it, "I'm happy you guys found me, too." She said in a low voice.

Marvin laughed and leaned back in his chair, "Well, I hope to have a long and profitable relationship, Miss."

Jessica smiled and nodded at Marvin, then put the money she'd earned in her purse. She then looked at Marvin again, and held out her hand, "That is my hope as well. Oh! Actually, I just remembered. Josh said something about seeing if he could find an actual band for me so I could play my own music. Do you think that'd be possible?"

Marvin thought for a moment, then stood from his chair, "Well, I'll see what we can do. If we find a band, though, we'll have to cut your earnings. But that's your call."

"Mmmm...that's not an easy choice." Jessica said, standing from her chair, and shaking Marvin's hand. "Mind if we discuss this another time after I've had some time to think it over?"

Marvin nodded, and led the way to his door, and opened it, "That sounds like a plan to me. Have a good night, Miss."

Jessica nodded, "You, too, Marvin. And thank you for everything."

Marvin nodded, and closed the door behind Jessica as she walked out.

As Jessica made her way back to her friends, Ashton approached her, "So…how much did you make?" She asked curiously.

Jessica smirked and crossed her arms, "Wouldn't you like to know? Well, take a guess before I tell you."

Ashton thought for a moment, then made her guess, "Five-hundred dollars flat."

Jessica smiled and shook her head, "Close. But no. Tonight alone I made eight-hundred even."

Ashton's jaw dropped, and she stared at Jessica in disbelief, "E-eight-h-hundred? Just from tonight? Well, I'll take this as an indication that you won't be working at the flower shop anymore."

Jessica laughed, and motioned her head for Ashton and her friends to follow her. "Of course I'll still be working at the flower shop. I can't leave you guys behind!" She turned to face Ashton again, "And besides, this is really just for the weekends…at least I think so, anyway."

"So are you still in a money crisis after this? Will you still be needing help to pay the bills?" Ashton asked.

Jessica laughed as she started walking to the exit again, "I'm always open to donations, Ashton if you're ever feeling generous once every blue moon."

"Oh, ha-ha! Very funny." Ashton said with sarcasm in her voice. "Well, in the end, I'm happy your dreams are finally coming true. I wish I had your kind of talent. I could never get on stage and sing and dance like that."

Jessica turned to face Ashton, but continued walking, "Well, I have years and years of experience behind me. I first started singing when I was in kindergarten or pre-school, and I started learning how to play musical instruments in second or third grade."

Ashton nodded, and turned her attention to Krista as she started another topic. "So…who was this friend of yours you played for during the last song, Jess?"

Jessica's eyes widened, and she turned to face Krista, "Uh…well… that's actually a bit of a long story."

"That's okay. I like stories." Krista said.

Jessica smiled, and turned her attention to the door, "Well…I'll tell you a bit. He was an orphan my family took in when we first moved to Washington ten years ago. He wasn't treated very well, and the minister at the orphanage treated him poorly, and forced him to live in…what *should* be illegal situations. So…long story short, Chris, who was the orphan, and I became friends over a period of time. I eventually convinced my parents to take him in…and we grew a little…closer together after that."

"Ohhh! Jessica had a boyfriend." Ashton teased, nudging her elbow against Jessica's arm.

Jessica's cheeks turned pink as she blushed, but she didn't refuse it. "That's true. I did."

"So…what happened to him?" Krista asked curiously.

Jessica glanced at Krista for a moment, then lowered her head as she thought about the answer. "Mmm…I really can't say. Chris didn't exactly have the easiest life, and he didn't know a lot about his past. One day, he just up and left, only leaving us a note saying he'd be back after he found some answers." She closed her eyes as she continued thinking, *"Of course, the truth is a bit more complicated."*

"What? Really?! Well, what a jerk! Didn't he like living with you and your family?" Krista asked.

Jessica turned to face Krista, "He didn't enjoy living with us, Krista. He *loved* living with us. But Chris had a mission of his own, and he wanted nothing more than to learn the truth about his own past."

Krista looked at Jessica in confusion, and raised an eyebrow, "Learn the truth about his past? What does that mean?"

Jessica turned away as she tried to think of an answer, then looked at Krista again, "He was in an accident when he was eight, and he lost most of his memory from before…or so he told me."

Krista's eyes widened, and she lowered her head, "Oh…well…I guess that explains a little. What happened to his parents?"

"They died." Jessica said, keeping her attention on the door. "Anyway, I'd really rather not talk about that right now. It makes me feel depressed."

Krista smiled and nodded, "Sure, Jess. No problem."

Jasmine stretched her arms behind her back as she yawned, "Well, I think I'm going to go ahead and head home. I'm beat."

Krista nodded, "Me, too. Mind if I take a cab back home with you?"

"Sure. Safety in numbers after all." Jasmine said.

Once the girls reached the door, Jessica hugged Jasmine and Krista one last time before they parted ways.

"You two be careful on the way home, okay?"

Jasmine laughed, and rolled her eyes, "Okay, mother, we're not teen agers anymore."

Jessica chuckled, and said her final good-byes for the evening, then called her own cab to take her, Krista and Ashton back to their street

As the taxi pulled to a stop outside Jessica's apartment, Jessica handed the driver the due amount, and exited the vehicle with Ashton. Once they were out, the taxi driver sped off, leaving the girls behind.

"Well, I guess we put some over time in for him." Ashton said, watching the taxi drive off.

Jessica chuckled, and turned her attention to Ashton, "He's probably as tired as I am. I think I'll sleep in for a few hours later this morning. Maybe even until noon."

Ashton smiled, "Well, you certainly earned it." She covered her mouth as she yawned, and smiled at Jessica again, "Well, I'll see you again tomorrow night. I better get home and get at least *some* rest before I go to work."

Jessica nodded, and pulled Ashton into a hug, "Thank you for supporting me, Ash. I really appreciate it."

Ashton laughed, and separated from Jessica, "Hey, I can't just leave you hanging. Besides, if you're making *that* kind of money now…maybe I could learn how to perform, too."

"We'll see. I'm more than willing to teach you." Jessica said.

"Fair enough. I'll see you later." Ashton said as she started to walk away.

"Yeah. Be careful on the way home, Ash."

Ashton laughed and turned around to face Jessica as she walked backwards, "Hey, this is *me* we're talking about."

"I know. That's what concerns me." Jessica teased, winking at Ashton.

Ashton rolled her eyes, and turned away as she continued walking.

Jessica watched Ashton for a moment, but started for her apartment once she felt her eyes getting heavier.

As Jessica ascended the stairs to her apartment, she proudly hummed the songs she played to herself, and grinned as she thought about her future. *"Ohhh! I can't wait to tell mom and dad about this! They'll be so thrilled to hear about what happened!"* She thought. Her expectations were high, and she couldn't help but smile proudly.

As she stepped on the floor to her apartment, she felt her phone go off in her back pocket. She pulled her phone out of her pocket, and saw she had received a message from a strange number. Her eyes narrowed in confusion, and slid the screen over to check the message. When it came up, Jessica's eyes widened in shock and her hands started to shake.

"W-what the?! That's…that's the same writing that's on that ring!"

Tempted to run in the opposite direction, Jessica put her phone back in her pocket and started to go back down the stairs. But as she descended, curiosity started to kick in, and she peered around the corner to see her apartment. She examined the halls and saw nothing was out of the ordinary, but now that she was thinking about it, the atmosphere seemed heavy and alien. Almost as if she were in a completely brand new building. She slowly started to creep towards her apartment, and felt the air was getting colder and colder as she approached.

"I can't believe I'm doing this!" She thought as she crept up to her apartment door. She fiddled with her keys for a moment until she found the key to her apartment door, and slid the key into the door knob. She slowly started to turn the knob, and pushed the door open. When she peeked around the corner, her eyes widened in horror, and she screamed as loud as her lungs would allow and jumped away from the door.

With wounds that suggested he had been ripped apart by a large animal and a snapped neck with his eyes still open, Josh hung from the living room ceiling fan. Along the walls were letters written in fresh blood that matched the strange language on the ring with a pentagram directly under Josh's corpse. The letters went all across the room, and an evil presences lingered in the air. Despite the fact she couldn't read the letters, there was something ritualistic to them.

Jessica's eyes filled with tears, and she covered her mouth as she backed against the hallway wall and started to cry. Her mind was a mess, and reality slipped away from her. *"This has got to be a dream! This has got to be a dream!"* The thought as she fell to the floor.

Some of her neighbors came rushing out of their apartments, and immediately saw Jessica crying with her hands covering her face. They immediately rushed to her aid, but stopped once they saw what was in Jessica's apartment.

The air grew still, and time seemed to slow down. Some of the men stepped inside Jessica's apartment while a woman rested her hand on Jessica's shoulder, and tried to get her attention. Jessica lifted her head to look at the woman, but her mind was in a daze. Nothing seemed real to her.

"Jessica, what happened?" The woman asks softly, trying to snap Jessica out of her daze.

Jessica remained silent for a moment as she stared at Josh's corpse and watched the men examine the scene. She ignored the woman for what seemed like a long time, but turned her attention to the woman as she started shouting.

"Jessica…what happened?" The woman asked in a concerned but firm voice.

Jessica sank and shook her head as she tried to think clearly again, "I…I don't know. I was performing for a new job as an entertainer at the Silver Tab, and came home to find him there. He was *supposed* to be my boss." Her voice was still bumpy with emotion, but she was managing to keep herself together.

"What was his name?" The woman asked.

"Josh." Jessica answered. She thought for a moment, and continued on, "I'd been talking with him over the phone for the better part of a week trying to set up this performance, but he just stopped calling before yesterday. No one knew where he was. Not even his father."

The woman's eyes narrowed in sympathy, and she did what she could to comfort Jessica. Commotion filled the halls, and Jessica listened to the random conversations. More and more people crowded the scene, and after several minutes, a woman's voice echoes through, "Has anyone called the police yet?"

"Yes, they're on their way as we speak." A male voice responded.

"Good. Maybe we should seal this floor off until they get here." The woman said.

Some of the men nodded in agreement, and ran to the stairwells to stand guard as they waited for the police to arrive.

When the police finally arrived, they were just as disturbed to see what they were called for. The residents had left the scene mostly untouched, and left without argument when the police started asking everyone to leave. Jessica was still sitting in the hallway, but she had managed to pull herself mostly together, even though she had the look of depression and terror on her face. As one of the officers approached, Jessica shifted her attention to him, and stood up to greet him.

"So, this is your apartment, Miss?" The officer asked.

Jessica nodded, "Yes, sir. The man's name is Josh Day. He helped me sign up for a job as an entertainer at the Silver Tab."

The officer pulled out a pen and a sketch pad, and started writing down the information Jessica was giving him. "And what is your name, Miss?"

"Jessica Holland, sir."

The officer's eyes widened, and he smiled at Jessica a bit. "Ah! I know this isn't the time or place, but I *have* heard your name before."

Jessica smiled, but didn't look the officer in the eye.

The officer cleared his throat before he continued, and asked Jessica another question. "Do you know if Josh had any…suicidal thoughts or if anyone held a grudge against him?"

Jessica shook her head, "No, sir. I only knew him for a little less than a week, and I only talked with him about things related to my performance at the bar."

The officer nodded, and continued writing information down on his pad, "I see. I have one more question for now, Ma'am. Do you know anything about those symbols on the walls?"

Jessica thought for a moment, and looked up at the officer, "Actually...I received a ring in the mail a while back that has those exact same symbols on it. I thought they were a language of some kind when I first got it...it looks like I might have been right."

"And where is this ring now?" The officer asked.

"It's in the main desk drawer under my laptop computer." Jessica said, "I don't care if you take it."

"Okay. Well, do you mind if we search your apartment for anything that may help in our investigation?" The officer asked.

Jessica shook her head, "No, not at all. You're free to search."

The officer nodded in thanks, "Thank you, Ma'am. We'll be back with you shortly. If you need anything, let us know."

Jessica nodded in thanks, and moved out of the way as a few other officers came on scene.

CHAPTER 10

Time's up

Dallas FT. Worth, Texas: Carswell Rebel Supply Base, 0140 (1:40 A.M)

With an urgent message, President Davis rushed through the halls of the Republic's corridors to the command room where his superiors, the Seven Shadows, were discussing some future plans. As he barged through the door, he caught the attention of his main commander, and rushed down the stair well to him.

"General! I have an urgent message that requires your immediate attention!" Davis shouted as he jumped off the last bit of the stairs.

"What is it? We're in the middle of something important, President Davis." The commander said in a slightly annoyed tone.

President Davis looked around the room, and saw six out of the seven shadows were standing in the room, staring at him through their multi-colored hooded cloaks. A sense of uneasiness came over Davis, and he started to stutter his words, "F-for g-give t-the intrusion, G-General, b-but this is something you *want* to hear. It's from the Overseers of Death."

The commander waved his hand, "Fine. Put them on the big screen."

President Davis nodded, and connected with the Overseers of Death on the main screen in the room.

"So, you have something to report?" The commander asked, crossing his arms as he focused on the screen. The member he was speaking to was clothed in solid black body gear with a black helmet and face mask, leaving only his eyes visible.

"Yes, General. We found the girl you sent us to look after, and we've been observing her movements for the past several days. Nothing has been out of the ordinary until now."

"So, what's the problem?" The commander asked.

"Her apartment is now the site of a brutal murder. The woman is fine, but the victim is a man she met just recently, and invited her to perform at the local bar. We didn't witness the crime or see how this man ended up in her apartment, but there are symbols all over the walls written in the man's blood. It appears to be a language, but none of the letters are familiar to any of us. What makes this a concern, however, is the letters are a perfect match of a ring the woman came into possession of before we arrived."

The commander's tone changed, and he rested his arms at his side. He lowered his head to look at the ground before he continued, "Describe this ring, Captain."

"Mostly gold with what I think are red ruby's going around the bed, sir."

The commander's eyes widened, and he started backing up but kept his attention on the screen, "Captain, do *not* let that woman out of your sight! If anyone or anything suspicious approaches her, shoot to kill! I'll be there as soon as I can."

The captain nodded, "Yes, sir!"

The screen went black, and the other members of the Shadows turned to face the commander, "They've already made their move. This is too soon. We're not ready yet."

The commander faced the other Shadow, "Then we have no choice but to move quickly. So long as this ring remains in her hands, the enemy will know where she is at all times."

"But don't forget its value to us as well. It's a tool that can prove more valuable than any weapon." One of the shadow's said.

The commander nodded, "I know. But so long as that ring is in her possession I won't be coming back. Shadow Six, I'm leaving everything in your hands."

The Shadow nodded, "Agreed. I suggest you take the Falcon. It's the fastest plane within the Rebellion."

"I intend to." The commander said, turning his back to the others. *"I just hope I'm not too late."*

CHAPTER 11

Familiar Faces in Dark Places

After an interview with the police that lasted several hours, Jessica was led to the front of the police station where Ashton was sitting on a stool waiting for her. As Jessica approached, Ashton looked up from a book she was reading. Her eyes widened, and she darted over to Jessica.

"Oh my God, are you okay?! When I heard about this incident I feared you were injured or would be arrested for a crime you didn't commit! I was so worried!"

Jessica acted as if she were practically dead. A mix of fear, depression, and just plain fatigue had worn her down to the point she was just barely able to keep her eyes open. Despite how tired she was, however, Jessica still managed to smile a bit, "No, I'm fine, Ashton. I appreciate your concern." She lowered her head again, and wept a bit as Ashton pulled her into a comforting hug.

"I'm so sorry this happened to you." Ashton whispered softly in Jessica's ear.

Jessica remained silent for a bit, but wrapped her arms around Ashton's back, "Are the others coming?"

"I didn't call them." Ashton said, gently pushing Jessica back, "I was more concerned about reaching you and making sure you were okay. Do you want to see them, too?"

Jessica slowly shook her head, "No. I just want to go home… assuming I can."

Ashton smiled, and lifted Jessica's chin to meet her eyes, "I think you'd better stay with me for a while. At least until the police get this figured out."

Jessica nodded slowly, but hung her head again as a thought came to her, "Ashton…what will I say to Marvin about this? His son was found dead in my apartment! How can I ever show my face around him again?! Every time he looks at me, he'll see the woman that got his son killed!"

Ashton firmly rested her hands on both of Jessica's shoulders, and looked her in the eye, "That's not true, Jess, and you know it! What happened to Josh is *not* your fault, and Marvin will hold *nothing* against you! Don't even think like that! Nothing about this is your fault!"

Jessica sniffed and wiped some of her tears away, "I know. I just… I don't know how to say it."

"Well, you can think about it on the way home, okay? Anyway, it's super late. Let's hurry up and get out of here. I still have work tomorrow." Ashton said.

Jessica nodded and followed Ashton's lead out of the police station.

As they walked out onto the street, they found the city air was cool, and a cold breeze was making its way through the streets. The ground was turning wet as a light rain started to fall from the sky, and thunder erupted in the distance after quick flashes of lightning. The wind was slowly picking up, and before long, it was fast enough that it howled through the alleys and openings of buildings, making an eerie and haunting night time sound.

Ashton sighed as she looked into the distance after walking out of the police station, "**another** storm? I'm starting to think Poseidon is actually real, and has something against me."

"Doesn't everyone, though?" Jessica teased, despite her fatigue and depressed mood.

"Oh, ha-ha! Very funny, Jess. Admittedly, though, you're not that far from the truth." Ashton said.

Jessica chuckled a bit, and started walking in direction of Ashton's apartment, "I know you too well not to be. Anyway, let's just get to your apartment. I'm starting to think wearing this crop top was a bad idea."

"I doubt any guys you run across will say that, but fine. It's getting cold out here, anyway." Ashton said. She caught up with Jessica, and they walked side-by-side to Ashton's apartment.

Nearly halfway to Ashton's apartment, the rain was starting to come down harder, and the thickness of night grew darker as the rain fell. The air was getting colder, and the wind was getting stronger. The two girls had taken note of something that made them on edge, but also allowed them to feel somewhat safe. They were the only ones walking along the side walks on either side, and the streets were lifeless.

With Ashton following close behind, Jessica suddenly stopped walking, making Ashton run into her, and bump heads.

"Okay...what's up with the random stop, Jess?" Ashton asked in a slightly annoyed tone as she squeezed the bridge of her nose.

Jessica didn't answer, and she stood as still as a statue.

Ashton looked at her friend with a puzzled face, and reached out to grab her shoulder, but stopped when Jessica rose her fist in the air as a way of telling her to stop. She continued to watch Jessica as she observed every detail about the area around them, and her heart started to pound against her chest. "Jess, what's wrong?" Ashton whispered in a nervous voice.

Jessica remained silent for a moment, then looked back at Ashton, "We're not alone. Something's been following us since the police station."

Ashton's eyes widened in fear, and she turned her back to Jessica to watch behind them, "How do you know?"

Jessica pointed at the nearest street light, "Watch the light on the building."

Ashton turned her attention to the building and waited for something to happen. After several seconds, a shadow moved across the wall, making her take a step back, "What is that?"

Jessica shook her head, "I don't know...but it's big. It's probably what killed Josh."

Ashton put her back against Jessica's again, "Why didn't you say something sooner? We could have had the police escort us home."

"We probably should have done that to begin with." Jessica said, moving her eyes to check every inch of her surroundings, "What were we thinking? Two women walking home in the darkness of night. We could have been easy targets for a number of different things. None of them good."

"Yeah? Well, I'd rather take my chances with a rapist over whatever the hell *this* thing is." Ashton said as she continued to skim their surroundings. There was an odd silence between the two of them as they stood back-to-back for several seconds. Ashton turned her head to Jessica, "So what do we do? We can't stand here all night, and let that... whatever it is ambush us. What's it waiting for, anyway?"

Jessica remained silent for a few seconds, and looked up to check the walls of the building next to them, "It's waiting for us to make our move. It already has a plan. It will follow if we choose to either run for your apartment or back to the police station."

Ashton's eyes widened, and her jaw dropped, "Are you serious? So, no matter which way we choose to go, we'll be walking into this thing's trap. Great. Why don't we just kill ourselves and spare that thing the trouble?"

Jessica closed her eyes as she thought about what to do, and turned to face Ashton, "We won't do that because it's not after you...it's after me."

Ashton turned to look at Jessica, fearing she knew what Jessica was about to do, "You don't know that, Jess. And don't try to be a hero. You're going to get yourself killed."

Jessica smiled gently, "I have to do what I have to do, Ash. When I give the signal, we'll split up. If you make it to the police station, tell them what's happening."

Ashton thought for a moment, and raised an eyebrow from suspicion, "You know...you seem to act like you know what's happening. Care to explain?"

Jessica stared at Ashton in earnest, but tilted her head as she sighed, then looked at Ashton again, "The truth is...I know what this thing is.

I don't have the time to explain to you right now, but if I live, I'll tell you what you need to know."

Ashton's eyes curled, and she gave Jessica an angry stare, "You've been hiding something from me?"

"This isn't the time, Ashton."

"Fine. But I want an explanation if you live through this!"

"I'll explain everything…I promise." Jessica said, turning her back to Ashton and examined her surroundings. She spotted an alley to her right, and nodded to herself. "Okay, Ash. On my signal we split. One… two…*three!*"

Jessica and Ashton split up, and ran as fast as they could in opposite directions. Ashton headed back to the police station, and Jessica took the alley to her right. As Jessica ran through the alley, a loud, haunting and terrifying screech echoed behind her, a sound that would haunt her even in her worst nightmares. She didn't dare look back, and kept her eyes on the path ahead. She found herself in a maze of buildings, and zigzagged her way through the alleys, trying to lose the creature chasing her. She was running in near pitch blackness, and only the flashes of lightning lit up the alleyway enough she could see where she was going.

Despite how fast she ran, she could sense the creature was staying with her, but she still didn't dare look back. She took a sharp right into another alley, but her eyes widened the second she realized she had just made a fatal mistake.

"A dead end?!" She thought, terrified about the situation. She turned around, and slowly backed to the corner, and sat in the darkness, hoping the creature wouldn't spot her. She did her best to remain as quiet as possible. A few seconds passed, and the creature peered around the corner of the alley. Jessica's eyes widened in horror as a flash of lightning revealed what it was. It had the body of a giant centipede mixed with a man. Its arms were long, and turned into pinchers similar to that of a scorpion. It was at least twelve feet long, and the body stood at least seven feet off the ground. Its head was that of an alien. Misshapen with a massive overbite, but razor sharp jagged teeth that would be suitable for easily tearing through flesh.

Jessica covered her mouth as the creature entered the alley, and started searching for her. It sniffed the air, and threw a dumpster aside like it was nothing. The dumpster smashed through the wall of a building, and parts of the wall collapsed. With every step the creature took, it got closer, and closer to Jessica. It didn't take long for it to reach the end of the alley, where it stood over her, sniffing the air.

Jessica didn't look at the creature, fearing that looking at it would draw its attention. She covered her mouth as the creature released another loud and terrifying screech, and tried to keep calm, but she squealed slightly. She looked up to meet face-to-face with the creature, and became paralyzed with fear. The creature sniffed her for a few seconds, then released another screech. It grabbed Jessica by the neck with its pinchers and lifted her into the air where it held her back against the wall. It studied her for a second, growled, and started to turn its pinchers like it was going to snap her neck.

Jessica closed her eyes, and waited for the end to come. There was no point in trying to fight this creature. It was far stronger than she was. However, she opened her eyes again when the unexpected happened. The creature released her from its grip, and started to back away slowly. It looked around as if it sensed *it* had become the prey of something else.

Jessica remained speechless as she sat on the ground, watching the creature. A flash of lightning lit the alley, and behind the creature was a man in a hooded black cloak. The creature turned to face the man, snapped its claws, and bared its teeth to the man.

From what Jessica could see, the man didn't even flinch. She watched in awe as the man reached into his cloak, and pulled out two swords. Without warning, the creature charged at the man, striking at him with its claws. The man dodged the attack, and sliced the creature's arm with his sword. The creature screeched in pain, and immediately pulled its arm back. It retreated for a second, then charged at the man again. The man dodged the attack, and sliced an X on the creature's body, making it screech in pain again.

Jessica watched as the creature covered its wounds with one of its claws, and used the other to strike at the man again. The man dodged the attack, and jumped over the creature, sliding his sword through the centipede part of the creature's body, and pinning it to the spot.

The creature couldn't move, and was incapable of defending itself. With one final move, the man jumped on the creature's shoulders, and stabbed his remaining sword through the top of the creature's head. The creature screeched and squirmed, throwing its arms around as it tried to pull the man off its shoulders. The man twisted his sword, then retracted it as he jumped off the creature's shoulders. The creature remained standing for a few seconds, then collapsed on the ground.

Jessica stared at the scene before her in awe, amazed by what she saw. She pulled her legs back, and wrapped her arms around her knees as she watched the man approach her, twirling his swords around in his hands before sliding them into his cloak. She couldn't see his face, but she couldn't help but feel there was something familiar about him. She didn't feel threatened by his presence, and the man kept a comfortable distance from her as he looked down at her, checking for any wounds she may have gotten from the creature.

A flash of lightning lit the alley. The man quickly looked up at the sky, then turned his attention to Jessica again. Her eyes widened in disbelief as she caught the man's facial appearance, and she slowly stood off the ground, using the wall next to her to keep her steady. "Chris?" She asked, overjoyed to see him again, but almost too nervous to approach him.

Chris continued to look at Jessica for a second, but slowly started to back away, disappearing into the shadows.

Jessica started to chase after him, but tripped on something hidden in the darkness. "Chris! Wait!" She cried out as she looked up and reached her arm out to him. A flash of lightning lit the alley again, and Jessica could see him standing at the end of the alley, next to the corpse of the creature. She watched as he grabbed the creature and started to walk off. She stood still, before chasing after him again. When she reached the end of the alley, however, Chris was gone without a trace. Even as a flash of lightning lit the alley, she saw no sign of her long lost friend.

Saddened at the fact that he didn't speak to her, she hung her head, and thought about how things could have gone differently. *"Was it something I said?"* She thought as she started to cry, *"The first time we see each other in over ten years, and you don't say a single word to me? What did I do wrong?"*

"Ching"

Jessica looked up to see a knife sticking to the wall next to her with a note attached. She wiped the tears from her eyes, and reached for the note.

"It's good to see you again. Unfortunately, it's not time for us to meet yet. After the Republic takes control of Washington, seek me out at the National Mall. The soldiers will know what to do. The civil war is over, but the real enemy has already made their first move. Your apartment is no longer safe. Stay with your friends until Monday."

Jessica grinned slightly, and turned to look in the direction the knife came from. Chris was gone, but there was an exit further down the alley. She held the note close to her chest, and her grin turned into a huge smile. She laughed in joy for a moment, unable to contain her excitement about seeing Chris again for the first time in what seemed and felt like an eternity. She folded the note, and carefully shoved it in her pocket, then made her way back to the street where she met up with Ashton who had managed to convince the police station to send out a SWAT team. They both hugged each other, but as Jessica looked over Ashton's shoulder, she could just make out the figure of a man standing on the ledge at the top of the building across the street. She smiled softly, and broke away from Ashton.

"I think I owe you some answers, Ashton." Jessica said.

"Indeed you do. But let's wait until we get back to my apartment before we talk." Ashton suggested.

Jessica nodded, "Sounds good to me."

Ashton led Jessica back to the SWAT team where Jessica was searched and examined for any injuries, but was released from custody when they found nothing was wrong.

CHAPTER 12

Warnings and Explanations

Arriving at Ashton's apartment, Ashton let Jessica in first, and locked the door behind them after she walked in. Jessica wandered into the living area of Ashton's apartment, and lay her purse down on the kitchen counter. She looked down as she twiddled her thumbs for a moment, then looked back at Ashton, "I owe you some answers, don't I?" She asked, turning to face Ashton.

Ashton nodded and walked up to Jessica, "Indeed you do. What secrets have you been hiding from me all these years? How do you know what that…that thing was?"

Jessica lowered her head as she tried to think of an answer, and looked up at Ashton again once she decided to just tell the entire truth. "I'm going to tell you some things I really probably shouldn't, but there's no point keeping them hidden from you anymore since you've seen one of them."

Ashton's eyebrows raised in curiosity as she watched Jessica walk over to the main window of her apartment, "Why, what are you, some kind of government agent?"

Jessica laughed a little at Ashton's joke, but turned to face her with a serious face, "I wish it were that simple…but no." She paused for a moment as she thought about something, then continued, "Ashton, did you ever hear anything about a military project called "Experiment 2025"?"

Ashton thought for a moment, then shook her head, "No, I can't say that I have. What does that have to do with anything?"

"I'll put the pieces of the puzzle together piece by piece for you." Jessica said, "Remember that boy I was telling you about at the bar when we were leaving? The orphan my family took in when we first moved here?"

Ashton nodded, "Yeah."

"Well, I didn't tell you the entire truth." Jessica continued, "See, I have a certain…gift, I suppose you could say. It's called Forayer's Sight. Basically, I can look into your eyes and learn about your past as if I'm watching a movie about you. I've only used it on a few certain people because I don't know what effects it has on me, but Chris, the orphan my family took in, was one of these people."

"Wait…you can see peoples past…just by looking into their eyes?" Ashton said, hardly able to believe what she was hearing.

Jessica nodded, "I know it's a little hard to believe, but I've never lied to you before, so why would I start now? Anyway, when I used Forayer's Sight on Chris, I wasn't able to see his entire past. Everything before the age of eight was completely pitch black. It took me a while to figure out, in fact, it wasn't until he told me what happened to him in his younger years that I was finally able to put everything together. The point I'm getting at is – Chris is this Experiment 2025."

"So, what does that mean, exactly?" Ashton asked, still a little skeptical of the story Jessica was telling her.

"It means nothing good." Jessica answered, "I was never given the details of how they accomplished this, but somehow the military sealed the spirit of the Grim Reaper inside Chris hoping it would allow them to control the deadliest weapon on the face of the Earth. The ability to control the elements like its child's play along with supernatural strength. A weapon far more deadly than any nuclear weapon."

Ashton's eyes widened in curiosity, and she uncrossed her arms, hanging them at her sides, "What happened to him, then?"

Jessica sighed before she continued, "Well, for a time, it was believed the experiment failed. Chris had his memory wiped, and he was forced out onto the streets with no idea who he was or how he got to D.C. He was only eight at this time. Can you imagine how terrifying the world must have been to him then? It makes me sad just thinking about it."

"So how does he connect to that thing we saw?" Ashton asked.

Jessica thought for a moment, and turned away from Ashton to look out the window, "A few weeks after we'd met, and I finally convinced my parents to let him live with us, I saw what kind of power Chris had sealed within him. There was an…incident at Washington High, and that's when Chris unleashed the Reaper's power for the first time."

Ashton's eyes widened, and she took a step back, "Y-you don't mean h-he was…"

Jessica turned to face Ashton, "That's right. Neither history nor the media actually wrote down what happened correctly. There was a fight that took Chris to his limit, and that's when his anger finally snapped. I've forgotten just exactly how many people died during this outbreak of the Reaper's power, but I *do* remember half the school was reduced to rubble."

"So…what happened, then?" Ashton asked.

"Well, I tracked Chris down and learned the truth about him. Or… at least what *he* knew, anyway." Jessica replied, "However, it wasn't long after this that we met a man who called himself Night Hawk – one of the pre-ranking members of the Seventeen Assassins from the Land of the Unknown."

Ashton crossed her arms and stared at Jessica in disbelief, "Land of the Unknown? That's just a myth, Jessica. It's something from an old child's novel, used to put kids to sleep. It doesn't exist." novel, used to put kids to sleep when they got to bed. It doesn't exist."

Jessica smirked, and turned to face Ashton, "How much are you willing to bet? I know who and what I saw ten years ago. If you think the Unknown doesn't exist, you're in for a serious surprise when the Rebels take D.C…and after that."

"What's that supposed to mean?" Ashton asked.

Jessica sighed, and looked down at the floor for a moment, then looked back up at Ashton, "We're heading for another war. Not against terrorists, not against communist countries, but against something far, far worse. That thing that was following us was a member of the Agroneese – a demonic cult that worship's the demonic lord of fear, Agromon. From what I can remember, they've returned, and are building an army large enough to declare war on the entire world."

Ashton's eyes widened in fear, and opened her mouth widely, "S-seriously?! So...well, wait. I thought the legend was the Unknown defeated the Agroneese at the end of the first war."

"They nearly did." Jessica replied as she nodded at Ashton. "The Agroneese were on the very brink of annihilation from the advance of Unknown troops, but a volcanic eruption destroyed the capital city at the last moment, forcing troops to withdraw back to the Unknown. I'm not sure where the Agroneese went after that, but now they're coming back."

"Oh, good. So now we have this stereotypical Hollywood and Disney movie scenario where the bad guys are coming back for revenge on the guys who nearly killed them, and want to rule the world." Ashton said in a sarcastic tone as she rolled her eyes. "I am so glad there's still originality in the world..."

Jessica laughed, "It certainly seems that way." She said in a serious voice "After Chris turned into the Reaper, we met Night Hawk who told us everything I'm telling you now. He told us a number of different things that I shouldn't really go into detail about. To cut a long story short, he told Chris his true origins, and took him away to train and learn how to control the Reaper and his powers."

"A pre-ranking member of the Seventeen?! You're seriously telling me these people exist?!" Ashton asked, unable to make up her mind on whether she should be scared or amazed at the fact.

"It would seem they do. And I think they're these Shadows that are in command of the Republic." Jessica said, "In fact, I know for a fact now that Chris is one of them."

"*What?!*" Ashton yelled in a mix of disbelief and awe. "A-are you certain? How could you know that?"

Jessica started to rub her chin, and turned to look out the window as she replied, "I should have seen it sooner. I knew there was a sense of familiarity about the tactics the Republic had started using lately, but I couldn't place my finger on it. My dad was an undefeated Chess champion for years. He was so good no one would even try playing him anymore. Then, the first night Chris spends with us, he wins every single game he and dad played. No matter what my dad tried, Chris saw right through it. He was a military and economic genius, but people didn't give him the credit he really deserved." She turned towards Ashton as she continued, "When it became clear to us that Chris was a lot smarter than he let on, we set up some simulation games for him. Certain economic building games, and military strategy games set at the hardest difficulty. He built the most prosperous cities and provinces I'd ever seen, and his military strategy was second to none. My dad even said Chris would be the last general anyone in his right mind would want to go up against, and he was a Captain in the Marine Corps when he said this."

"That's amazing! Do you know what his I.Q is?" Ashton asked curiously.

Jessica shook her head, "No. I never really got the chance to test him. However, I can almost guarantee you is was over two-hundred. He was too smart for his I.Q to be any lower."

"So…do you *really* know it's him, or are you speculating at this point?"

"No…it's him." Jessica said in a slow but reassuring voice, "I know because I saw him earlier. He saved me from that Agroneese scout. Were it not for him…I'd be dead right now."

"Wait. He's *in* the city now?" Ashton nearly yelled, "It's not that I'm not happy that he saved you, but doesn't that mean the Rebels are likely on their way now, too? If he's the head general of the Republic… the army must be moving in, right?"

"I have no idea. He didn't say." Jessica said as she shook her head, "He didn't even say a word to me, but he did leave a note for me. He said it's not time for us to meet yet, but he wants me to seek him out after the Rebels take the city… My God, it's all starting to make sense."

167

"What is?" Ashton asked. She watched as Jessica started to pace back and forth.

"Again, Chris just shows his brilliance. I wondered what was taking so long for him to return. Washington against seven or eight pre-ranking members of the Seventeen? The city would be in ruins by the time they finished. But had they taken over by force, they would have been seen as the bad guys. The world wouldn't have listened to them when they told us about the coming Agroneese threat. So they had to plan out this entire civil war, split the country, and make the Rebellion a much larger force than the media lets on. I'd even be willing to bet they have control of the media, which is why they haven't told us anything. I bet they know a lot more than they're being allowed to tell. At least FOX and CNN, anyway. The others I'm not so sure about."

"So what do you think is going to happen after the Republic wins? They'll have to reveal themselves sometime." Ashton said.

Jessica nodded, "That's true. If I had to guess a time they come out and reveal themselves, it'd be after President Lane and his administration are removed from office. I have no idea what's in store for them after that, though. Chris hated politicians for what they did to him and his family. I can't blame him, but I fear he won't be the same as he was when he left. President Lane may be living on borrowed time for all I know."

"How could Chris be the same, though?" Ashton asked, "It's not like one spends ten years with the most dangerous people, learn what happened to him and his family, and continue to be a very friendly person. By what you're telling me... I think the Chris you knew all those years ago may be dead, Jess. I hate to say it like that, but..."

"No. You're right, Ash." Jessica said, "I know Chris has changed a lot. He'll not only be a completely different person, but a seasoned killer at this point. You don't earn the title of "Assassin" by sitting around doing nothing for ten years."

"And you're okay with this? Weren't you in love with him?" Ashton asked.

Jessica's cheeks turned pink, and she scratched her cheek as she looked down, "Well...yeah. We had a very close bond when he left, and I think that even after all these years he'll still be loyal to myself and my family." She stared at Ashton with serious eyes as she continued, "But if you're asking whether or not I support what he's doing or may do in the future... If there's anything I learned about Chris when we first met, it's that he's unstoppable when he sets his mind to something. It's Washington politicians that made him what he is now, who ordered the military to experiment on him, sold his family to the Muslim Brotherhood... there's a list a mile long of reasons he has to hate everything about this city, and I can't blame him for seeking revenge. They did *terrible* things to him for their own selfish and greedy agenda, and I think whatever Chris does to them will be perfectly justified. As the saying goes, Karma's a bit of a bitch."

"Hmm...well, if the government really did all the things you say they did to Chris, then I suppose he's not in the wrong. I just hope he's not, like, *really* bad when he reveals himself to the world." Ashton said.

"Well, truth be told, Chris has more people to hold grudges against than Washington's politicians." Jessica said sighing. "But I think some of what I know would be easier to explain when you see it yourself. I'm sorry for keeping this a secret from you and the others, Ashton, I really am. But I promised the others I wouldn't tell anyone about this stuff because they feared it'd start a panic, and the element of surprise, their only real advantage over the Agroneese would be gone. Can I ask you to keep what I told you to yourself?"

Ashton smiled and nodded, "Oh, don't sweat it, Jess. I admit I'm a little...sad at the fact you didn't trust me enough to tell this stuff to me, but I understand why you didn't. My mouth is sealed. What happens in my apartment stays in my apartment."

Jessica smiled, and nodded at Ashton in thanks, "Thank you, Ashton. Well, I suppose we better call it a night. You still have work tomorrow, after all."

"Yeah, don't remind me."

CHAPTER 13

Ring of Xzerriph

Hidden in the mist of the rain, and the shadow of the night, Chris watched Jessica and Ashton talk in Ashton's apartment from the top of a building across the street. His face was hidden entirely in the shadow of his hood, and his cloak made him impossible to spot even to the sharpest eye. As he observed the girls, he could see a mix of emotions in Jessica's eyes. She was overjoyed to have finally seen him again, but she was also scared and worried. By reading the movements of her body, and reading her lips, Chris could tell she hadn't forgotten about their secret. She was scared of the Agroneese, yes, but he could also tell she was scared of what he'd become within ten years of training with the assassins.

Chris watched over the girls for a time, making sure nothing else unplanned came along and spoiled his entire scheme. He'd waited ten years to take his revenge on those who did him and his family wrong. The last thing he needed was some Agroneese filth coming along and making a mess of things. He continued to monitor Jessica's lips. She was now telling her friend about what happened ten years ago, and revealing her secrets. He didn't mind this much. From the info he'd already gathered on Ashton, he knew she was a loyal friend to Jessica, and wouldn't reveal any of what she'd witnessed. She was safe...for now.

It wasn't long before the girls called it a night, and turned in. They had no idea they were being watched, and Chris wanted to keep it that way. When the lights in Ashton's apartment went off, he turned away from the apartment, and walked to the center of the roof. He pulled out a communication device that he designed and made for him and the rest of his order. He pushed a button, waited a few moments, then the hologram of one of the other assassins came up.

"I take it your mission was a success, Night Walker?"

"Yes, master. She's safe for now. There's no question about it. The Agroneese have found her." Chris replied.

The other assassin grabbed his chin as he continued, "Hmm…this complicates things. How much flexibility did you give your overall plan?"

"Enough that the Agroneese won't be a problem so long as we take Washington by Monday evening. Anything later, and we'll have a problem. That's why I personally stepped in to speed things up." Chris replied.

"I see. We received word from our troops on the Eastern war front. Your new toys arrived within the last hour, and troops are arming them as we speak. Richmond will be surrounded by tomorrow afternoon." The assassin said.

"Good. I'm leaving you in command of the mission for now. I have some business I need to attend to here in the city." Chris said.

"And what of the Overseers of Death? I take it you'll be staying in the city until our mission falls into place?"

Chris nodded, "Yes. You can dispatch the Overseers to wherever they're needed now. Their mission here is finished. I was able to inspect the apartment where this all began. There's no doubt in my mind. She's come into the possession of Xzerriph's ring. How this happened, I have no idea."

"We *need* control of that ring! Where is it now?"

"It's in the custody of the D.C Police Department." Chris growled, "It's a minor setback. The police in this city have gotten clumsy and corrupt. Stealing from them will be easy."

"See that it gets done! That ring *must* be in our possession before the Agroneese can recover it. Kill the cops if you have to, just get that ring back!" The assassin demanded.

"With pleasure."

Chris ended the conversation, and slid the communication device into an inside pocket in his robe. He looked back at Ashton's apartment building for a moment, then jumped down to the street and disappeared into an alley.

CHAPTER 14

Besieged

Jessica's eyes snapped open, and she shot up from her sleeping position, screaming as loud as she could. She was drenched in sweat, and panting heavily as she looked around, relieved to find she was safe inside Ashton's apartment. She held her hand over her chest as her heart beat against her chest with the strongest beating she'd ever experienced. Once the knowledge that she was safe sunk in, she laid on her back again, wiping the sweat off her forehead.

Not ten seconds later, Ashton came barging into the room with a look of worry and rushed to Jessica's side. "Are you okay? What happened?"

"I-it was nothing. Just a nightmare." Jessica said, still breathing heavily.

"Some nightmare. Look at you! You're covered in sweat! Do you remember anything about the dream?" Ashton asked.

Jessica took a moment to catch her breath and reflect on what she saw in the dream. "I saw that...thing again. That being I told you about not too long ago. You know, the one that held me against a tree?"

Ashton's eyes widened, and she stared at Jessica with concern, "Can you describe it for me again?"

"I don't think I want to." Jessica replied, "Besides...this time it was...different. These dreams. They feel too real to be just regular nightmares, and I've run into that being more than twice now. He gets scarier every time he reveals himself to me." A shiver ran down her spine, and she curled her knees and wrapped her arms around them, "Those eyes. Redder than the hottest fire, but colder than the coldest ice. All I see is murder and a thirst for blood when I look into them."

Ashton rested her hand on Jessica's closest shoulder for a moment, then started to rub her back, "Well, it's over. For now at least. I made some Green Tea for when you woke up. You want any now?"

Jessica curled her lips into a small smile and nodded, "Sure. What time is it, anyway? It feels kind of late."

"A little past ten."

"And you're not at work?"

Ashton shook her head, and stood from where she was sitting. "Work was cancelled after Shelby saw the news about what happened last night. It seems as though you've gained a bit of fame after last night's...incident. Krista and Jasmine are on their way to see you as we speak."

Jessica's eyes widened, and a look of guilt grew on her face, "Oh, blast and dammit, I never called my parents! They're probably worried sick about me! Mind if I borrow your phone, Ash?"

Ashton nodded and handed Jessica her phone, "Take as much time as you need, Jess. This probably won't be easy. In the meantime, I'll start making us something to eat for when the others get here."

Jessica took the phone, sat up in the bed, and dialed in her mom's cell number. "C'mon, c'mon pick up the phone!"

While Jessica talked with her parents, Ashton left the room and started preparing some food for when the others arrived.

Not long after Jessica ended the call with her parents, Krista and Jasmine came through the door.

"Ah! There you two are. I was wondering if you'd gotten lost." Ashton joked.

Jasmine smirked as she kicked off her shoes and walked into the kitchen, "Me?Get lost? Humph! You don't me at all."

"I think she knows you perfectly." Krista murmured as she walked past Jasmine.

Ashton glanced at Krista for a second, then rolled her eyes back at Jasmine curling her lips into a grin.

Jasmine sighed, and hung her shoulders, "Alright, fine! I took a corner too early and didn't realize my mistake until twenty minutes later. Are you happy now?"

"Overjoyed. Now, I made some food for us to eat. Come and get some when you're ready." Ashton said.

Jasmine rolled her eyes and made her way to Jessica.

"We heard about what happened, Jess. I'm so sorry that happened." Krista said, offering her comfort to Jessica.

"Thank you, Krista. But if it's alright with you, I'd rather not bring that topic up any more than we have to." Jessica replied.

Krista gave Jessica an understanding nod, and claimed her seat in the main room, next to the TV.

The others grabbed their snacks before claiming their seats, and Ashton put on the movie.

A few hours passed. The girls, weary of watching movies, agreed to get out of Ashton's apartment for a while. But as Ashton took the movie they had watched out of her Blu-ray, disturbing headlines were at the bottom of the screen.

Richmond Besieged by Heavy Rebel Forces

The girls' eyes widened, and they slowly stood up from their seats.

"I-is this for real?" Krista asked with hints of fear in her voice.

The others were too shocked to answer, but Jasmine was able to slowly nod.

"It's finally happening." Jessica whispered. "Richmond is about to fall."

The others glanced at Jessica for a moment, then turned their attention back to the screen as a FOX reporter started talking.

"It's like waking up and being on a completely different planet, Rhonda. One moment they weren't here, and the next they've got the entire city surrounded with artillery. Military personnel are trying to lock down fortifications and prepare for an immediate attack on the city, but they're severely outnumbered."

The TV switched back to the reporter at FOX HQ. "It's amazing to think they pushed that far that fast. Are civilians being let out of the city, or is the military escorting them to safer places deep inside the city?"

There was a brief pause before the second reporter started talking again, "Uh, it's going a bit of both ways, actually. For those living in the suburbs closer to rebel positions, Republic troops are allowing civilian vehicles to get out of the city, but the military is escorting others who are deeper inside the city to safer locations. I'm not sure when the attacks will begin, but we had a talk with one of the soldiers here, and he says hell is literally about to break loose. This is the single largest Republic army that has merged together since the assault for Hoover Dam over two years ago."

"That's absolutely incredible. Rob, keep your head down and get out of there when you get the chance."

"Oh, believe me. I don't plan on staying."

The screen cut the reporter from Richmond off, and focused on the woman at HQ. "This has been a rather interesting – if not terrifying change of events. Republic forces practically popped out of nowhere and surrounded the city of Richmond, Virginia. We've also received reports that the Republic Navy consisting of two aircraft carriers and their flagship now known as the "Rogue Wave" is making its way into the Atlantic with the old Navy moving to intercept them. The end of the war is closer than it has ever been. How much longer until this war is over? I give it a month at most."

Ashton turned off the TV, leaving the girls with blank faces of shock and awe. There was a long silence before Jasmine finally spoke. "So that's it, then. The Rebels have finally made it to Richmond."

"And it won't be long until they make their way here." Jessica said. "With Richmond fully blocked off, Washington can't send or receive reinforcements. The Rebels don't even have to attack Richmond now. They can just send strike forces around the city and straight into D.C"

Ashton swallowed nervously, and looked at Jessica, "So...what do we do now?"

Jessica looked at Ashton for a moment, returned her attention to the black TV screen, "We wait. It's all we can do."

CHAPTER 15

Capitulation

With media stations from all around the globe reporting on the besiegement of Richmond, almost everyone could agree on one topic: it was finished. The war was as good as over. With the number of troops growing by the day, it was obvious the Republic was far larger than it actually attested to. The original troop count at the beginning of the siege was over forty-thousand, but thousands more troops arrived with each day, bringing more vehicles and supplies with them.

While more Republic reinforcements arrived, Republic artillery surrounded the city and began what would become a three day constant bombardment of the city, demoralizing the military, and destroying key installments such as machine gun nests, and barricades the military built to block off streets. The Republic also sent in waves of carpet bombers that would wipe out entire streets, and helicopters with specially designed equipment hovered over the city taking photos and downloading coordinates for the artillery the fire on.

Republic snipers and spotters surrounded the city in ghillie suits, preventing military scouts and infantry to give away the locations of Republic artillery, and the spotters helped spot infantry setting up defensive areas.

Across the rest of the state, Republic troops took control of the railways and highways, and the Air Force ruled the skies. Convoys of Rebel trucks transported soldiers, tanks and AFV's to Richmond where they were unloaded and prepped for battle. Older vehicles were replaced, and sent back to Republic bases to be worked on or scrapped for new designs the Republic had planned.

These events went on for three days. On the fourth, Republic troops armed themselves and prepared to march into the ruins of the city. But as they readied themselves, their minds looked past Richmond and focused on Washington D.C. Their goal was in reach, and being so close to it after almost five years of fighting, their morale was higher than ever.

Despite the danger and the city being placed under Martial Law, Jessica and her friends were scheduled to work, even though the Rebellion was less than one-hundred miles out. To say they were unhappy with their boss's decision would be an understatement. Jessica worked the counter again while the other girls took over the rest of the store. It was an unnerving atmosphere. Not a single customer entered the store the entire day, but soldiers outside the store were setting up walls of sandbags and placing machine gun installations just outside the shop. It was a terrifying thought for the girls to think they could come back the next day and see the blood of these soldiers scattered all over the walls of the building. The scariest thing wasn't the fact the Rebellion was almost to the city. It wasn't the fact Martial Law had been declared for the first time in U.S history. It was the suspense of hell finally opening its doors and unleashing its fury. Every second seemed like a minute, and every minute felt like an hour. Every tick of the clock could mean the beginning of an assault from Rebel troops coming from a completely different direction than expected.

Every once in a while, Jessica would glance up at the TV in the far corner of the store with the urge to turn it on and see how things were going, but she convinced herself not to.

"What would be the point?" She thought as she leaned on the counter, resting her head in her right hand. She glanced to each of her friends, observed their body movements, and then continued her thoughts, *"We're all scared enough as it is. Turning on the news would only make the situation worse. Ashton's hands are trembling, Jasmine has been unusually*

quiet, and Krista looks as though she could have an anxiety attack any moment." Her eyes drifted to the door of their boss's office, *"Damn you, Shelby. Why would you call us in on a day like this?! I understand you want the store to do well, but what good does it do if we're all dead? If you think I'm coming in tomorrow you've got another think coming."*

The day slowly ticked by, and aside from the military building defensive points outside, the streets were as silent as a ghost town. Not one car or civilian passed by the shop, despite it being in one of the busier parts of the city. Every now and again some military personnel would enter the store, only to leave shortly after. They wouldn't look for anything or talk to anyone, but would stand next to the door. After a while, the girls just figured they were coming in to get out of the humidity for a while. However, the fear and anxiousness was visible on the faces of the soldiers that entered the store. They weren't ready to make a final stand, and it was obvious some of them didn't even know what they were still fighting for.

Jessica pondered for a while as she watched the soldiers outside. She couldn't hear what they were saying, but she could hear their muffled voices talking about something. She saw how tired, scared and anxious they were. A sadness came to her as she realized these men were unlikely to survive the final assault. They were sons, husbands, fathers and brothers to someone out there, and just men that were fighting on the wrong side. As a final act of kindness for these soldiers, Jessica and her friends brought the soldiers some crates of bottled water, and a jug full of ice cold water. The soldiers didn't expect this kindness, and some of them broke down in tears as the girls thanked them for their service. The soldiers thanked and saluted them before returning to their jobs. The girls went back inside the shop and finished their day.

After what felt like eternity and the day after, their shift finally ended, and the girls clocked out. Usually, they would be talking, laughing and debating where they should eat. This day was different, however. The girls acted like they were strangers to one another, and could barely look one another in the eye. One by one they clocked out and exited the store where they were greeted by the soldiers who thanked them for their kindness earlier. The girls thanked them for their service again, shook their hands, and walked away. Ashton and Jessica walked side-by-side as they usually do, but neither of them spoke a single word to one another. Ashton kept her eyes facing the ground as she twiddled her thumbs while Jessica scanned the skies. The Rebels had superior air power, and it wouldn't take much for the Rebellion to launch waves of fighters at the city. It was a bright sunny day with clear skies, but it definitely wasn't the opening to some kind of Fairy Tale.

The walk home seemed to go on forever, though Jessica couldn't decide if it was the awkward silence between her and Ashton, or if it was the suspense of the impending Rebel attack. She occasionally glanced at Ashton to try and get an idea of what she was thinking, but her mind was all over the place, and no doubt dwelling on what the future would bring. She wanted to stop and reassure Ashton everything would be okay in the end, but she didn't want to make the situation worse and give Ashton something else to worry about. Sometimes silence speaks the loudest.

What was usually a fifteen minute walk seemed more like thirty. However, it wasn't the threat of the Rebellion being so close, it was the quietness of what was usually a bustling city, turned into a ghost town. She couldn't shake the eerie Silent Hill vibe she got from the stillness of the city, especially after her recent run in with an Agroneese scout. Just dwelling on the memory of that night made a chill run up her back and her hair stand on end. What haunted her the most, however, was that nightmarish screech that seemed to nearly rip apart reality itself. She forcefully closed her eyes and shook her head, trying to find another topic to think about. The next thing that popped into mind was that quick glance of Chris she'd gotten from a lightning strike, and the note he left her.

"Seek me out at the National Mall after the
Republic has taken control of Washington"

She couldn't help but see the irony of the situation. For the majority of her life she wanted nothing but for Chris to return. But now that he was finally within reach, she wanted it all to go away.

When the girls finally arrived at Ashton's apartment, there was a sudden change in atmosphere. The air suddenly felt breathable again, and the tension between them came to an end. Ashton returned to being her normal self by tossing an apple over her shoulder at Jessica. "Here, eat this. Your stomach was growling half the way here."

Jessica caught the apple and took a bite, "It wasn't *that* bad. Besides, it's not my fault you're the worst cook ever. That meal you made for lunch today...what was that?"

"Something I will *never* make again is the answer to that question." Ashton replied as she kicked her shoes off and hurled them to the door, "It was an experimentation gone wrong."

"What were you trying to make?" Jessica asked before taking another bite.

"It was supposed to be a casserole. But it didn't taste like any casserole I've ever eaten before. I doubt even a dog would've eaten that!"

"Well, I dunno about that. Dog's will eat just about anything."

"True. Well, what do you want to do now? Should we watch the news and see how things are coming along?" Ashton asked, grabbing the remote to the TV.

"Might as well, I guess." Jessica said, taking another bite of the apple, "If it looks like the Rebels may attack tonight or tomorrow, I want to be ready for it. But first...I'm going to make some food that's actually *edible* if you don't mind."

Ashton smirked as she turned the channel to CNN, "Well, you've proven your worth with cooking before. I won't mock you for this."

"If you want anything I make you'd better not."

As day turned to dusk, and dusk turned to night, the two girls watched the raging battle of Richmond in awe. Several videos of military troops holding out against the Republic had been aired, and even more photos of the destruction of the city had been revealed as well. The reporters of each news station were going insane, and the tone in their voices was enough for anyone to tell they were anxious for it to be over. The reporters had debates, showed maps of what could be Republic strategies, and argued whether or not the military should just surrender. Eventually, everything got to the point the news was just a repeating circle.

As Ashton prepared to change the channel, the screen went black for a moment, then a close up shot of a man wearing a face mask in a dark green hooded robe appeared on screen.

The appearance of the man nearly made Jessica spit out her drink, but she managed to hold it back. She stared at the man in awe as she wiped the escaped liquid from her lips, and her heart started pounding against her chest as she realized who it was.

"Night Hawk?" She whispered in a soft voice.

Ashton glanced at Jessica for a moment, "Huh? You say something?"

Jessica quickly glanced at Ashton, then shook her head, "Uh, no. No. It's…it's nothing."

Both of them focused their attention on the man as he started talking. "President Lane. Allow me to introduce myself. I am one of the Seven Shadows in command of the Rebellion, and I'm demanding the surrender of your armed forces. Your strategies have failed, your defenses have fallen, and now you waste the lives of innocent soldiers who have no choice but to continue fighting for your own selfish agenda."

The man's voice was cold, and was obviously filled with hatred. It was enough to make Ashton shudder.

"If you will not surrender, President Lane, perhaps your military will think otherwise." The man stepped out of sight from the camera, revealing four heavy armored tanks being unloaded off trucks. "Behold our new prototypes: the HA2T12GVST, our newest combat tank. Allow yourself to observe these machines for a moment."

Jessica studied the tanks as the camera showed them off. Her eyes widened in amazement, and it became clear why the Rebellion was so secretive of their weapons. The tanks had a body structure arguably similar to an Abrams. However, they required four sets of tracks, had spikes circling the body, and had three rotating machine gun turrets on each side. The main cannon was long and narrow with multiple anti-air weapons on top of the main turret. The tank was painted in a solid black, with the words "Viper Striker" painted on them. The vehicle was obviously highly computerized, and required two 18-wheelers with specially designed trailers to transport it.

"Holy mother of...those things alone would wipe out what remains of the military. They don't have anything left that could withstand that kind of power!" Jessica thought. She silenced her thoughts as the man reappeared on the screen.

"Now, Mr. President, you have been warned. Surrender! This is your last warning. If you fail to comply, we *will* send these to greet you in D.C!"

The screen cut back to the news station where the reporters had blank faces as they tried to wrap their heads around what had just happened. There was an awkward silence for a few moments before the reporters started talking, but Ashton turned the TV off before they could say a word.

"I think I've seen enough." Ashton said as she stood up, "Those tanks will completely destroy what little is left of the military with ease. Is there any point in watching anymore? If President Lane doesn't surrender, it's not going to be a final battle. It'll be a mass suicide."

"So what do you want to do instead?" Jessica asked.

Ashton closed her eyes and rubbed her forehead, "I...I don't know. I'm not really in the mood to do anything. I think I'm just going to take a shower and go to bed. Hopefully the city will still be here tomorrow."

"Well, if that's what you want to do, go ahead." Jessica said. She stood up and walked to the kitchen where she poured herself a drink. "In the event Shelby calls us in, however, I won't be going in tomorrow. It was foolish of her to have us come in today as it was, but after seeing those tanks? No way am I going *anywhere* near that part of the city until the war is officially over."

Ashton nodded, "Agreed. If we're fired, I'll find a new job. With the Republic in control then, it should be somewhat easy."

"True. Especially considering the Agroneese will be next. You wouldn't have a problem working an assembly line, would you?" Jessica asked.

"For the amount the Republic pays people to build their weapons? Where do I sign up? Get me some on the job training, and get me to work!" Ashton said excitedly.

Jessica laughed and walked back into the living room with her drink, "Well, hey. At least you'll have a change of scenery from flowers. Now you can watch military grade weapons and vehicles come off the assembly lines."

"*And* maybe even drive them!"

Jessica froze for a moment, glanced at Ashton a few times, then sat in her chair. "You... in the driver's seat of a Republic tank... I immediately regret bringing up this conversation."

Ashton chuckled a little as she rolled her eyes, then proceeded to the bathroom.

Once she was finished with her shower, Ashton came back into the living room to find Jessica was still watching the news. She watched the TV for a minute, but noticed things were changing. The fighting was becoming more intensive, and the atmosphere seemed uneasy. "So, what's going on now?" She asked curiously.

Jessica looked over her shoulder for a moment, then returned her attention to the TV, "The Rebellion sent in those tanks along with another thousand troops. The military is being overrun in several different locations across the city, and they've lost some of their most defended places."

Ashton's eyes widened, "Are you serious? Those tanks are seriously that powerful?"

Jessica nodded, "The military has tried everything to destroy them, but they lack weapons powerful enough to get through their armor. They've already lost four tanks, and anything that hits them just bounces off."

"And the military has little air support, too." Ashton said. She started walking across the room so she could sit in her chair.

"That's not even the half of it. Infantry can't go anywhere near these things because of the rotating turrets on each side of the main cannon.

Some soldiers tried flanking one of the tanks while you were in the shower, but they got mowed down immediately."

Ashton only stared at the TV in awe as another video of one of the new tanks came up. "Damn. The military has literally been bested." She remained quiet for a moment, then looked at Jessica, "You think Chris is there somewhere?"

Jessica shook her head. "I doubt it. There's already another member of the Seventeen commanding the battle. Chris is probably seeing to other things here in the city."

Ashton remained silent, and returned her attention to the TV. The two of them stayed up for a few more hours, but were eventually forced to call it a night.

Jessica's eyes snapped open as the thundering sound of low flying jet engines echoed in the distance. She immediately threw the covers off her, and rushed into the living room where Ashton was already watching TV. "What's going on? Have the Rebels invaded the city?"

Ashton glanced in Jessica's direction, then returned her attention to the TV, "No. It's about the worst thing that could happen for President Lane at this point. Watch."

Jessica focused on the TV. A reporter from FOX was in the National Mall with the White House directly behind her. Armored vehicles from the military *and* the Republic were in the shot, and Republic helicopters hovered in the distance. *"What in God's name...?"* Jessica thought, thoroughly confused about the situation.

"It...it's amazing how things turned out just over the course of last night. Two warring factions that have been going at each other's throats for nearly five years now suddenly join forces? This was completely out of nowhere!" The Reporter on the TV said.

Jessica's eyes widened, "No way! The military surrendered?!"

Ashton nodded, "You missed the video they showed earlier, but last night, military personnel came to Republic positions waving white flags, or doing anything that could show they had the intent to surrender. I guess they decided they were tired of fighting a losing war, and didn't see the point in throwing their lives away."

"So the Republic and the military are allies now?" Jessica asked with a hint of excitement in her voice."

Ashton shook her head, and looked at Jessica, "No. The military *is* the Republic now."

Jessica's lips slowly curved into a grin, and she found a place to sit where she continued to watch the reporter.

"And for those of you who may just now be turning in, the military *has* surrendered to the Republic. I repeat. The military *has* surrendered to the Republic. After the Republic released their latest combat tanks in the field, the military found themselves severely outmatched. They took heavy losses in Richmond, and were constantly losing ground to the Republic's new weapons. Eventually, the military's numbers grew too few to keep fighting, and they threw down their weapons. Now, as you can see behind me, the military has not only allied with the Republic, but they've *become* the Republic. Most of what remained of the military has surrounded the White House while other units have gone off to the Capitol Building and the Pentagon. It's unknown what they're waiting for. I don't think they have forces storming the White House right now, but I don't think the Secret Service has left the building yet. I don't even know if they've surrendered with the military or not."

"Well, this is good news to wake up to." Jessica said.

Ashton nodded in agreement, "Yeah, no kidding. It's nice to know the city will still be standing after today. I wonder what's going to happen now."

Jessica smirked a laugh as she shook her head, "Your guess is as good as mine. Let's just keep watching until it seems relatively clear for us to go check things out. Besides...there's someone I'm dying to meet again."

CHAPTER 16

Retribution

Republic fighters soared through the skies above Washington D.C, making the Republic's presence well known as their engines tore through the air like rolling thunder, and sent a message to the world: It was over. The Republic had won. On the ground below, Republic personnel and what remained of the old military took the National Mall, and sent battle groups across the city to every capitol building, including the Pentagon. The streets were empty of any civilians with the exception of the media, who desperately tried to get into the National Mall to get footage of what was happening. However, Republic infantry blocked their paths, and forced the media back. Lightly armored vehicles blocked the streets, preventing any vehicles from entering the area, and transport helicopters were landing within meters of each other as they unloaded Elite forces such as the Cobras, regular infantry, as well as a few armored vehicles before lifting off and making room for the next wave of choppers to land. Within mere minutes, the Republic had a force that vastly overwhelmed the Washington police and security forces, forcing them to stay away from the area.

The Republic's presence was heaviest at the Pentagon. Helicopters and lightly armored vehicles surrounded the building, making sure the remaining Generals couldn't bring any reinforcements from the North. If Republic soldiers intercepted any message leaving the Pentagon, it was to be destroyed.

The White House was the second most concentrated area in the city. President Lane and the rest of his administration were believed to be hiding within the walls, presumably the fallout bunker deep within the building, believed to be impenetrable from the outside. Helicopters outfitted with advanced infrared technology hovering above the building spied on the Secret Service as they moved around the building. They had not surrendered to the Republic yet, and pilots of the helicopters reported the Secret Service were setting up defenses in the hallways. Automatic machinegun turrets were being armed in several hallways, bombs were being placed in random locations, and several men were grabbing more ammunition and automatic weapons from the armory.

Republic officers armed with speakers repeatedly called to President Lane, demanding him to surrender. They received no compliance, despite having tried for multiple hours. The intention of Republic Generals was to take Washington without having to fire a single shot now that the military had sided with them, but as time went on, that hope seemed to dissipate. Eventually, the commanding officer in the field got tired of waiting, and ordered several Cobra squads to check their gear. But as he started to plan his strategy on how to take the building, a huge double bladed black helicopter emerged from over the rooftops as if coming from nowhere, and landed near the White House. The commanding officer recognized the helicopter, and immediately realized who had just arrived. He stopped what he was doing, and rushed to the helicopter as quickly as he could. Just as he arrived, the doors on the side slid open, revealing the man inside: The main commanding General of the Republic, and third member of the Seven Shadows – Chris Lynheart. He was dressed in his infamous black hooded robe, and the look on his face was far from amused.

The commanding officer waited for Chris to step out of the chopper, and then greeted him. "Welcome to Washington D.C., General. Our forces have overrun the city, but despite our greater numbers, the Secret Service are refusing to surrender. They've set up several defenses in the White House which will make it difficult for our troops to storm the building."

"I suspected as much. That gutless coward Lane was never going to surrender, no matter how desperate his position became." Chris said as he walked away from his helicopter, "I suspect they're setting up turrets and mines all throughout the building?"

"Yes, sir. Their defenses will be tough to breach, and they've chosen their positions well. We may take more casualties than we originally expected…wait, what's that?" The officer asked as he pointed to the roof of the White House.

Chris looked up to see a massive turret emerging from the roof of the White House, something he expected, but didn't think Lane would be stupid enough to use. *"You gutless idiotic coward!"* He thought as he took the officer's radio out of his hands, "All aircraft retreat!" He ordered.

Just seconds after, the turret unleashed a volley of bullets at the Republic's orbiting aircraft, killing both pilots in one chopper, sending it crashing to the ground, and disabling the rear propeller on the second. Having lost its stabilizer, the chopper started to spin out of control as it descended towards Chris and the officer. The officer ran in a random direction to escape its path while Chris stood his ground. The helicopter crashed into the chopper that brought Chris to the area, causing them both to explode, and engulf Chris in the flames of their explosion.

The officer who retreated froze in awe as he tried to make sense of what just happened. He began to tremble as he realized he left his superior to die, and that the Republic had just taken a massive loss. Troops from all over rushed to the scene, and medics checked the officer, who still couldn't believe what he had just witnessed. But just as the reality of what had happened began to set in, Chris emerged from the flames with no visible harm, brushing a piece of debris off his shoulder as he casually strolled away from the flames.

Nearby troops cheered, whistled and shouted as they saw their General walk away from the crash and give his next orders, "All guns, open fire! Reduce that building to a pile of rubble!"

Every tank and armored vehicle within range turned their turrets to the White House, and began a ruthless bombardment on the building. Shell after shell, and round after round tore through the walls, destroying the interior, and killing multiple Secret Service. The turret took a direct hit from an AT (anti-tank) round, permanently disabling it. Multiple helicopters returned to the area, and rained down their rockets into the building while their guns fired randomly into the building. Multiple jets flying overhead rained down their own rockets from afar, destroying what was left standing. After several minutes of a continuous bombardment, Chris ordered the cease fire and waited for the smoke to clear.

Minutes passed, and the smoke cleared enough for Chris to see the destruction. The White House had been reduced to ruins with only a few small portions of wall still standing. *"So much for that plan, you piece of filth."* He thought. He growled angrily, and radioed several Cobra squads, "Cobra squads one through twelve, advance to the White House. If you're met with resistance from the Secret Service, kill them. When you find President Lane and his administration, I only care about Lane. If the others refuse to surrender, kill them, but I want Lane alive."

The Cobras acknowledged their orders, and proceeded into the ruins of the White House where they split up and searched in different sections. All around them was destruction and the torn bodies of Secret Service who perished in the barrage. The smell of death was already strong in the air, but the Cobras continued on. Occasionally, they found a Secret Service who was still alive, but severely injured. The Cobras did what they thought was most merciful, and put them out of their misery.

A short while later the Cobras found the fallout bunker where President Lane and the rest of his administration were presumed to be hiding. They made sure the area was clear, and the commanding lieutenant contacted Chris, "General, we've found the fallout bunker. No signs of President Lane or his administration so far. They must have sealed themselves inside."

"Acknowledged, Lieutenant. Keep the area secure. I'm sending Engineers to your location to blow the door open." Chris said.

"Copy, General. We'll hold down here."

When the Engineers arrived they drilled holes into the walls of the fallout bunker, and placed several explosive devices in the holes. It took around thirty minutes for the Engineers to finish and fall back to a safe position with the Cobras. Once the blast zone was clear, the lead Engineer remotely detonated the explosives, triggering a chain of explosions throughout the area. Once it was safe for the Cobras to proceed, the commanding Lieutenant signaled his men to advance into the bunker.

"Move it, troopers! Go, go, go!"

The Cobras stormed into the room, emerging through the smoke, and firing multiple rounds at the remaining Secret Service before they could get a shot off. Within seconds, the last man defending President Lane and his administration fell, ultimately ending the Second American Civil War.

"Stay where you are and keep your hands where I can see them, Lane!" One of the Cobras demanded while aiming his shotgun point blank at President Lane.

President Lane, too stunned by the circumstances to talk, did as he was told, and watched as several Cobras grabbed the remaining people in the bunker, and forced them out of the room. Before he had a chance to react, the Cobra in front of him grabbed him by the shirt and dragged him out of the bunker and up to the surface. "Our commander would like to have a few words with you, Lane."

When they reached the surface, the Cobras took Lane and his administration to the yard of the White House, and forced them on their knees side-by-side each other – practically execution style.

The former president was shaking. He felt like his heart could pop out of his body at any second, and he constantly fought back the urge to gag or puke. He glanced over to each of his former administrative members, and could see they were just as terrified as he was. As much as he didn't want to admit or see it, his plans to crush the Republic were just wasted time and words. Now that he was away from the safety of the White House, and had no military to protect him, his eyes were opened to reality for the first time. He finally saw that he had lost before the war ever really began. As he dwelled on his thoughts, and feared for the future, he heard the sound of grass crunching as someone approached. He looked up to see a figure approaching him, but he was blinded by the sun directly behind the approaching person. When the person's face was no longer hidden in shadow and could be made out, Lane's eyes widened, and he started to tremble with fear. But this was a different fear than what he was dealing with earlier. He now had a vague idea about what lay in store for him, and it wasn't anything good. Pain was all he would experience until this man was finished with him.

"Y-you…it can't be. You're supposed to be dead!" Lane shrieked.

"So you remember me, do you?" The person asked.

"Y-yes! Y-you're Experiment 2025! You were presumed dead years ago! How have you survived?!"

"Experiment 2025? That name passed on long ago. I am no longer one of your toys that has a serial number for a name." The person said coldly. "I gave myself a real name after you and the rest of your ilk threw me to the streets and left me for dead all those years ago. Did you really think I would never find out what you did to me in the past? What you put the rest of my family through. My hatred for you has only strengthened as time went on. I would kill you right here if you did not have any useful information for me. Unluckily for you and your administration, however, we'll be seeing each other a lot over the next few days."

Tears formed in Lane's eyes, and he clapped his hands together as if he were praying and begged the man standing before him, "Please, sir! Have mercy! I beg of you! Don't do this! Please!"

The person narrowed his eyes at Lane and swatted his hands away. "I'll give you the same mercy you gave me and my family. None!" He struck the former president with the back of his hand, forcing him on the ground, and turned to the Captain next to him. "Captain, take these people into custody and prepare them for transport to our prison in Oklahoma. The former president and I have…some catching up to do."

The Captain nodded, "Yes, General!" He stepped aside as his superior stormed off and turned his attention to the Cobras behind the former administration. "All right, you heard the General. Get these prisoners to a chopper! Move it!"

The Cobras pulled the prisoners to their feet, then escorted them to a Republic Black Hawk for transport.

CHAPTER 17

Reunion

"Jessica, are you sure this is such a good idea?" Ashton asked as she and Jessica cautiously made their way to the National Mall. "I mean, I know the Republic just won the war and set up a camp and everything, but this may be a little soon to...you know...approach them."

"Look, Chris told me to seek him out after the Republic had taken Washington. I'm going to assume these soldiers know he's looking for me, or he gave them a description to look out for. I can't turn back now. This is what I've been waiting for for over ten years. *Ten*!" Jessica said.

"I get that, I just...I'd rather not have to look down the barrel of a really big gun when and if these soldiers tell us to back off." Ashton said.

"Okay, if they tell us to leave, we'll leave. But I can't turn around without trying. Besides, haven't you been saying you want to meet a few Republic soldiers just to see what they're like?" Jessica asked.

Ashton opened her mouth to say something, but stopped herself. She thought quietly for a few moments as she stared at the ground, then looked at Jessica again, "Fine. But I'm warning you...I'm pointing at you if these soldiers yell at us."

"Oh? And here I thought you were the brave one." Jessica jokingly mocked.

"I am brave! But I confess I really, really hate being so sometimes." Ashton said.

Jessica smirked and rolled her eyes, "And here I thought you were the tough one."

"There's a difference between tough and severely outmatched against well-trained and battle hardened soldiers, Jessica."

As they approached the National Mall, the girls realized the media hadn't given the Republic justice in just how strong their presence was in the city. The Republic had completely dominated the D.C area with several hundred troops already on the ground, and transport helicopters continuing to bring more. Every few seconds a helicopter would land in the National Mall with reinforcements, bringing the Republic's body count up another sixty soldiers. Fighters and bombers ripped the distant sky apart like thunder, and orbiting helicopters sliced the air as they flew overhead. At every intersection, the Rebels had stationed light attack vehicles with fifty caliber machineguns, and the occasional medium tank on the larger streets.

As they got closer, the girls were approached by a number of soldiers armed with the Republic's most common weapon – the M86 – a more advanced version of the M16 the military was still outfitted with. The girls stopped and slowly raised their hands in the air as the soldiers approached.

"This is a restricted area. State your business or turn around and go back the way you came." One of the soldiers demanded.

Now that they had an up close view of Republic soldiers, the girls started to wish they hadn't come. Most soldiers wore a solid black or dark grey uniform with matching body armor. Their faces were also covered with ski masks that had terrifying designs drawn on, and were more intimidating than either of them cared for.

"Speak!"

Jessica tore herself from her thoughts, shaking her head a little. She took note of the soldier's badges, and saw that he was a Captain or even higher ranking. She took a deep breath to calm her nerves, then started talking, "Excuse me, sir. I'm not quite sure how to say this, but I'm a friend of who I believe to be your highest ranking General. I...I was wondering if I could speak with him."

The Captain crossed his arms and some of the soldiers raised their weapons, forcing Jessica and Ashton to move back slightly, and making their tensions rise. "Now that's a bold claim if I've ever heard one. Two female civilians come walking down the street towards a highly concentrated Republic military position, and claim to know our General. You must have some nerve. What is the name of the General you're wanting to speak to?"

"Um…Chris Lynheart." Jessica said nervously.

"Who the heck is that? Look, lady, my patience is wearing thin. I'm going to give you the count of three for you two to start walking and get lost." The Captain said.

"But, sir! The General I'm talking about is one of the Shadows!" Jessica yelled with a hint of fear in her voice. She noticed the Captain's eyes widen for a split second before he turned to face one of the other soldiers.

"One of the Shadows…could she really…"

"I find it hard to believe."

"But what if she's telling the truth? All our heads will be on spikes. We'll be stationed in the Mess Hall for a year if we're lucky."

"I suppose if she's telling the truth and he's actually looking for her, we won't get in trouble for contacting him. But who's going to do it? I'm sure as hell not contacting him."

"Rock, paper, scissors anyone?"

"You're the highest ranking, Captain. It's kind of your job."

"Shit. I better not get demoted for this."

Jessica watched as the Captain faced her again and approached, "Let me see your I.D.'s."

Jessica and Ashton both handed the Captain their I.D.'s, and the Captain examined the names. "Jessica Holland and Ashton Hoy…I don't recognize Miss Hoy, but the General did say something about a Jessica Holland." He looked at Jessica for a brief second, then used his radio headset to contact his superior.

"General…it's Captain Lovelace, sir. I…I know, sir. Yes, sir. I have a woman here who goes by the name of Jessica Holland – she matches the description of the woman you've been looking for…yes, sir. She has a friend here, too... yes, sir." The Captain folded his microphone away from his mouth and looked at Jessica, "Ma'am, I need you and your friend to follow me right now."

Jessica smiled softly, but her cheeks turned bright pink as Ashton wrapped her arms around her neck and jumped on her back, "Awwww! Someone's about to meet their boyfriend!"

"Oh, hush, Ashton."

Republic flags – a flaming eagle wrapping its wings around a wooden cross as if protecting it and glaring straight ahead trying to intimidate – flapped in the wind across the Capitol city as Republic troops lowered the American flag. A symbol that once recognized freedom and prosperity for all, turned to corruption and greed. It would go down in history as one of the greatest meaning symbols of all time, but was met with a tragic end.

"So it's true, then. The United States of America is a thing of the past." Ashton said in a quiet tone.

Jessica nodded in response, "It's a funny feeling, huh? To think that flag once represented the most powerful country on Earth. Hard to believe it's actually just another part of history now."

Ashton watched some soldiers handle an American flag as they lowered it. Though it represented a legacy lost to history now, they still treated it with the upmost respect expected of a soldier. They folded it slowly and carefully as if there was still something precious or personal to them.

"I wouldn't be too confused, Ashton." Jessica said, taking Ashton away from her thoughts, "You have to remember a lot of these Republic soldiers were in the United States military before the war. That flag is still personal to them...even though it represents what they've been fighting against."

"I understand that. I just...you can tell it definitely bothers some of the soldiers." Ashton said.

"It was never going to be easy to do, Ashton. That flag used to mean something personal to a lot of people, even on the Republic's side. It deserved a better end to its legacy than this." Jessica said.

"It will take some getting used to. Now the country has to come up with a new pledge to the flag, a new national anthem and who knows what else." Ashton said with a hint of sadness.

"I know. But considering how things will be going in the near future...I think that may be the least of our worries." Jessica said.

"True. Let's just keep pressing on, shall we?"

Arriving at the Capitol building, Jessica and Ashton followed Captain Lovelace through the main entrance and through several different hallways. Awestruck by their surroundings, it dawned on them that they had never even attempted to visit the capitol buildings even though they were more or less open to the public and tourists. They wanted to stop and look at the art work and read the rich history, but Republic soldiers were everywhere, which forced them to stay with Captain Lovelace. Eventually, he led the girls to a large open room where a large number of senators were being held at gun point while a man in a solid black robe spoke to them. Lovelace turned to them and raised his hand, telling them to stop. They did so, and watched over his shoulders as the man started to rip the senators apart.

The man in black robes paced back and forth across the room, looking directly at the senators as he walked. The senators kept their heads down in an attempt to not make eye contact with him, but it was obvious they were terrified of him. "I'm going to make this short and to the point, and speak in tiny little words since that seems to be the extent of your brainpower, despite being senators for what was once the United States of America. You are all traitors to the Republic and its people. Every one of you has committed crimes that should ultimately be punished by death. You've lied, corrupted, and made unfair deals with our enemies. You ignored the oaths you took when taking office, and stabbed the American people in the back when they weren't looking. You illegally intervened with foreign countries' affairs, you created terror organizations, conducted illegal experiments and you intervened with elections that weren't in your favor by cheating in the voting booths. For these crimes, you are immediately being stripped of your political ranks, and your bank accounts will be wiped out. Your money will be given back to the people you stole it from, and you will be forced to publically announce your crimes. Then, you will be stripped of your freedoms and forced to work in Republic factories manufacturing weapons, ammunition, gear and vehicles for our army. You will work fourteen hour shifts six days a week, and work overtime as needed. For the crimes you've committed, death and prison are too forgiving. I'll make sure you come to resent your own mothers for bringing you into this world. Now get out of my sight!"

Ashton leaned over and whispered in Jessica's ear, "If that's your boyfriend...I like him already."

Jessica giggled quietly and whispered back, "How long have we been wishing someone would do that to Congress? It's about time they got what's been coming to them." She turned her attention back to one of the congressmen as he rose his voice.

"You have no power here, Experiment! The American people..."

"The American people will learn of your atrocities whether you like it or not, Congressman!" The man in robes barked back in a terrifying voice, snapping at the congressman, even Jessica and Ashton stood at attention. The robed man stormed to the congressman and got in his face, "You will do well to remember your place, scum bag. The lives of politicians are worth less than ants to me, and the lives of corrupt politicians such as yourselves aren't worth batting an eye over. Maybe I need to break down the food chain for you. At the top there's the Shadows, then there's the Republic military, then the people it protects. Skip forward a bit and you have whale shit, then there's your worthless hide. Your lives and the lives of your families are forfeit as far as I'm concerned. Now, for the final time...get out of my sight." He quickly walked off to another side of the room to speak with some Republic soldiers, leaving the Congressman traumatized and in fear for his future.

Several Republic soldiers pointed their guns at the Congressmen and ordered them to get moving. They all raised their hands in the air and marched out of the room with ten soldiers escorting them.

Ashton and Jessica stepped out of the way and watched as the soldiers walked by. One of the Congressmen tried speaking to one of the soldiers, but he was poked in the back with the muzzle of the soldier's gun, "Keep moving!" The soldier yelled forcefully.

The Congressman stumbled a bit, but managed to catch himself before falling. He quickly scrambled back to his feet and got back in position. He glanced over his shoulder at the soldier, but turned away before he was spotted.

Jessica and Ashton watched as the Congressmen disappeared around a corner, and started to laugh.

"Okay, whoever this guy is, he is *officially* my new favorite person!" Ashton managed to say, even though she was still laughing.

Jessica leaned against the wall and covered her stomach, "It's…it's about time something like that happened! I think I can say my life is officially complete now having watched that."

They stopped laughing for a moment, looked at each other briefly, and then started laughing again. However, they quickly regained their composure as Captain Lovelace approached them.

"Miss Holland…the General is ready for you."

Jessica stared at Captain Lovelace for a moment, then looked at Ashton. "You know…I told myself I would always be ready…but now… I'm starting to panic."

Ashton gave Jessica a comforting smile, and rested her hands on Jessica's shoulder, "You've come this far, Jess. You can't turn and run now, especially after waiting this long. No matter what happens, I'll be waiting right here for you."

"But what if he wants me to stay with him for a while?" Jessica asked.

Ashton smirked a laugh and rolled her eyes, "Girl, I've lived in this city most of my life. I think I know my way back home. If he wants you to go with him, then by all means! Besides, do you really think I'm going to voice an objection to *that*?" She asked as she pointed at the robed man.

Jessica looked over her shoulder and saw the man was standing in the middle of the room waiting for her. She turned to look at Ashton again, who nodded for her to go. She took a deep breath, turned around and started walking to the man. As she got closer, she felt her heart skipping every three beats, and she found herself walking faster and faster as the man started to lower his hood. Once his face was visible, her eyes widened, and tears quickly blinded her vision. She started to walk faster and faster until eventually, she was in a full sprint to the man, but each step she took seemed to make a bigger distance between them as if the room was growing to keep them apart. Once she was close enough, she leaped at the man, and wrapped her arms and legs around him, clinging onto him as if her life depended on it. Now sobbing and sniffing, she buried her face in the man's chest and cried out his name, "*Chriiiiiiiiiis!*"

Chris wrapped his arms around Jessica, and held her tightly, "It's good to see you again, Jessica. It's been...too long."

Jessica sniffed, and continued sobbing, taking in as much of the moment as she could. "Ten years. Ten years you made me wait. Ten years I've dreamed of this moment ...and now it's finally here. I...I don't even know what to say. I have so much to tell you. So much to ask. I've missed you so much, Chris." She unwrapped her legs and stood on the floor again, but hugged him even tighter. "I just want to savor this moment as much as possible. If time suddenly froze right now, I would gladly welcome it."

Chris stood in place, allowing Jessica to enjoy the moment. Seconds went by, then he gently pushed Jessica away, and she looked up at him as he talked, "Believe me, Jessica, there is nothing I would like more than spending some time together and catching up, but I'm afraid time is a luxury I don't have."

Jessica smiled and nodded in understanding, but also noted how Chris had changed over the years. He now towered over her at a height of 6'6 with a body build that matched the reputation of the legendary Seventeen Assassins. His hair was solid black, cropped, and he maintained a clean shave, meaning he kept a "professional" look. Another change, and one Jessica liked very much, was his voice. It was dominant and demanding. Forceful, yet still somehow quiet with a mysterious tone to it. Almost like an aggressive and angry whisper. But as she saw just moments ago, he could also yell in an even more demanding tone, making his presence much more dominant, and a voice that could possibly even snap a seasoned war veteran to attention.

"Will we have time to talk soon, at least?" Jessica asked, desperately hoping for a reasonable answer.

"We will. But right now is not a good time. Now that the civil war is over, the Republic must put its laws into effect immediately before things become too chaotic. Riots are expected to break out soon. Anyone still foolish enough to believe Lane was a worthwhile leader is bound to cause trouble."

"Riots? Even with several hundred well-armed and war hardened soldiers parading the streets, tanks and air craft, you're expecting riots?! People can't be *that* stupid." Jessica said.

"I beg to differ." Chris said, catching Jessica's attention. "Remember how chaotic and out of control the left was when Donald Trump won in 2016? Riots broke out all across the country day after day. Monuments were destroyed with little or no remorse, and the media tried their hardest to erase parts of American history because their precious Hillary Clinton lost the election, and Obama's 'presidency' was brought to an end. The police were able to do very little because the governors of leftist states didn't give them the power to fight back. Bear in mind, this is Trump winning the election fairly. He won both the popular vote, and the Electoral College. Now, that that worthless coward, Lane, is being forced out of power because of his incompetence during the civil war, the public will be brought under Republic law whether the like it or not."

"So…what's the plan if a riot does break out?" Jessica asked.

"They will be arrested and forced to face the consequences of their actions." Chris said harshly, "The days of the media permitting these younger generations to commit crimes to attack their enemies are over. From now on, illegal actions will have consequences. Any governor who openly supports criminal movements will be removed from office just like the senate. Any media that celebrates or defends these crimes will be terminated."

"Oh, I like where this is going. It's about time someone grew a backbone to handle these issues." Jessica said.

"Indeed. Anyway, I should go. I still have a lot of work to do." Chris said. He turned his back and started to walk away from Jessica.

Jessica quickly glanced over her shoulder at Ashton, who smiled and waved for her to pursue. She smiled softly and nodded, then chased after Chris, "Hey, wait!"

Chris turned to face Jessica as she walked up to him.

"I…I don't suppose I could…you know…accompany you?" Jessica asked nervously.

"Hmm…that actually would be useful. Some of the other assassins wanted to see you when they were ready." Chris said.

Jessica's hair stood on end and her face went pale. "Wa – wait a minute. Members of the Seventeen want to see *me*?! I'm not sure if I like the sound of that."

Chris crossed his arms as he continued talking, "You're in no danger. In fact, it would not be wise to keep them waiting any longer than you have to."

"What do they want to see me for?" Jessica asked.

"It's about the ring you received a while back. I don't want you to panic, but you're in a considerable amount of danger now." Chris said.

Jessica's eyes widened a bit and she started to hesitate, "W…why? What does that ring have to do with anything?"

"The short answer is this: it's a trinket that's basically a double edged sword. As a Daughter of Forayer, you can naturally see people's past just by looking in their eyes. That ring allows you to do the exact opposite. You can see the future through your dreams and see events almost exactly how they'll play out." Chris said.

"That's amazing! But what's the bad side?" Jessica asked.

"It attracts the Agroneese to you. So long as that ring is in your possession, you are basically a human magnet for them. Which is why we took it from the police force." Chris said.

"Is there anything else to it?" Jessica asked.

Chris nodded, "There is, but I'm not the one to tell you. You'll want to speak with Silent Arrow when you get the chance."

"Silent Arrow? Who's he?" Jessica asked.

"He's one of the Seven Shadows, and the smartest of the Pre-ranking Seventeen. He's basically a library on legs. Anything about the history or legend of Atlassia, he knows like the back of his hand. I suggest you speak with him the second you get the chance." Chris said.

"I'll...I'll do that." *"As terrifying as it might be."* Jessica thought.

"Good. Anyway, if you're coming, we need to move now. The others will be waiting." Chris said.

Jessica nodded, and followed closely behind Chris, but looked over her shoulder again to see Ashton smiling in approval before she turned and walked back the way they came.

CHAPTER 18

The End of America The Birth of the Republic

Jessica followed Chris throughout the Capitol building, eager but nervous for what the future now held in store for her since she was about to meet with pre-ranking members of the legendary but deadly group of assassins known as the Seventeen. Though she had lived in D.C for a long time, she never had the opportunity to visit the capitol buildings, so she took in as much of the scenery as possible. Chris walked at a very brisk pace, which made it difficult for her to keep up with him. She had to basically jog to match his speed.

Chris led her through multiple hallways and corridors of the Capitol Building, even through areas that would normally be off limits to the public. Eventually, they came to a large open room where many Republic soldiers were standing guard, but more importantly, President Davis and several Republic Generals were planning their next move. Jessica continued to follow Chris as he walked over to one of the large tables where a presumed General left something for him to look at.

Jessica stayed glued to Chris since she was now surrounded by armed soldiers, but listened to a conversation between President Davis and one of the Generals.

"Now that we've captured the former president, Lane, we can focus on our plans for the future. Right now, I think it's best that we address the Elephant in the room, which is going back to the Middle East. I think it's safe to say the public isn't going to be happy when they hear about this, Mr. President." The General said.

President Davis nodded in understanding, "I know. But this isn't my plan. The Shadows believe it's a necessity to go back to that part of the world and prepare for...something. They won't tell me what, though."

"Well, if that's the case I'll leave the conversation there. However, there is the case of our economy. With the war finally over, we will be able to mine for resources unrestricted. We've had full control of the Rocky Mountains for the majority of the war, but there are still places in western states we need to take advantage of. Those new tanks proved to be invaluable during the battle of Richmond. If we can continue to open mines along the Rocky's and other mountain ranges, we'll be able to produce those things by the hundreds." The General said.

"There's still the case of organizations such as PETA and other groups getting in the way. This may be a new country, but those mind sets will not go away without a fight." President Davis said.

"True. How do you want to handle this issue, then? We *need* more of those tanks." The General said.

"This is beyond my line of work, I'm afraid. This is something the Shadows will have to discuss." President Davis said.

The General looked over at Chris for a moment, then turned his attention back to President Davis, "Well...I guess we'll just go ahead and plan to have those tanks, then."

President Davis smirked and nodded, "Indeed. However, we'll need to also focus more on building better roads and railways across the country and into Canada. They've proven to be a very useful ally."

"Indeed. Well, I'll talk with the other generals to see what our next plans are. If you'll excuse me, sir."

President Davis nodded and turned to face Jessica as the General walked away, "I'm sorry, ma'am, I don't believe I know your name."

Jessica glanced at Chris for a second, then walked around the table to President Davis, "Oh, my name is Jessica Holland, sir. It's a pleasure to meet you." She said as she shook Davis's hand.

"Likewise. But what are you doing here?" President Davis asked.

"That is information you needn't worry yourself about, Mr. President. This is a matter concerning only the Shadows." Chris interrupted.

"Uh…of course, sir."

Jessica glanced at Chris, then looked at President Davis again, "I must say, sir, it's an honor to meet you. I'm glad this war is finally over. My friends and I have been eagerly waiting for the Republic to restore order."

"Thank you, ma'am. But I'm not the one you need to be thanking. The ones who deserve your thanks are the ones buried underground." President Davis said.

"Very true. Their sacrifices will not be in vain so long as the Republic keeps its word and doesn't turn its back on the people it serves." Jessica said.

President Davis nodded in agreement, "You won't have to worry about that, miss. People like your friend over there make it very clear what happens when politicians step out of line. They hold the real power, and they've done well for Republic and its people."

Jessica looked over her shoulder at Chris again, then returned her attention to President Davis, "I see. Well, no offense intended, Mr. President, but I think it's good we finally have people keeping a tight leash on politicians. Ever since Trump left, the 'swamp' has been filling itself up again."

President Davis chuckled a bit before replying, "Oh, you won't have to worry about that. Our higher ups won't tolerate career politicians. Once our terms are up, we're done."

"Good to know."

Chris walked around the table, and approached President Davis, "Given your lack of activity, I take it you're ready to address the public with our new laws, Mr. President?"

"Yes, sir. Once the rest of my administration and your order arrives, we will be ready for the media." President Davis said.

"Good. It's nice to see you've actually taken the initiative for once in your career." Chris said. He continued walking past Davis to another table where he started reading a stack of papers that were presumed reports from other Generals.

"Sir, what about the expected protesters?" President Davis asked.

"Protesters or rioters, President Davis? There's a difference between the two. Actual protesters who just want to have their voices heard, still have that right. The people of this country still have their constitutional rights, so they keep their freedom of speech. As for rioters…the shadows have plans for them."

"What kind of plans?" Jessica asked, curious about what Chris meant.

Chris glanced over his shoulder at Jessica for a moment, then continued reading the papers, "Some things are better shown than told, I think. When the riots break out, which they will, those people will get a taste of what's been coming to them. That's all you need to know for now."

Puzzled, Jessica looked at Chris for a moment, then shrugged her shoulders, "Well, if you insist."

"Anyway, the last of my order will be arriving soon. So, I suggest you prepare to meet the former assassins, including Night Hawk." Chris said.

"I figured I'd be seeing him again. When he came on TV last night to reveal the Republic's new super tanks, I knew I'd be seeing him in the near future." She sighed deeply before continuing, "You know, you can tell me to not be nervous meeting these people as much as you want, but it's not going to change anything. Although, I think terrified is a better word to use here."

"Well, there's a reason you'll be speaking with them. The Shadows, let alone the Assassins, don't take time out of their day to speak to just anyone. Just keep a cool head and don't do anything to provoke them. You'll be fine." Chris said.

Jessica released another deep sigh, "If you say so."

A short time later, President Lane's administration came into the room, escorted by several Republic Cobras and Phantoms. They all gathered in the center of the room where they started discussing the best way to start President Davis' speech. As they chatted, Chris remained in the back of the room, keeping a close eye on them while Jessica only observed what Chris was doing. She couldn't get over how he had changed over the years. He was no longer a jokester or prankster, and had matured into a very attractive, though terrifying young man. She couldn't wait to have some one on one time with him and learn what the ten years was like for him. If his attire said anything, he had it rough, and the training he went through wasn't easy by any stretch of the imagination. Just by looking in his eyes, she could see he was no longer scared or afraid of what the future held for him. He was no longer the soft or lost boy she found all those years ago. Now the look in his eyes was dangerous. He was angry, filled with hatred, and he wanted bloodshed.

Suddenly, the air went cold as if the heat had just been sucked out of the room. Jessica quickly wrapped her arms around her in an attempt to keep herself warm, but she started to shiver regardless. In the corner of her eye, she saw movement, and turned to see six men entering the room. These men, however, were not politicians. Each one wore a hooded robe that differed in color. One even kept the most terrifying k-9 animal she'd ever seen by his side. These were the pre-ranking assassins of the Seventeen, or the Seven Shadows as the majority of the public now knew them. The overseers of the Republic's government.

Jessica quickly made her way over to Chris and stood behind him, but she wasn't unnoticed. Several of the assassins had already seen her, which was a feeling she wasn't too keen about.

"President Davis. The public is waiting. Finish working on your speech swiftly so we can carry on with our plans." One of the assassins said.

"Ye-yes, sir!" President Davis and his administration quickly added any last touches to their speeches, then joined up with a number of Republic soldiers who escorted them outside.

The assassins turned their attention to Chris then one in a dark green robe approached him, "Well done, Night Walker. You managed to speed up the war effort and finish it quicker than we expected."

"I did what had to be done. But this is far from over. Our struggles are only beginning." Chris replied.

"Indeed. But you have done well. I suggest you allow yourself some time off and take some time to think about your next move." The assassin said.

"I'll think about it."

The assassin nodded, then turned his attention to Jessica, "And what do we have here? She's grown into quite the attractive woman since I last saw her."

"Indeed. I told her to meet with Silent Arrow once Davis has finished his speech. She needs to know what we'll be dealing with in the future, or if it's even safe for her to remain on the surface." Chris said.

"Very well. For now, I think an introduction is in order." The assassin approached Jessica and held out his hand, "It's been a long time, Jessica. I trust you remember me."

Jessica nodded and shook the man's hand, "Of course. It's good to see you again, Night Hawk."

"Good. I can tell you're confused about the situation, but we will explain all you need to know in due time. For right now, it's probably best that you learn our names." Night Hawk said before stepping off to the side and introducing the other assassins. "In the dark purple robe to the right is Telikee. He's a higher ranking assassin, and the one who trained Chris to control the element of air, hence his name is a reference to telekinesis magic. Then, standing next to him, is Widow Maker. He trained Chris with the element of Shadow, which leads to some...rather unique abilities. Next in line is Silent Arrow, the one in the darker colored green robe. He taught Chris the Atlassian language and our way of life. It's with his help Chris built a number of different businesses that rapidly turned into large companies. He also trained him with the element of sound. Up next, in the yellow robe is Electric. The man who trained Chris with the element of lightning. In the dark red robe is Magnis. I'll let you guess which element he instructed Chris with. And finally, in the dark blue robe is Aqua, who trained Chris with the element of water."

Jessica greeted the assassins by nodding at them, then looked at Night Hawk, "So, I take it you were Chris's main teacher in the long run?"

"More or less. We all taught him in equal amounts of time, but I oversaw his training from start to finish." Night Hawk said.

"I had a feeling that would be the case. But I never imagined you guys would come back…well…like this. Were you always in command of the Rebellion?" Jessica asked.

"That's simple enough to answer. I'm the one who started it." Chris said, catching Jessica's attention.

"But how? To produce the quality of troops and technological weapons you guys have…you would have needed tremendous amounts of funding. Far more than what the United States could ever produce." Jessica said.

Chris grinned a little and smirked, "It's actually quite simple, really. I can give you the full rundown when we're finished, but right now, we need to move. It's time we introduce ourselves to the public."

Jessica thought for a moment, and watched Chris turn and walk down the hallway. The assassins followed, but Night Hawk gently shoved Jessica forward. "You'll want to see what happens next. Don't fool yourself into thinking this is the same Chris you knew ten years ago."

"What do you mean?" Jessica asked curiously.

"If our expectations are met with the rioters, you'll find your answer." Night Hawk answered. The tone in his voice took a sudden turn from fairly friendly to a chillingly icy cold tone that had a thirst for blood.

A shiver ran down Jessica's spine and she gulped. She nervously turned her attention ahead of her, hoping things weren't going to get as ugly as she feared.

When the assassins made their way outside, they saw President Davis and his administration had already been ambushed by the media. They were being asked a thousand questions at once with cameras flashing their lights with every picture, and video cameramen were doing their best to get a good shot at the administration.

A chilling breeze started to blow, just enough to gently blow a person's hair. But there was something different about this sudden breeze, making every reporter stop, silencing the rambling noise of a hundred people in a small area. Every media person slowly turned to see seven extremely dangerous looking men overlooking them from atop the stairs of the capitol building. The air grew more and more still with each passing second, and many reporters struggled to keep their breath. Some struggled to breathe while others were frozen in fear. Nervous whispers slowly started to spread through the ranks.

"It...it's really them."

"The Seven Shadows...they're really real."

"How can this be possible?"

"Are we really supposed to be here?"

Night Hawk made his way in front of the assassins and looked down at President Davis, "President Davis, take your position and prepare yourself. As for you, ladies and gentlemen, spread out! I warn you now that our patience is very limited and I will not ask this a second time."

The media personnel all looked at each other nervously, then slowly took several steps back, allowing President Davis and his administration to reach their positions. The assassins then descended the steps and took their positions between each member of the new administration, keeping a firm eye on the small, but growing crowd below.

The administration started to deliver their speech, and the media started filming and snapping pictures again. Meanwhile, the assassins stood in position, keeping a sharp eye out for any potential trouble. Armed Republic soldiers were scattered around, but most had gone off to the Pentagon or to direct traffic now that civilians were starting to come and see what was going on.

As time went by, the new administration finished their speeches one by one. They were being televised all across the globe with billions of people watching. The assassins continued to stand in place, eagerly waiting for something to happen, but the day was quiet so far. However, they could see trouble was brewing in the distance.

"So they've come after all. Good." Chris thought.

By the time it was President Davis's turn to speak, a large group of protesters approached the area, screaming and swearing at President Davis's administration and the assassins.

"Well, well, what have we here?" Night Hawk asked, intrigued by the sudden appearance of protesters.

Jessica, who was standing and watching behind Chris, stepped forward as the apparent leader of the group made his way to the front of the crowd, "People, listen to me. This is not the time to protest. Go back to your homes for now. You don't want to do this."

"Yeah, shut up, bitch and go back to hiding behind your boyfriend." One of the protesters demanded in a nasty tone.

Jessica's eyes widened in shock, but she tried again, "Please! Listen to me! You don't want to be here!"

Some of the protesters laughed as they continued to approach, "Why? What's going to happen, bitch? You ganna cry when we chase these guys out of the city?"

Jessica felt her heart sink a little, and she opened her mouth to say something, but decided against it. "If you're going to be like that, fine. But don't say I didn't warn you."

The protesters laughed at Jessica as she retreated back behind Chris and the other assassins, "Yeah, whatever, bitch. Take a hike."

President Davis looked at the gathering crowd, "Are you people here to protest or just cause trouble?"

"What do you think, dumbass? We want our elected officials back! President Lane was twice the man *any* of you will ever be!" A woman in the crowd shouted.

"We won the war. Not Lane..."

"That's President Lane, you moron!" The same woman shouted.

Chris smirked and crossed his arms as he thought to himself, *"Fools. Showing their true colors already."*

An intense argument between the new administration and the protesters broke out and lasted for several minutes. But the protesters started to turn violent, and eventually the mob turned into a riot. One person in the crowd threw a rock directly for President Davis's face, but it was caught by Chris just before it struck its target.

The crowd quickly settled down now that one of the Shadows had moved after standing guard for so long. Chris's eyes were fixated on the person who threw the rock, forcing the man to take a few slow steps back.

"You've got some nerve, kid." Chris said in a low chilling voice. He held the rock in front of him, making sure the person who threw it had a good look at it. He then started to squeeze it, and the rock was quickly reduced to dust as he crushed it with his hand. "You just attempted an assassination of the Republic's president, and you will face the punishment for it."

Suddenly, a group of young men who appeared to be in their late teens or early twenties got between Chris and the suspect, trying to block Chris's vision.

"Is there something you would like to say?" Chris asked. He clapped his hands together to brush off what remained of the rock, then crossed his arms.

One of the men stepped forward, "Yeah, I got something to say. How about you ass holes go back where you came from? You white trash redneck hillbillies got no place in this city!"

"And who's going to make us?" Chris asked, not taking the man seriously.

The man laughed and looked around him and laughed with his friends before looking back at Chris, "What? You really think you can take us on, cracker?"

"I recommend you hold your tongue." Chris responded coldly.

"Oh, a tough guy, huh?" The man asked as he and his friends laughed in a mocking manner. They laughed for a few moments before the man got serious again, "Well, if you're so bad, why don't you just prove it to us? Show us how big and bad you really are you bitch ass coward."

"To challenge an assassin is a fight to the death. I advise you to walk away. Now." Chris's tone grew hostile and impatient.

"Bitch, me and my friends ain't goin' nowhere until we beat you and your worthless friends, and take that bitch behind you for ourselves to play with." The man said.

A sudden strong gust of wind rushed forward, knocking the punks off their feet, and blowing them several feet away into the crowd of rioters. Everyone watched in shock at what they saw, and their ideas of causing more trouble quickly faded from their minds.

The voice of the man who threatened Chris a few seconds ago could be heard behind the dust cloud as he begged and pleaded for mercy. What followed was anything but. The sick slashing sound of flesh being sliced open was followed shortly by an eerie scream of terrible and dreadful pain that only grew louder and louder as time went on. When the dust settled, the crowd backed away slowly and grew more silent by what they saw.

Chris had the loudmouth leader of the group of thugs hanging by his neck several inches off the ground with the spikes on his gloves buried deep in the man's throat. The man screamed and screeched in unimaginable pain as he held Chris's arm and tried to pull himself off the spikes, only to have Chris slice the spikes on his other hand up the man's stomach and torso, ripping a sizable chunk of flesh from his body. His screams went from painful to that of a nightmarish horror. His hands slipped off Chris's arm, making his weight pull his neck even further up Chris's spikes. Blood poured and shot from his mouth and wounds, but he wasn't able to scream any longer since the spikes went through his larynx. Now, all he could do was twitch, but eventually he stopped moving all together.

Chris glared at the group of men who were yelling at him earlier, and grabbed the man trapped on his spikes by the neck, and lifted him even higher in the air. "So this is what passes as a thug these days? This is what passes as killers, rapists and robbers anymore? I think I've been more intimidated by boxes full of clawless kittens. You people are no killers. Just a bunch of brats who managed to stumble their way into the big leagues." He snapped the man's neck and threw the corpse at the crowd of rioters who were starting to slowly back away, "Now that I have your attention, know this. So long as the Republic's government is in command, the laws will be followed accordingly. The days brats like you got away with crimes because you were part of a political party are long gone. From this point on, any crime will be punishable. Any threat will be taken seriously. Any idiot celebrity who makes a bold claim will be held accountable. Unlike before, your actions now have consequences. I suggest the rest of you go home while you still have the chance."

The crowd slowly backed away, allowing President Davis to continue, and Chris returned to his original position. Once there, Jessica, still trying to wrap her head around what she just witnessed, stared at Chris with a sense of awe. "I…I tried to warn them." She said with a hint of self-guilt in her voice.

"Yes, but there is nothing you could have done. People like that have nothing but hatred, and can't settle things peacefully when they don't get their way. They would rather riot and cause trouble." Chris said.

Jessica released a depressing sigh and looked at the ground, "I guess so. But what happens now that the war is over? Are you going to focus your attention on the Agroneese?"

"We still have Lane to deal with. He's on his way to one of our prisons in Oklahoma, where we're also going to meet with a man I need to speak with."

"Who would that be?" Jessica asked.

"Robert Vype. One of the men who helped supply and arm the Rebellion. He's currently working on the next phase of our newest combat tanks." Chris said.

Jessica's eyes widened, "You mean those monstrosities you guys rolled into Richmond last night?"

Chris nodded, "Indeed. He's the one who designed them. He recently asked me to visit him."

"For what reason?" Jessica asked.

"I guess we'll find out soon enough. However, that will have to wait. The assassins have some things they want to discuss with you first." Chris said.

CHAPTER 19

Daughter of Forayer

After President Davis finished his speech, the media surrounded him and his administration once again, trying to get as many questions answered as possible. The assassins remained standing watch for a short time, but eventually disappeared from the area when they felt enough soldiers had reinforced the area, and shoved their way through the media to guard President Davis and his administration.

Jessica was still disturbed by what she saw happen earlier with the thug, and his screams still haunted her. She knew things were going to end badly, and even though she tried to not think about it, she couldn't help but feel she didn't do enough to prevent that man from dying. She kept her head low and played with her fingers as she walked. In a way, she was relieved because it was one less thug in the world, and anyone in that crowd was bound to change their ways after witnessing what had happened. But she still couldn't shake the feeling of guilt for not trying a little harder.

She followed the assassins back into the capitol building where they led her to a large meeting hall. They closed and locked the doors behind them, then walked by her as Chris started to talk.

"Now, Jessica. We have some things we need to talk about."

"L-like what?" Jessica asked. She claimed a chair at one of the tables, and kept her attention on Chris as he spoke.

"Some time ago you somehow came into possession of a ring. I need to know where it came from and how you got it." Chris said. He stood in place with his arms crossed, waiting for her to respond.

Jessica lowered her head for a moment as she thought, then looked up at Chris again, "How did you know I had a ring in the first place? Were you spying on me?"

"In a manner of speaking." Night Hawk said, catching Jessica's attention, "We sensed the Agroneese had already made their first move, so we dispatched a sniper team to keep an eye on you so we knew when you were in any kind of danger."

"And they told you about this ring I had?" Jessica asked.

Night Hawk nodded, "Yes. Did this ring seem a little strange to you when you had it?"

Jessica stared at Night Hawk for a moment, then sighed and turned her attention forward again before lowering her head, "'Strange' is only the simplest way I would put it. I received that ring as a package in the mail. It had no name or return address on it, which raised a red flag for me from the very beginning. But my curiosity got the better of me, so I opened it. Well, then the blasted thing became a minor obsession of mine. The language that was written around the bend…I tried *everything* to find out what language it was, but it never came up. I researched ancient languages, modern languages, and even some extinct languages trying to figure it out."

"And did you ever experience anything weird with it?" Chris asked.

Jessica looked up at Chris with a blank face, then rested her chin in her palm as she thought back, "Actually, yes. Every time I wore it…I had a nightmare. But it was the weirdest thing. These nightmares seemed to act in a pattern of some kind. The first one I was in Tehran, Iran. The Republic was fighting the Iranian military, then a nuclear warhead went off. After that…there was some being who haunted my every step. He started off as a Skeleton, but he eventually took form. All I remember seeing about him was pale white, or maybe even greyish skin with long black hair. He tormented me in every dream I had after he made himself known."

"Grey skin…long black hair…" Night Hawk's eyes shot open, and he rushed over to Jessica and started shaking her, "What was that being's name, Jessica? Did he tell you his name?!"

Stunned from Night Hawk's change of attitude, Jessica froze in fear for a few moments until he stopped shaking her. She paused for a few moments, trying to pull herself together, then tried to remember her dreams, "Mmmmm…I don't really remember. All I know is he was evil. And I swear I felt the pain in my arm after the first night. I fell down a hill and broke my arm in the dream, but even in real life my arm hurt."

Night Hawk and the other assassins stared at Jessica with a hint of fear in their eyes, "It can't be. They can't be trying to bring him back."

Jessica looked at Night Hawk, terrified by his tone of voice, "H-he? Who's 'he'?"

Night Hawk returned his attention to Jessica and shook his head, "No one good. We have to move fast. Things are far worse than we originally thought. They're already three steps ahead of us."

"What? Who is this person?" Jessica asked, her voice giving away her fear.

Night Hawk sighed, and turned his back to her, "Never mind that. This is a problem for us to worry about. Silent Arrow, I think you can take things over from here."

Silent Arrow nodded and approached Jessica while the other assassins, including Chris, left the room, leaving them alone.

Jessica watched Chris disappear through the door, then turned her attention to Silent Arrow as he came closer to her. "So, what's so important about this ring?"

Silent Arrow remained silent for a moment, then spoke, "Perhaps it would be better if we just start from the beginning. Night Walker tells me you have the gift of Forayer's Sight. Is this true?"

"You're asking if I can see another's past by looking in their eyes? Then yes." Jessica answered.

"And do you know the history of this gift, or the potential of its power?" Silent Arrow asked.

Jessica shook her head, "No. I haven't used it that much because I don't know what costs it may have. As far as the history goes, I kind of assumed I was the only one to have it."

Silent Arrow shook his head, "No. You're not the only Daughter of Forayer. Not by a long shot. You may be the only one of this life time, but not in recorded history."

"What? How many has there been?" Jessica asked.

"In recorded Atlassian history, there has been at least twenty, and each one was around during specific times. Daughters of Forayer are spread few and far between, with only one being born every two to five-thousand years. The last one was a Greek woman during the beginning of the Roman Empire."

"So…what exactly does this have to do with me?" Jessica asked.

Silent Arrow remained silent for a moment as he thought, then started speaking, "An ancient legend written long ago has all but come true. It says the defeat of the Agroneese was only delayed, that they would come back when countries of free men and women spill their own blood, and when a daughter and an assassin sync in time. Night Walker is Twenty-four, as are you. You share similar birth dates. He was born the tenth of October. You were born the seventeenth of October. A long story cut short, you may be the most powerful daughter that we've ever recorded."

Jessica's eyes widened in interest, "H-how do you mean, exactly?"

Silent Arrow reached into his pocket, and pulled out the ring they were talking about earlier, "This ring was a gift from the Agroneese. It is a ring of Xzerriph – the Atlassian demon of nightmares. This ring, if worn by a daughter, allows her to see the future through her dreams while she sleeps. In a sense, her spirit leaves her body and flies to wherever a big event is going to happen. You said a nuclear bomb will go off in Tehran Iran at some point in the future, which indicates you know about things we have yet to discover. However, this gift comes at a cost. It is double edged. Whenever you wear this, the Agroneese will sense you, and they will start hunting you. Just like the assassins, the Agroneese are somehow drawn to Daughters of Forayer. We have no idea why, and may never know, but it is a fact we have to deal with."

Jessica stared at the ring with a look of amazement, then looked at Silent Arrow as she thought of something, "So…what does it say on the bend? Is that the language of the Agroneese?"

Silent Arrow nodded, "It's Aggronniss. A language thought to have died out over six-thousand years ago. After the first Agroneese war when the Atlassians drove them to near annihilation."

"And how long ago was this war, exactly?" Jessica asked.

"Three millennia before the Egyptians built their first pyramid." Silent Arrow answered.

Jessica raised her eyebrows in amazement, "Damn. That was a long time ago."

"Indeed. But we're getting off subject. I have a theory we can turn this ring into a lethal weapon with the right kind of training." Silent Arrow said as he walked by Jessica.

With a puzzled look Jessica turned to watch Silent Arrow walk by, "W-what kind of training? You want to turn a piece of jewelry into a weapon? Short of blinding my enemies with a glare from the sun, I don't see how that will be possible."

Silent Arrow looked over his shoulder, "That's because you don't know our history."

"But…how can this even work? I mean…it doesn't make any sense to me." Jessica said.

Silent Arrow turned to face Jessica again, "You surface dwellers have a very limited way of thinking. No wonder your countries are constantly at war. You rely on your governments to tell you what's right and wrong, but when has the government of any nation been more concerned with the wellbeing of its people and not lining their pockets with the money they made by pillaging other lands?"

Jessica opened her mouth to say something, but couldn't argue against Silent Arrow's point. His statement was far from untrue. She thought for a few seconds, then focused on Silent Arrow again, "So what's your plan? If I'm going to receive some kind of training from you guys, wouldn't that technically make me an assassin?"

Silent Arrow smirked, and started walking to her, "It takes more than just some training to become an assassin. Until you can openly take another's life as your profession, you haven't earned the title. And based off what I've seen of this surface world so far, let alone what was America, you never will be an assassin. You surface dwellers, especially those in Western culture, have grown too weak and feeble. Your attachment to technology is harming you more than it's helping you."

"So what's the plan, then?" Jessica asked.

"While you may not become an assassin, you still have the potential to become a formidable foe to your enemies." Silent Arrow said, "When I learned of Night Walker's plans to take down the old country, I immediately started researching all the old myths and legends of past Daughters of Forayer. I knew his plans would, in one way or another, lead him back to you, so I wanted to make sure my own plan wasn't a waste of time. Night Walker spent many years going over his plans for the civil war day in and day out. For every minute he spent planning the war, I spent theorizing potential future plans for you. I have reason to believe that with the right kind of training, you can wear that ring and use it as a tool to see into the future without having to sleep."

"You mean…I could actually see into the future…as far as I wanted?" Jessica asked.

Silent Arrow nodded, "In theory, at least. The length of time you may be able to look forward to may be limited, but the short term could prove to be far more valuable. Especially now that we're going to war against the Agroneese for the second time. If you can learn to use the ring like that, you will prove to be more than just the Daughter of Forayer of the present, you could prove to be a valuable ally. You could warn us of surprise attacks from our enemies, you could give us information on an approaching disaster, and you would be nearly unstoppable in a fight. You would know your opponents move before they did, and you would know how to counter every one of their attacks. You wouldn't be able to last against an assassin, or stronger members of the Agroneese, but you could comfortably hold your own against most opponents."

Jessica stared at Silent Arrow with great interest and was eager to know more, "Okay, so how do you plan to train me?"

"We'll need to start with you being able to control your dreams." Silent Arrow said, "Given your current state, I doubt you're able to sustain your visions for very long. Is this true?"

"They seem long enough to me. Every time I have one of these dreams it's a nightmare." Jessica said.

"So is the reality of war, and the mess your world is about to find itself in." Silent Arrow said.

Jessica sighed and lowered her head, then looked at Silent Arrow again, "Fine. But once I'm able to stay in these dreams for extended periods of time, how can I train myself to see the future?"

"That's a far distant future. One you needn't worry about right now." Silent Arrow said, "Once you're able to control these dreams and remain in them for extended periods, we can move onto the next phase: daydreaming."

"Daydreaming?" Jessica asked.

Silent Arrow nodded, "Once you become skilled enough, I believe you will be able to have visions of the future just by daydreaming. I'm not sure what kind of effects this will have, as you are the only Daughter in this world's history that will have accomplished this. It's in one of the oldest Atlassian legends that says when a Daughter of Forayer is in possession of Xzerriph's ring and holds a bond with an assassin, darkness will surround them. The enemy will invade and spread across their lands like wildfire. Cities will burn, alliances will crumble at the hands of defeat. However, within the same legend, it says another force will come into play."

"Another force? What does that mean?" Jessica asked.

"I...I am unsure. In the first Agroneese war, there were only two contenders. Atlassia and the Agroneese. I am unaware of any third party that came into play at that time." Silent Arrow said.

"And you never thought this third party was odd to begin with?" Jessica asked.

"No. It's possible it refers to Night Walker's ancient ancestor, Night Blade. The most powerful member of the Seventeen Assassins in the history of our order. His enemy, Shadow Snake, sided with the Agroneese and wreaked havoc on Atlassian forces a number of times throughout the war. So the military called for the aid of Night Blade to chase him off. To make a long story short, Night Blade defeated Shadow Snake a number of times, but he always managed to slither away from their fights and continue his reign of destruction. In order to keep Shadow Snake emerging from his hiding places, Night Blade took on entire armies of the Agroneese by his self, paving a road to Attinimas, or what you call modern day Iran. So it's possible the legend refers to another powerful assassin coming into play towards the end."

"Wonderful. Yeah, I was hoping for the day I'd see two men capable of wiping out entire armies on their own duke it out somehow. That's not going to be terrifying at all." Jessica said in a sarcastic tone.

Silent arrow smirked and turned away from Jessica, "Well, I think we've gone over enough for now. I believe Night Walker will want to speak with you in the near future. So be prepared."

Jessica nodded, "That's something I can handle." She stood from her chair and made her way out of the room.

CHAPTER 20

Necklace of Sealing

As Jessica left her meeting with Silent Arrow, Night Hawk caught her attention as she looked down a hallway and saw him leaning against the wall as if he were waiting for her. Before she had a chance to do anything, he pushed himself off the wall and walked to her.

"Jessica, there is something I need to speak to you about. Privately." Night Hawk said.

Jessica stared at Night Hawk with a curious look for a moment, then nodded.

Night Hawk turned and led the way to another room where he waited for her to enter first, then closed the door behind him.

"So what is this about?" Jessica asked as she turned to face Night Hawk.

"It's about Chris. I wanted to make sure you knew he isn't the same as when he left all those years ago." Night Hawk said.

"How do you mean? Are you asking if I realized he's probably a very dangerous person by now? Then yeah, I kind of pieced that together when he dealt with those thugs outside." Jessica said.

"Yes, Chris has earned his place as a pre-ranking member of the Seventeen. Which means the Chris you knew ten years ago is gone. However, part of him remains."

Jessica raised an eyebrow and stared at Night Hawk with a confused look, "What do you mean? How can the old Chris be gone, but here at the same time?"

"Remember when you first met him? His only dream at that point was to meet his mother and family. That's all he wanted in life back then. Now…he's different. I am unsure what hopes he has for the future outside of defeating the Agroneese and avenging his family's death, he more or less just shut the rest of the world out from himself. But still, he continues to wear the necklace I gave him, thinking her spirit still lives with him."

Jessica lowered her eyes in sadness for a moment as she thought back to that day that seemed so long ago. She remember Night Hawk giving Chris the necklace he spoke of, telling him his mother was still with him in one way. She sighed quietly, and looked at Night Hawk again, "So… is there some other reason you gave him the necklace outside of a gift?"

Night Hawk remained silent as he thought of a way to respond. But rather than beating around the bush, he sighed and went straight to the truth, "Back when I told you the power that necklace had, I spoke the truth…but I didn't tell you everything. Chris has grown powerful since you last saw him. He's starting to take after his ancient ancestor's ways, and becoming more and more powerful with each passing day. The Reaper, however, is growing in power, too. We've all sensed it. It's growing impatient, and desperately wants to escape its cell. That necklace is a magical trinket made specifically to keep the Reaper's power at a minimum, and to ensure it never escapes."

"What happens if it does escape?" Jessica asked.

"Nothing good. The Reaper is far more powerful than all of us assassins combined. Should it manage to escape entirely, it may mean the end of this world. The Agroneese will be the least of our concerns should this happen." Night Hawk said.

"And…what happens to Chris?" Jessica asked, fearful of the answer.

"You've already seen what a small outburst of the Reaper's power can do. Not only to those in his vicinity, but to Chris himself. That first outburst wasn't even a fraction of the Reaper's potential. He destroyed the school and other parts of the city, yes, but things could have been much worse than they were. Chris suffers immensely when something like that happens. With just that small breakout, Chris's body suffered severe burns, cracked bones and many other injuries. But the Reaper also heals him. Because if Chris dies, then the Reaper disappears as well."

"So...they're connected in certain ways?" Jessica asked.

Night Hawk nodded, "That's putting it simply. Chris can use the Reaper's power to use some...other worldly techniques. But at a cost of his own life."

"So, if he uses those types of powers, he could literally die?" Jessica asked.

Night Hawk nodded, "Yes. Rather painfully, in fact. But this is not all I wanted to talk to you about. You and Chris developed a rather strong bond all those years ago. You said you would do whatever it took to keep him safe, and that his dreams were also yours."

"Yes. And I still stand by what I said." Jessica said.

Night Hawk remained silent for a moment before he continued, "While Chris may no longer wish to meet his mother due to the unfortunate mess the old government made of his family, he still secretly cares about his family's past. And in a sense, his mother still lives in you, too."

Jessica's eyes widened, and memories of one of her past dreams came to her. She remembered sitting in the orphanage with Chris, and speaking to a woman who looked very similar to her. Even to this day, the final words she said haunted the back of her mind,

"Please, watch after my son."

A tear slid down Jessica's right cheek, and she wiped the tears from her eyes. "I know this. I met his mother in one of the dreams I mentioned. She looked exactly like me with a few minor exceptions. Why?"

"If I had to guess, I'd say it's because you're this time period's Daughter of Forayer, and she was drawn to you knowing you would end up meeting her son eventually." Night Hawk said. "But I can't say for certain."

"What do you want me to do?" Jessica asked.

"First off, Chris has worked hard to become what he is today. He is the primary General and economic advisor for the Republic. He has earned the title as the most fearsome General in history, and his enemies fear him for it."

Jessica smiled softly, and turned to face another part of the room, "I don't doubt that. I assume it was his idea to target the Washington Monument?" She asked, turning to look at Night Hawk again.

Night Hawk nodded, "It was."

"I figured as much. I thought I recognized his tactics as the war went on, but I wasn't sure." Jessica said, "He's always been a great tactician. Even my dad, who was Chess champion back in the day couldn't beat him."

"And now you understand why he has his reputation." Night Hawk said, "He's a General out of his time. He cares nothing for collateral damage. Once someone declares him an enemy, he treats them as such."

Jessica smirked, "So *that's* how the Republic made its reputation with the rest of the world. Russia respects you, China fears you. The EU wouldn't dare oppose you. Just because of him."

"Most countries around the world do support the Republic for a number of reasons. China is our biggest contender, and we're increasing relations with Russia." Night Hawk said, "Chris has proven to be an excellent leader."

Jessica blushed slightly, and smiled softly as she lowered her head, "I always knew he would. The moment I met him I knew he was destined for something big."

"But despite his accomplishments, Chris has little companionship. He never openly admitted it, but he was looking forward to seeing you again for a long time." Night Hawk said.

Jessica's blushed again, and she turned to look at Night Hawk, "I always wondered if he wanted to see me again. He never wrote or tried to contact me at all."

"A lot of that is just because we were always traveling. When we first started training, he said he had a debt to repay you and your family." Night Hawk said.

"He owes us nothing. I was proud to have taken him in, and so was my family. They missed him just as much as I did." Jessica said.

"I can imagine." Night Hawk said. He remained quiet for a few moments, allowing an awkward silence to build between them. "Well, I think we've covered everything I wanted to. I suggest you head home now, Jessica. We have a lot of work to do. You'll find your apartment is safe to return to. The Agroneese won't dare come near you with seven assassins within the general area."

Jessica nodded, and walked out of the room when Night Hawk opened the door for her.

CHAPTER 21

Reunification and Admiration

The buzzing of Jessica's alarm clock woke her up. In total disbelief, she rolled over to look at the time and saw it was in fact 7:00 A.M. She growled quietly, and moaned as she sat up in her bed, rubbing her eyes. She stared at the far wall on the other side of her bedroom, waiting for her vision to clear, and for her head to stop spinning. When she was ready, she stepped out of bed, and started her morning stretches, bending and popping her back, and reaching for her toes. Once she was finished, she grabbed some clothes from her drawers and closet, and proceeded to the bathroom where she took her morning shower. After that, she proceeded to the kitchen to make her breakfast.

"Ugh! One would think mornings would eventually become tolerable." She thought.

She quickly decided on what to have for breakfast, and started gathering what she needed. As she cooked, she kept an eye on the news, but had to laugh at how hysterical the media and public were. Protests and riots broke out across the country, but were of little use in the long run. The Republic had won, and that was the end of it. However, politics were not something that interested her anymore. Now that Chris had come back, she was more than content to know he was safe and they were, in one way or another, together again.

When Jessica finished making her breakfast, she sat it on a plate and sat down at the bar so she could keep an eye on the TV as she ate. But she was caught by surprise as someone knocked on her door. She looked over her shoulder at the door for a few seconds, waiting for another knock.

"*What in the world? Who could possibly want to see me at this ungodly hour?*" She thought.

She waited a few moments for another knock, but nothing happened, and she eventually shrugged it off and dismissed it as her just hearing things. However, the knock came again when she returned her attention to the TV, and she immediately rushed over to the door. But when she saw who it was, she instantly regretted not coming sooner. She immediately unlocked the door, and opened it. "C-Chris! Uh...what are you...I mean...how did you...hi."

Chris, who was wearing his black tattered cloak stared down at Jessica with a pleased face. "May I enter?"

"O-of course! Please, come in!" Jessica said. She stepped aside, allowing Chris to enter through the doorway, and closed the door behind him. Once she had the door locked again, she turned to Chris with a delighted look on her face, "You'll have to forgive me. I wasn't expecting company so my apartment's kind of a mess."

"I would expect nothing less. Despite being raised by Marines, you never really were that neat." Chris said.

Jessica playfully slapped Chris's arm and laughed sarcastically, "Ha, ha, ha! Very funny! Ha, ha, ha!"

Chris smirked at her, and turned his attention to her unfinished breakfast sitting on the counter, "I guess I caught you as you were eating..."

Jessica nodded, "Yeah, but that's okay. Um...it's not that I'm not happy to see you, but what brings you here? I wasn't expecting to see you so early."

"I thought about what the others said, and allowed myself a day off. It's been a long time since we've actually talked." Chris said.

Jessica nodded in agreement, "It's been too long, Chris. Far, far too long."

"I hope I'm not getting in the way of any big plans you may have had for the day." Chris said.

Jessica shook her head, "Don't worry. Any plans I may have had, including work, were cancelled the second I saw you standing at the door. Which actually reminds me..." She rushed over to the counter and grabbed her phone. Then called the flower shop, and waited for Shelby to answer.

"Hey, Shelby, it's Jessica. I'm afraid I won't be able to come in today. Something unexpected has come up. ...Well, an old friend of mine I haven't really seen in a long time just came to my door this morning, and I'd like to spend some time with him. ...Uh...are you sure? I mean, I can come in tomorrow... Well, if you're sure. ...Okay. Thanks, Shelby! Bye." Jessica ended the call and sat her phone down, then looked at Chris and leaned on the kitchen isle, "So, with that out of the way, may I interest you in anything to eat or drink? I was just getting ready to have some French toast."

Chris was about to answer, but something familiar caught his attention. He looked around the room for a moment, but couldn't spot what he was looking for. "That scent...what is it?"

Jessica looked at Chris with a puzzled face, "Scent? Do you mean the candles or my perfume?"

Chris shook his head, "I'm unsure. But it smells just like the old house."

"Oh! That would be the candles I had burning throughout the night. Does it bring back memories for you?" Jessica asked.

Chris remained silent for a moment, then looked at Jessica and nodded, "Yes. It brings back memories. Things just seemed... simpler back then."

"If you call getting beaten within an inch every day of your life 'simple', then I guess I can't argue with you." Jessica said.

"I meant after you got involved." Chris replied.

Jessica smiled softly and lowered her head for a moment, then looked up at Chris again. "I know. You know, the house got dreadfully boring after you left. I no longer had someone to play games with, swim with, or watch movies with. You owe me big time, buster."

Chris smirked, "And here I thought you didn't collect debts."

Jessica smiled innocently and put her arms behind her back, "Only when things matter, Chris."

"I figured as much." Chris said.

Jessica giggled and approached the refrigerator again, "Anyway, can I get you something? I can make you breakfast...or just get you something to drink."

Chris remained silent for a moment, thinking back to Jessica's cooking in the past. "You always were a good cook, and I haven't had an actual home-made meal in a long time. So...sure. I'll have what you're having."

Jessica smiled kindly and nodded, "That won't be a problem. Give me just a few minutes and I'll have it ready."

She proceeded to walk around the kitchen, gathering the ingredients and pottery she needed. Once she was ready, she started making Chris a French toast breakfast. As she cooked, Chris took a moment to look around her apartment again, but turned his attention to Jessica as she sighed and lowered her head.

"Chris, I...I just don't even know where to begin. There are so many things I want to ask you. How your training went, how you got involved with the Rebellion...I can't make my mind up."

"Well, we have the entire day." Chris stated.

"I know, but...sometimes days just aren't long enough." Jessica said.

"Well, pick a topic and I'll answer while you're cooking, then." Chris said, continuing to stand in place.

Jessica looked over her shoulder at Chris for a moment, then turned her attention to her cooking, "Alright. Let's start with the training. Where all did you go, and how intense was it?"

Chris took a moment to think about the best way to answer, "My training took part all across the world. I traveled with the assassins to remote locations on every continent, including Antarctica just to tone my body to deal with natural environments of all types. But the environments on the surface were nothing compared to what I had to face in Atlassia. You think the Gobi gets hot? Try spending a day in the Bamah sometime."

Jessica looked over her shoulder, "The Bahmah Desert? What's that?" She asked curiously.

"The largest and second hottest desert in Atlassia. It lies on the eastern coast of the continent, and is surrounded by mountains in the north, south and west with what would be the ocean to the east. Temperatures on a good day reach one-hundred twenty. On a bad day they can stretch up to one-hundred fifty degrees." Chris said.

Jessica's eyes widened in shock and amazement, "Really?! Good grief! Why didn't they just toss you in an oven?"

"It would have been more convenient, I'm sure."

Jessica giggled, and returned her attention to the food she was making, "Jokes aside, tell mem more."

Chris thought for a moment, then continued, "Well, as I said, I ventured all over the world to adapt to extreme environments, but add in having to do endless amounts of workouts, sword fighting, and learning to control the elements in each of those environments."

"That...sounds like it wouldn't be easy." Jessica said.

"Physical training was tedious at best. A minimum of five-hundred pushups, a thousand sit ups and crunches and a twenty mile run before lunch if I was lucky enough to have it."

Jessica rolled her eyes to look back at Chris, "What do you mean "lucky enough to have it?""

"I'll put it this way: training to be an assassin takes your body to its very limits. The assassins often go without food for extended periods, so they accustom themselves to hunger just not being a thing they have to worry about. The best assassins were often able to survive three weeks without actually having to seek out food, and they also managed to survive up to four days without water, depending on the environment they were in."

"Do you think they could have pulled it off in the Bahma?" Jessica asked.

Chris shook his head, "No. Nothing lives in that desert with the exception of a few animal species. That desert is the most unforgiving place on Earth. Well, maybe with the exception of the northern most region in Atlassia – the Land of the Seventeen."

Jessica looked over her shoulder at Chris again, "Land of the Seventeen? What's that?"

"It's a volcanic plain. The history behind it is it was once the fourth desert of the land. Then two extremely powerful assassins declared war on each other, and they made the landscape unstable. Now its scorched lands are littered with rivers and lakes of magma." Chris said.

Jessica's eyes widened in amazement, "You're kidding. Those assassins weren't Night Blade and Shadow Snake were they?"

Chris shook his head, "No. Those events took place long before either of them existed."

Jessica turned around entirely to face Chris, "But…Night Blade and Shadow Snake were the most powerful assassins to have ever lived, right?" She exclaimed.

Chris only nodded in response.

"Then…their power must have been terrifying to witness." Jessica said in a quiet tone.

"No assassin has ever achieved the amount of power those two possessed. They were literal breathing gods among mortal men." Chris said.

"But…where does their power come from in the first place? I would assume these people start off as just regular human beings, don't they?" Jessica asked.

Chris thought for a few moments, then replied, "Typically, you're correct. Most assassins do start off as just normal men. But there are others who…weren't necessarily human to begin with. Atlassia – more commonly known as the "Land of the Unknown" didn't earn its name for nothing. There are sources of power in that land you would only think existed in a fairy tale. However, the Blihkt Ritah has more to do with assassins gaining their power than magical trinkets and other devices."

"Blihkt Ritah?" Jessica asked.

"It's the final test a pre-ranking assassin must take before he can actually call himself a true member of the Seventeen. It's the last, but most difficult part of training." Chris said.

"Why is that?" Jessica asked.

"Because it feeds on your worst fears, and it will force you to experience the most painful scenario you can think of. Imagine being eaten alive by a lion, but you never die. You're alive and you feel everything. From it pulling out your organs, ripping off your limbs, chewing your flesh, and snapping your bones. Then multiply that pain by a thousand." Chris said.

Jessica froze in place for a moment, then quickly turned away to focus more on her cooking, "I would rather not have to imagine that. Just hearing it gives me goosebumps!"

"Well, just to give you an idea to work with." Chris said. He paused for a moment, then continued, "The plus side of it is, is that it only lasts a few seconds in reality. Seventeen seconds. A second for every demon from Atlassian mythology. If you survive the test, you're gifted with unimaginable power. The power to crumble entire nations is in the tip of your fingers."

Jessica stared at Chris with a look of amazement for a moment, then thought of another question, "But...how are we supposed to counter one of these guys? If an assassin can truly be as powerful as you say, what's to stop them from ruling the world with no competition? We would need God himself to get involved."

"Or another assassin." Chris stated, catching Jessica's full and undivided attention, "The assassins are called the "Seventeen" but that's mostly because they represent the Seventeen demons from Atlassian mythology that's still around today, despite the land being more or less a Christian-like nation."

"What do you mean by 'Christian-like'?" Jessica asked.

"Basically they have their own beliefs in the Bible. There are some things they saw as...basically made up crap, so they took it out." Chris said.

Jessica raised a suspicious eyebrow and gave Chris a funny look, "And an example of this would be...what, exactly?"

"I haven't given it a huge read over, myself. I was never really that into the Bible. But one thing I know for a fact is they took out Adam and Eve. They found it ridiculous to think humanity started off with one man and one woman. Which, if you ask me, is fair game."

"Well, as a Catholic, I'm not really sure if I ever really bought into the Adam and Eve thing, either." Jessica said.

"Well, regardless. Religious beliefs aren't important to me. I only care about winning this damn war." Chris said.

Jessica smiled and nodded, then turned around to continue cooking, "Anyway, tell me how you got involved with the Rebellion."

Chris sniggered a little before replying, "As I told you. I'm the one who started it."

Jessica looked over her shoulder again, "But how? I mean, building an army like the Republics can't be cheap."

"The assassins had a fair play in it as well, and I managed to come up with the idea of three companies that took right off." Chris said.

"Companies? What kind of companies?" Jessica asked.

"Let's just say they're political benefits to the three political factions that make up Atlassia's politics. They make billions each year, and I turn the wealth I make off them into American dollars. Just one Atlatii is equal to seventy-five U.S dollars. It doesn't take long to reach a billion dollars when you're making billions of Atlatii." Chris said.

Jessica's eyes widened in amazement and she turned to face him, "Then…if I'm hearing this right…that would make you the richest man in the world!"

Chris smirked and shook his head, "No. The richest man on the surface is nothing but a mere peasant compared to a middle wealth Atlassian. The richest Atlassian would easily be a trillionare were he to move to the surface."

"And how do you compare to him…or her?" Jessica asked.

"Poorly." Chris answered. He thought about what to say next as he looked into the other room, then looked at Jessica as he continued, "My companies merely serve as a means to an end. Nothing more."

"You mean you…don't want the wealth, and to live a life of luxury?" Jessica asked.

"Wealth is a drug, Jessica. It's something very few people know how to control. It amounts to power, and power corrupts who you are as an individual. Even a die-hard Christian could not turn down the gift of ultimate power if given the choice. They may hesitate at first, but they will eventually take it. Then, the power consumes them in a way that changes who they are. The religious claim the devil is the greatest evil in the universe. I say it's money." Chris said.

Jessica turned back to cooking again, "Well, I suppose that makes sense. It's…also a very wise way of looking at life, actually." She paused for a moment, then thought of something else to ask, "But how did you actually start the civil war? I mean, you would have had to have governors willing to turn on their country, and politicians prepared to lead the way. How did you manage to pull that off?"

"Careful planning for one thing. I didn't spend my entire time with the assassins just training to be a brainless brute with an unhealthy obsession of blood." Chris stated, "I studied the tactics of famous generals from all over the world. Romans, Greeks, Arabs, Chinese, Napoleon, British and American generals, I read them all. War is something I understand very well, which is more than I can say for anyone else at this point in time. The world has grown too soft."

"You're a general out of your own time according to Silent Arrow." Jessica said.

"The people of this world aren't ready for someone like me. They'll view my coming actions as war crimes, but I'll let them live in their delusions. At least for the time being." Chris said.

"War crimes? Why would anyone accuse you of doing that?" Jessica asked.

"Because the Muslim Brotherhood, the people the government sold my parents to, are about to find themselves dealing with a very pissed off military experiment they'll wish they'd never messed with. I don't care about making deals with them, they can serve as food or playthings for the Agroneese as far as I'm concerned. And until the leaders of that bunch of cowards are kneeling before me, I'll reduce their countries into ruin."

Jessica remained quiet as she looked over her shoulder with a concerned face, "Technically, that's inevitable anyway, isn't it? Isn't that part of the world where the Agroneese are already gathering their strength?"

"Yes. In the deserts of Iran where they were defeated long ago." Chris said, "The Iranians are blindly thinking these beings are their allies and they can use them to restore the Persian Empire. They are very mistaken, however. Once the Iranians are no longer of any use, they'll be brushed aside and the Agroneese will flood the lands like a virus taking over a body. Between them and me, the Muslim Brotherhood will have nowhere to run."

"So…you're using the deaths of millions to accomplish your goal of revenge?" Jessica asked.

"There is no 'using' to it, Jessica. Millions would die, even if I wasn't looking for the Muslim Brotherhood. And the way I see it, they're the next problem the world needs to deal with. I've already taken down Washington. The vermin of that pathetic part of the world are next." Chris said.

Jessica remained quiet, but kept her attention on the food she was making. Eventually, another question came to her, "So…what's the plan for alliances? You can't expect to fight this war on your own."

"No. Soon we'll be calling for a meeting of world leaders. We expect most of Europe, Russia, Japan, China, Australia and many other countries to attend. This is where we break the news about the Agroneese to the world." Chris said.

"And you expect the public to just accept another war is right around the corner? People are tired of war, Chris. People are looking for peace and prosperity. Not more war." Jessica said.

"If humanity emerges victorious, our numbers will be so small we won't have need for war for a long, long time. If we win, everyone will have to worry more about rebuilding their countries and getting over what will likely be the bloodiest event to ever exist in human history. On top of that, if things start looking too bad for us, the Atlassians will likely get involved. They have no love for the surface world, and they view surface dwellers as scum and unpunished children. But they have no desire to see the surface world die, either. If they get involved, they will likely remain the dominant superpower for years to come." Chris said.

"Well, that's a lot of 'ifs'." Jessica said, "I have to admit that just hearing the numbers of these monsters is terrifying enough. But to know what they'll do to us when we're dead…I just want to wrap myself in a ball and cry."

"Well, I think you may be lucky in the end, actually." Chris said, making Jessica look over her shoulder at him again, "The assassins and I…we have a plan that involves you. We haven't decided on it yet, so I won't tell you the details yet."

Jessica stopped what she was doing, and turned to face Chris, "Wha-what do you *mean* you have a plan for me? What can I be, some kind of secret weapon to you?"

"Actually…that is a suitable title for you." Chris said.

Jessica blinked a few times, and stared at Chris with a confused face, "And you can't tell me the details because…?"

"I'd hate to get your hopes up." Chris said.

Jessica rolled her eyes and turned around to the food she was making, "Fine. Be that way you little jerk. Anyway, enough about that. Your food's ready, so dig in!" She sat the food on a plate, handed it to Chris, and they sat down at the bar on opposite each other.

Jessica took the first bite of her breakfast and looked up at Chris, "So what happened to Lane after the invasion ended? I never heard."

"He's in Oklahoma City now in the Republic's maximum security prison waiting for me to come and entertain him and his administration." Chris said.

Jessica looked at Chris with a curious face, "Why? What's so important about him that you need to see him yourself?"

Chris paused for a moment as he took another bite of his food before answering, "He has information I need, and I know for a fact that he is not what he claims to be. I have reason to believe he is actually an Agroneese infiltrator that was sent here to weaken the country. If I'm right, this will be an eye opener for people across the world On top of that, I have my own personal vendetta with him."

"How is that? Have you met him before?" Jessica asked.

Chris lowered his head for a moment as he thought, then looked at Jessica again, "I'll...tell you that when I feel it's time. I think we've talked enough about this stuff."

Jessica smiled and nodded, "Agreed. Forgive me, I was just a little curious about you is all. Anyway, how is your breakfast?"

Chris nodded and gave a thumbs up, "It's good. Your skills as a cook dramatically increased over the years."

"Good answer. I was afraid I might have to throw something at you if you said anything else." Jessica giggled.

Chris glared at her in a firm, but bouncy way, "I would not advise it."

Jessica laughed and stuck her tongue out, "Fine. I'll behave myself... for now."

As the day went on, the two enjoyed their time together welcomingly. Jessica showed Chris around her apartment, and offered him samples of some of her more famous foods. When she ran out of things to cook, she showed Chris her collection of guitars and even sang a few songs to him, most notably was one of her favorites: "Song on Fire" by Nickleback. In return, Chris showed her the swords he trained with and went into more detail about the training he had to endure. Jessica told him what it was like watching the Republic grow and move closer and closer to the city each day, which amused him when she started overreacting. She also told him about her friends and what it was like working at the flower shop, and Chris told her what it's like being the main General and economic advisor of the Republic.

They visited through most of the morning, and played a number of card and board games through the afternoon. Then, when evening came, they settled down on the couch in the living room where Jessica ordered several movies to watch. She sat curled in a ball with her arms wrapped around Chris's and her head resting on his shoulder. But despite all the fun they had throughout the day, she could sense something was wrong. She glanced up at Chris's face, and sat up to face him, "Chris...you seem a little...tense. What's wrong?"

Chris looked at Jessica for a moment, and sighed before answering, "It's nothing. I just don't remember the last time I allowed myself a day off like this. Just to kick back and relax for a while. Now that I'm not doing anything, my mind is racing. I could be planning future strategic battles, I could be making sure the economy doesn't dip down overnight, I could be doing this or that, or a lot of other things."

Jessica remained silent for a moment, then slowly placed her hand on Chris's opposite cheek and turned his head her direction where she spoke to him in a soft and gentle voice, "But you're not doing those thing right now, Chris. You're here with me. Forget about the rest of the world for now. Even God had to rest eventually, there's no shame for you to have a little time to yourself or with me. You're always welcome here, so just relax, okay?"

Chris sighed and tried to relax a little, but still found it a little difficult. "I guess I can try."

Jessica looked at Chris for a moment, then softly kissed his cheek, "I know. My brother and dad had similar problems when they came back from tour. I know adjusting back to a civilian life isn't easy, but I imagine it's completely different to what you're used to."

Chris only looked at Jessica in silence for a moment, then turned his attention back to the movie.

When Jessica decided it was time to call it a day, she gathered some blankets and made a place for Chris to sleep on the couch, and wished him the best of dreams when she went back to her bedroom.

When Jessica woke the next morning, she quickly rushed out her room to the living room, expecting to see Chris had left, but she found him leaning against the wall in the kitchen as if he were waiting for her.

"Ah. You're finally up." He said.

Jessica, though happy he was still with her for the moment, looked at Chris with a slightly confused face, "Well, good morning to you, too. I have to say, I was expecting you to be...you know...gone when I woke up."

Chris smirked and approached her, "I thought about what you told me yesterday. About how it was a struggle for you to make ends meet, so I thought I'd leave you with a parting gift until I got back." He reached into his pocket, then handed Jessica a narrow piece of paper.

"A check?" She asked as she took the paper from him. Her eyes widened and her body went into a state of shut down when she saw the amount written on the check. She nervously looked up at Chris and smiled, "I, uh…I think you may have made a mistake. Surely you're not giving me *that* much."

Chris smirked a little, "I had a feeling that was going to be your reaction. But no. That's for me not writing to you, and helping you make ends meet."

Jessica stared at the check in amazement. Her face was beaming, and she started to shake with excitement, "And to think if I started going out with someone else. I mean, I don't want you to think I only want you for your money or anything like that, but…this is a huge amount to take in all of a sudden."

"You act like you've never seen two-million dollars before." Chris said in a teasing tone.

"Well, that's because I haven't, ya dumb, dumb!" Jessica playfully mocked back. She took a seat to calm herself, and took several looks at the check to make sure she wasn't hallucinating. "Chris, I…I promise I'll find a good use for this. With two-million I could do all kinds of things for charity. I could help wounded soldiers on both sides, I could start a business of some kind, I could…well, I could blow it all on clothes that I'd just forget about, but I'm not that kind of girl."

"You mean you're going to use it for other people besides yourself." Chris said.

Jessica nodded, "Of course! I mean, I'll keep a little for myself just to make ends meet, but I'm not one to just sit around while people need help."

"I see. Well, I guess I'll be expecting some kind of fundraiser for wounded soldiers when I get back." Chris said.

"And where are you going?" Jessica asked.

"Telikee and I are going to Oklahoma City to deal with the former president and his administration. Then, there's also another man I need to meet. Says he has a few new toys for the Republic's military." Chris said.

"Already? Didn't you guys just unleash absolute Hell with those new tanks? What else could you possibly need?" Jessica asked.

"Those were just prototypes. They did their jobs, but they're nowhere near as powerful as the final product will be." Chris said.

"So...how long will you be gone?" Jessica asked.

"A few days at most. But when I get back I'll have that meeting of world leaders to attend. So I won't be seeing you for a while yet." Chris said.

Jessica lowered her head for a moment, then looked up at Chris again as she thought up an idea, "I don't suppose I could...you know... go with you?"

Chris paused for a moment, and looked back at Jessica, "Hmm... having you around could be useful with your Forayer's Sight. Are you sure you can stomach being around when Lane decides he doesn't want to cooperate? We're not known for being subtle when someone's hiding information we want."

Jessica thought for a moment, then nodded, "Yes. So long as I'm with you, I'll be fine."

"Very well. You may want to take some time to say farewell to your friends, though. You may not see them for quite some time."

Jessica nodded, and rushed to pack her suitcase.

CHAPTER 22

Terrifying Presence

Escorted down through the halls of the Republic's super maximum security prison near Tinker Air Force Base in Oklahoma City, former president of the United States of America, Lane, followed the guards of the prison. His hands were handcuffed behind his back, a belly chain kept him from moving his arms, and his ankles were tied as well.

The prison housing him was the Republic's newest and largest super maximum security prison, nicknamed Haunting Silence by the prisoners. Those sentenced here were corrupt politicians from the old government, deserters and corrupt government and military officials from the Republic. The guards operated as their own entity, and answered only to President Davis or members of the Seven Shadows. The Warden was handpicked by the Shadows due to his loyalty to the Republic, and he followed every one of their orders without question. Neither he nor the guards had any sympathy or empathy for the prisoners sentenced here.

This prison in particular operated outside the jurisdictions of the Department of Corrections. Guards here were always armed and wearing combat gear rather than just law enforcement uniforms with handcuffs and pepper spray. With the guards being armed, and the fact they only answer to people as unforgiving as the Shadows, prisoners either learned to keep a cool head, or they were executed for being stupid.

While he was being escorted, Lane remained silent. He knew what was coming, who he was about to face. His body was shaking, and his thoughts were racing. Eventually, the guards brought him to the intimidation room where they shoved him inside, then locked the door and stood guard just outside. Lane looked around for a few moments, then sat down in one of the corners. After several minutes, he heard the guards talking. His eyes widened with fear, and he anxiously waited for the door to open. He was here.

"Good day, General. We have the rat from the old country locked inside and waiting for you."

"Good. Open the door." Chris ordered.

The guards nodded, and pushed the door open, then stood aside, allowing Chris through.

Before he entered, Telikee turned to face Jessica to ask her a question, "What you're about to see may become a little...intense. Are you absolutely sure you want to come in?"

Jessica thought for a moment, but slowly nodded, "Y-yes. I...I think so."

Telikee studied Jessica's eyes for a moment, but could see she really wanted to go in. "Very well. But don't say I didn't warn you." He said. He then turned around and went through the door. Jessica followed, and immediately saw Lane sitting in a corner shaking with fear. She turned as she heard the door shutting behind her, then turned her attention to Chris as he started speaking.

"Well, well, well. Fate certainly is a cruel mistress, wouldn't you agree? We have a number of ways we can do this, Lane. I suggest you just cooperate."

Lane only stared at Chris with fearful eyes. He nervously swallowed before speaking, "Y-you're supposed to be dead! How have you survived all these years?!"

"I had some help. Now, tell me. I know you're a member of the Agroneese, so what was your plan with Experiment 2025?" Chris asked.

Jessica's eyes widened from shock, *"Wait...he knows about..."*

Lane remained silent for a moment, then stood up as he replied, "Before I tell you...how did you find out about me?"

"Do you think I'm stupid? Ever since I learned the truth I've studied you and your history. You were hard to follow at first, but I eventually started piecing the puzzle together. Ever since you got into politics, you've made all kinds of friends in high places, even the Soros family backed you. You played a 'yes man' with the most powerful people in politics until it was your turn, but every single one of your policies was damaging for the country. And let's not forget about that tattoo you have on your chest, either." Chris said.

"Tattoo? What tattoo?" Jessica asked.

Chris glanced at Jessica for a moment, then used the spikes on his knuckles to rip Lane's shirt apart, exposing his chest. With ink as red as blood, Lane had a symbol that resembled a pentagram, but it had an A with several slashes going through it carved on his chest.

"What…what is that?" Jessica asked in a fearful tone.

Telikee growled, and used his telekinetic power to push Lane against the wall, "It's the Agroneese symbol of acceptance. Apparently, he somehow learned of them and went through their initiation process. That tattoo on his chest symbolizes he's an accepted member of their order. So tell *me*, Lane. How does it feel to know your soul is forfeit?"

Lane started to laugh maniacally and stared directly at Telikee, "Forfeit? My soul is saved! Those disgusting creatures you mortals call 'gods' have no power over Agromon! Soon, our armies will flood your lands, burning your cities and feasting on your mortal flesh! The time Agromon rules this pitiful world is nigh! Nengushail will reign supreme while your gods cower in fear! Hahahahahaha!!!!"

Telikee growled, and pushed Lane even harder against the wall, "You seem very sure of that."

Lane smiled, and turned his attention to Jessica, "Ah, and the Daughter of Forayer joins us. How quaint. It seems the prophecy has finally come! Agroneese, Assassins and the Daughter of Forayer all cramped into one space. How fitting."

Chris put himself between Lane and Jessica, then stepped forward and dug his spikes into Lane's throat, "Your soul may not be forfeit. But I can make your life a hell far worse than you'll experience. Now tell me what I want to know, and *maybe* I'll make your passing easier."

Lane faced Chris and laughed, "You haven't learned a thing have you? Yes, I'm the one who took you from your family and sold your whore of a mother to the Muslim brotherhood. They've served as such adorable pawns for years, so I thought it was time to give them someone to play with."

Jessica stared at lane with disgust, and stepped away as Chris started lifting him further in the air, allowing his spikes to rip through his neck, "So that's it. You created me because you thought you'd be able to control me and use me to weaken the military." He started to twist his wrist, slowly turning his spikes inside Lane's neck, "Tell me this. How does it feel to die at the mercy of the thing *you* created?" He pulled his spikes out of Lane's neck, allowing him to fall, but slashed his face, ripping out one of his eyes before he hit the ground. He ignored Lane's screams of agony, then grabbed him by the face and sent electricity coursing through his body before lighting him on fire.

Lane rolled around screaming on the floor for a while before his body eventually came to rest. Once he wasn't moving anymore, Chris took one of the short swords around his waist, and stabbed it through Lane's brain to ensure he was actually dead.

"Piece of filth." Chris said, sheathing his sword. He turned away and started walking for the door.

"Why did you do that? He still had information we could have used." Telikee said.

"I learned enough. As it turns out, I answered my own questions." Chris replied.

Jessica stared in horror at Lane's corpse, then slowly turned to look at Chris, "S-so wh-what happens now?"

Chris looked over his shoulder as he replied, "You and I will remain in the city for a while. Telikee, you can go back to the city and prepare our meeting with the world leaders."

"Do you really think they're going to be eager to get into another war? America doesn't exactly have the cleanest reputation." Telikee said.

"Which is precisely why I kept that body of the Agroneese Centarritess that came for Jessica. If they need further convincing, we'll allow them to…observe an example of what's coming." Chris said.

"Very well. I guess I'll see you in a few days." Telikee said.

Chris nodded, and watched Telikee vanish from the room before looking at Jessica, "I guess now you know what I wanted to know from him."

Jessica looked at Chris with sorrowful eyes, then lowered her head with a sigh, "Chris, I'm…I'm so sorry. I…I didn't know he was the one who did all of this to you." She remained silent for a moment, watching Chris's body language. She could tell it was a powerful moment for him by looking at him. Her frown slowly turned into a gentle smile and she took a step forward, "So how does it feel to have revenge?"

Chris didn't answer, and started walking forward again, "Let's just get going."

Jessica nodded and followed closely behind Chris as the guards led them out of the prison.

CHAPTER 23

Vype Brothers

After they left the prison, Republic soldiers transported Chris and Jessica to another part of the base where Chris was supposed to meet a man named Robert Vype, one of six brothers the Shadows recruited to aid them in the civil war.

The soldiers drove Chris and Jessica to a hangar at the far end of the base where they dropped them off. The two exited the vehicle and made their way inside the hangar where a man dressed in a suit and tie with short dark brown hair was waiting for them. He waved his hand at Chris and ran over to meet him and shake his hand.

"Ah! It's good to finally see you again, General. I was starting to wonder if you got my request." Robert said.

"I take it you've made some progress on the new designs, then?" Chris asked.

"Yes, actually. Soon, these new tanks will be unmatched by any other weapon in the world. Shall I explain on the way? The flight isn't very long." Robert said.

Chris nodded and followed Robert to a nearby Republic helicopter that would fly them from Oklahoma City to a rural field near Weatherford, Oklahoma.

While flying over rural Oklahoma to a secret Republic base, Jessica remained quiet as she listened with interest to the conversation between Chris and Robert.

"I think you'll be quite pleased with the progress we've made since your last visit, General. Our new weapons and vehicles have come a long way since you first saw them." Robert said.

"I hope so. I didn't recruit you and your brothers for nothing, Robert. Your skills as designers and engineers were severely underrated." Chris said.

Robert nodded, "Thank you. We've made tremendous amounts of progress in all fields. Our weapons are stronger, our vehicles are faster, and the secret organization you requested is nearly ready to produce its first graduates. We call them the Vipers."

"Organization? What do you mean by that?" Jessica asked.

Robert looked at Jessica for a moment, then turned to Chris, "Should I tell her? Or would you rather wait?"

"She's going to find out either way. Don't keep her wondering." Chris said.

Robert nodded and looked at Jessica, "To put things simply, the Shadows of the Republic asked us to design a training course to make the ultimate soldier. Each of these soldiers goes through rigorous amounts of training only the bravest and the strongest can stand. We're tearing apart the factions of the old military. What we've created is something that never would have existed without the constant funding from the Republic. We've made the ultimate killers. Spartans in today's modern age. The Republic Vipers."

"Vipers?" Jessica asked curiously.

Robert nodded, "These men are not recruited by normal means. One cannot come off the streets and request to be a Viper. With so many young strong men wasting their lives behind prison bars with life in prison sentences, the Shadows thought of a way for them to redeem their crimes. With the threat of a new enemy on the horizon, they saw it best that the country use all its available resources, even ones people didn't even know it had. My brothers and I went to prisons all over the country meeting men sentenced to either life or death in prison. We offered them a choice: either waste their lives rotting in the prison, or make up for their crimes fighting for the Republic. In return for their services if they survive the war, their crimes will be forgiven, and any criminal record will be erased."

"But...aren't these people killers, rapists and who knows what else? How can you control them?" Jessica asked.

"The soldiers watching them act as their own security force. They only answer to me, my brothers or the Seven Shadows. Not even President Davis has any authority over them. In the event one of these prisoners...revolts, they are immediately terminated. We make it very clear they are not the top dogs and that they control nothing." Robert said.

Jessica's eyes widened in amazement, "Wow. So after all is said and done, you end up with a very disciplined, combat hardened and just badass soldier, huh?"

"Putting it mildly, yes. The Vipers are not "free" until they've completed their contract, however. They may be soldiers of the Republic, but they are not free men. They are specific men who have nothing left to lose, but saw it more fitting to die in the heat of battle than to waste away in a prison cell. You may think many of them to be the lowest type of scum, but many of them are thankful for the opportunity and view it as a gift from whichever god they believe in."

"I see. Do these guys cause trouble very often?" Jessica asked.

Robert shook his head, "Not as often as you might think. Most of them are smart enough to know they could be shot at any time if they try something stupid. And by the time their training is complete, they've been disciplined enough to know bad actions will cost them their lives."

Jessica sat back in her seat and looked at Chris, "I suppose *you're* the one who came up with this idea to begin with?"

"That's on a need to know basis, actually." Chris said.

"What? I'm your girlfriend, I need to know!"

"Oh, you do?"

"Yeah, is there anything else I should know?"

"No, I'd say you're up to speed."

"Okay, thank you."

Jessica watched out the window of the helicopter as it slowed to a hover over a field somewhere between Oklahoma City and Weatherford, Oklahoma. She looked around, confused that there wasn't any sign of a base anywhere, then looked at Robert, "Um…where is this base, exactly?"

Robert looked at Jessica and smirked, "You're looking right at it."

Jessica stared at Robert with a confused look for a moment, then looked at the pilots as they started pushing certain buttons in the cockpit. Suddenly, in the corner of her eye, she saw movement, and looked out the window again to see the field splitting apart. Her eyes widened in amazement as two gigantic mechanical doors open up a huge hole in the ground and the helicopter started to descend. She blinked several times, unable to believe what she was seeing, and turned to face Robert again, "This…this is for real. What the hell have you guys been up to?"

Robert chuckled a little before replying, "We're not called the best engineers in North America for nothing, Miss. And by the way, this is just the doorway for helicopters to land."

Jessica looked out the window again and stared in awe at the hidden base below. Her mind was racing back to war movies and old sci-fi comic books where super villains had built underground bases to remain hidden, except she was living it.

When the helicopter went passed the doors, they started to slowly close again, and the walls lit up to reveal the landing area where another six helicopters were parked. It took five minutes to reach the bottom, but Jessica could hardly believe her eyes. Beneath the walls were entire sections of the base where Humvees, tanks, and trucks were moving supplies around. Hundreds if not thousands of soldiers were standing guard all over the place, each one armed to the teeth with a deadly variety of weapons.

When the helicopter landed, Robert opened the door, allowing Jessica and Chris out. Jessica was beside herself; observing the sights before her and staring at her surroundings in awe. When she heard the door to the helicopter close, she turned to face Robert, "I'm going to take this as an indication the Republic's military might is far more powerful than what the government indicated."

Robert looked at Jessica and smirked, "You have no idea, miss. The Republic's military may not quite outrank China in terms of population, but even China and Russia combined could not stop our troops in a full on war. Thanks to the Seven Shadows allowing us to research whatever we please and giving us the resources to do so, the Republic is well on its way to being the dominant superpower in the world without question."

"Are you developing nukes at all?" Jessica asked.

Robert shook his head, "No. Nukes are being developed by a different team. My brothers and I specialize in weapon and vehicle design."

"I see. So, what are we seeing first?" Jessica asked.

Chris looked at Robert and crossed his arms, "And spare me the toys. Your weapons are good, no question, but I came here to see the weapons, not the play things."

Robert chuckled a little, then started walking, waving for the two to follow him, "I wouldn't dream of wasting your time, sir. First stop is our new attack helicopter."

Robert led Chris and Jessica through the base, and took them to an enormous production line where hundreds of people were assembling new helicopters of a design Jessica hadn't seen before. She leaned over the guard rail of the platform they were standing on for a better view, then looked to her right where she saw a completed model. The new helicopter was painted in solid black, and had two sets of propellers as its main set. The rear propeller was protected by an armor plating that was strong enough to deflect rocket propelled grenades or RPG's. The cockpit was a two seater, and its overall body was long and narrow with several weapon's bays that could open from the sides or bottom of the craft, each carrying at least ten missiles or rockets. Under the nose was also a mini-gun the co-pilot would operate similar to an Apache. The turret would be linked up with the co-pilot's helmet, and would follow his head movements.

"We call this the Wraith. Armed with not only a variety of weapons, but is resistant to EMP, can reach speeds up to 270 miles an hour and is undetectable by radar, this is the most modern helicopter in the world." Robert stated, "This came after our invention of the Republic's new heavy combat tanks that won the battle at Richmond just the other day, which we'll get to shortly. Those tanks are powerful enough, there is not a single weapon that can answer back to them in the world yet, and there won't be for quite some time. But my brother wanted to experiment with ideas and create the ultimate anti-ground helicopter that would reign terror on the battlefield. Thus, the Wraith came into existence. Its main armament comes from the four missile bays on the craft's side and belly. The ones on the side are meant for taking out bunkers and infantry in mass groups, and the ones on the bottom of the craft are meant for taking out tanks and other armored vehicles. The mini-gun…well, it's pretty obvious what it's for. It can shoot eighty rounds per second, which will rip any infantry unit to pieces. These helicopters are expensive to make, but my brother is more than confident they will make up for it on the battlefield."

Jessica watched the assembly line for a moment, then looked at Chris, "So is this how the Republic's economy became so strong in such a short amount of time? These weapons…they're not being made by machines, but people. Actual working people."

"It's one of the ways the economy rocketed, yes. The other members of my order, including myself, didn't care for the automated industry. It was faster, yes, but it also meant less jobs. The Republic's mechanized army isn't assembled by other machines, but is carefully constructed and observed by hard working people thankful for the opportunity." Chris said.

"And I'm sure you've noticed the Republic constantly produces new vehicle designs on a regular basis." Robert said, catching Jessica's attention, "Any destroyed vehicle isn't just taken to a junk yard. It's taken back to a factory where it's disassembled, and parts are stored for extra supplies. This allows people like my family and other designers to observe the weaknesses of these vehicles, and see what could be done to strengthen them. So, in the end you have a much more powerful vehicle that's capable of withstanding even more punishment."

"So, you let no resources go to waste, then." Jessica said.

Robert nodded, "Indeed. That was always something that got under my skin when I was younger. When vehicles are destroyed, they're often just sent to junk yards to rot. People may buy spare parts off them time to time, but they're never really recycled. My brothers and I changed that when we got into the rebellion. However, we rarely ever reuse parts of downed aircraft unless we are one-hundred percent certain they're safe to reuse."

"Impressive. So do you and your brothers make other equipment as well?" Jessica asked.

"A few things, but we're mostly devoted to weapons and vehicles. There are some new...rival families if you like, that have recently grown into power who focus more on the defensive side of a soldier. Since my brothers and I focus on offense, we didn't have much room for defensive projects in the near future, so the Shadows sought out someone who had the potential to meet their demands." Robert said.

Jessica turned to Chris and smirked, "Giving these guys some competition, huh?"

"I'm only doing what has to be done. Our troops need better protective and defensive equipment to improve their survivability in hostile conditions. I would hardly call this a "rivalry"." Chris said.

"I suppose that's true." Jessica said.

Robert cleared his throat, getting Jessica and Chris's attention again, "Well, I think we've seen all there is to see here. Shall we move on?"

Jessica nodded and followed Robert closely as he led them to another part of the base. They got in a Humvee where the driver transported them to the completely opposite side of the base, and took them down an elevator to another level of the base. When they reached their destination, Robert exited the vehicle and led Chris and Jessica to another assembly line, but this one was far larger than the previous.

"Miss Holland, I'll take a wild guess and say you've seen these tanks before." Robert said, leaning against a guard rail.

Jessica stood next to him and looked down at the assembly line for a moment. Her eyes widened and she looked at Robert, "T-those are… those are the tanks the Republic used in Richmond!"

Robert nodded, "Indeed. These are the Republic's newest prototype of what will soon be the world's strongest tank without equal. They weigh in at one-hundred tons and require a crew of eight to operate. They're highly computerized on the inside, but they can easily withstand any EMP. There isn't a weapon in the world that can disable, let alone destroy these tanks. Nothing the Russians or even the Chinese have comes even remotely close to this. You're looking at a new era of tank warfare with these leading the charge."

"How much does one individual tank cost?" Jessica asked.

Robert passed for a moment before replying, "Each tank is roughly in the neighborhood of one-billion dollars. You may think it comes from the computers they're operated by, but no. The armor that protects them is very thick and very hard. It's a resource buried deep under the Rocky Mountains that had been unnoticed for years. It's a metal far stronger than Titanium."

"Wow! So what's their weakness?" Jessica asked.

"Mostly their weight and lack of maneuverability. These tanks are very slow, which can make them a good target, but the only way to "disable" one of these tanks is to get lucky enough to destroy their tracks." Robert said.

"What about mines?" Jessica asked.

Robert shook his head, "Useless. Each tank is heavily reinforced on the bottom, and their tracks are behind built in plows that are used for setting off mines before the tracks ever reach it."

"Ah! Clever."

"Indeed. Well, enough about that. I think it's time I show you what you really came here for. If you'll please follow me." Robert said.

On the final level of the enormous underground complex, Robert lead Chris and Jessica to a balcony overlooking an enormous training room where hundreds of men were in the middle of physical training.

"This is our newest group of Vipers who are currently in their second week of physical training. The first group will be parading for us when we reach them, but I wanted to show you what a full regiment of new recruits looks like before we send some away or they just quit."

Jessica looked down at the men training, and was amazed at what they were having to endure. Picking up logs, non-stop pushups, instructors getting in their faces, being tied to a post and repeatedly punched and kicked all over their body. It was easily the most brutal training she had ever seen. And just to add to the stress, they always had armed guards keeping their eyes on them.

The voices of the men were painful, and many had blood marks on their knuckles from punching wooden posts and dummies for so long. But as she continued to watch, she saw the physical condition of the men below and could tell they were destined to become super soldiers in the near future.

"How long does their training last?" Jessica asked.

"Thirty weeks just for basics. This is the hardest part for them. Here, they'll do sixteen weeks of physical training like you're seeing now. Then, it's another fourteen weeks of their drill instructors constantly beating them down and disciplining them as much as possible. This will include torturous scenarios to simulate them being captured by enemy forces and to build up their endurance. After all this is finished they'll go to weapons training." Robert said.

"So…how do you keep them under control when they have guns?" Jessica asked.

"Simple. They're always in controlled areas. Armed guards are behind them at all times with very good defensive cover, so these guys overthrowing the complex is impossible. And in the event they did get out of control, the facility would go into a full lock down, and automated turrets would eliminate everyone. We lose a few Vipers, but we also make it very clear to those in the future they have no control."

"I see. I was kind of curious about that part." Jessica said.

"Well, you have your answer now. Anyway, I suggest we move on to the next area where the first graduation is about to begin." Robert said.

Chris and Jessica nodded, and followed Robert to another part of the base.

The sound of marching boots and shouting filled the hallway Robert was leading Chris and Jessica through. The voices were strict and demanding, and the responsive shouting was almost deafening. At the end of the hallway, Chris and Jessica found themselves standing on a platform that overlooked an enormous room where the Vipers were marching in formation. Equipped with weapons and gear that far surpassed anything else the Republic had, Jessica knew these were the soldiers of the future.

"So how much does just one Viper cost?" Jessica asked.

"Around five-hundred-thousand per soldier." Robert answered, "The weapons and gear these soldiers carry are top of the line, and they are only outfitted with the best equipment the Republic can afford. Even the Cobras aren't as expensive."

Jessica turned to look at Chris, "What do you think? Impressed with what you see?"

Chris nodded and looked at Robert, "Well done, Robert. You've certainly proven your worth to not only the Republic, but my order as well. How soon can you have these men ready to deploy?"

"Soon. After their weapons training is finished, I'll see if they meet your expectations by putting them through obstacle courses. Also, our newest combat tanks will be ready within a few months' time, as well as our first Wraith. When do you expect the next conflict to arise?"

Chris remained silent for a moment as he watched the Vipers marching below, then turned to Robert, "Imminently. I need those weapons as soon as possible."

Robert nodded "I'll see to it. After what you did for me and my family, I owe you that much at least."

Chris nodded, and started to walk away, but Jessica remained. She slowly turned to face Robert and asked, "What did you mean by that? What did Chris do to make you indebted to him?"

Robert remained silent for a moment, then sighed as he smiled softly at Jessica, "He saved my three daughters from sex traffickers. I owe him more than I or my family could ever repay through means of material."

Jessica stood in shock for a moment, but her lips slowly curled into a soft smile, "Well…you have my sympathies, Mr. Vype. I'm glad you got your daughters back."

"So am I. Well, you better catch up to him before he leaves you here. I have a lot of work I need to see to." Robert said.

Jessica nodded and ran after Chris.

CHAPTER 24

International Negotiations

Back in Washington D.C, in the old Capitol building, the Seven Shadows had arranged a meeting with several world leaders from all over the world. Ministers and negotiators from many countries, including Russia and China had come to this meeting. Here the assassins would warn the world what was coming, and that it was time to prepare for a worldwide war against the most evil force in Earth's history. It was time for war against the Agroneese.

Thousands of Republic soldiers patrolled the grounds outside with armed security patrolling the halls. Light vehicles and armor were stationed at all entrances, and also Republic jets and helicopters patrolled the skies with orders to take down any aircraft that came into the restricted flight zone.

The meeting would take place in a large open room with a gigantic round table in the center of it. The flag of every visiting nation was on the back of their designated chairs. The world leaders stood silently, waiting for their que to be seated. As members of the Seven Shadows entered the room, tensions grew, and the air grew heavy. The assassins took their positions on each side of the room, and Night Hawk opened the meeting.

"World leaders, friends and foes, welcome to the United States of the Republic. I have just received word Night Walker has arrived in the city and is on his way. You may be seated."

The world leaders took their seats and returned their attention to Night Hawk as he continued, "By now most of you realize an ancient force is reawakening. One believed to have been destroyed long ago by Atlassian forces. For those of you who don't know, a demonic cult known as the Agroneese is reawakening. If we do not act swiftly, they will become a blight on your lands, slaughtering and feasting off your population like cattle. Politics and wars of the past must be set aside if we are to win this war."

The world leaders remained silent for a moment, then turned their attention to the Prime Minister of England as he spoke, "So, you Shadows...you're Atlassians, as well? Can we count on Atlassian assistance in this war?"

The minister from France smirked as he directed his attention back to Night Hawk, "Don't be a fool, Englishman. Atlassia is a myth. A fairy tale made up long ago by story tellers. There is no proof it exists or ever has. There are some who believe these "Shadows" are members of the legendary Seventeen, but I have yet to see any proof myself."

Night Hawk narrowed his eyes at the Frenchman as he spoke in a blood chilling tone, "Do you fear death, Frenchman? I advise you to watch your tongue if you intend to keep it by the end of this meeting. As a world leader you are safe for now, but know that no one on this planet is out of the reach of our order. There are large bounties on every single one of your heads, so unless you want us to forfeit the protection we offer you, I advise you to keep your mouths shut."

The French leader gulped, then turned his attention to the leader of Russia as he spoke, "So...this Agroneese cult. Can you tell us about them?"

"They're a demonic cult that worship the demonic lord of fear, Agromon. Their sole purpose in existence is to slaughter anyone and anything who is not a follower of their demonic master. They believe the people they kill in this life will be the souls they torture in the next when they become demons themselves." Night Hawk answered.

"So this isn't just a group of Islamic terrorists, then." The Russian leader stated.

Night Hawk nodded, "They are far worse than any terror group. Even ISIS pales in comparison to their evil."

Chatter broke out across the room for a while, but stopped when the Chinese leader spoke out, "What proof do you have they are coming, and how do you plan to stop it? Your western culture has gotten soft, and your parties focus more on political correctness than the greater good of your people."

The leaders directed their attention to the minister of England as he spoke again, "And what can we do about them at this point? Islamists have already flooded into our lands and damaged our economies. We can no longer field the armies we once could."

"Your political weakness has been the key for your downfall, Westerners. If you still had the same backbone you had back in the days of World War II you would not be facing such a crisis." The Chinese leader said.

The English minister sighed, and looked at the rest of the European leaders before speaking again, "We've closed our borders, we're trying to end the welfare state, we've set up checkpoints to keep them out of our countries...we don't know what else we can do."

"Perhaps that is the problem." A cold and terrifying voice said from the main entrance of the room. The world leaders directed their attention to the source of the voice and saw Chris standing in the door way. "You lack imagination, minister, when it comes to delivering results."

The Prime Minister of England remained silent for a moment, then finally built up the courage to speak, "General Lynheart...your reputation proceeds you. What would be your plan to deal with this issue, then?"

"You can start by growing a backbone, Prime Minister. With the elites out of the picture, there is nothing stopping you from taking your country back in force. Unless you want to live under Sharia law, I suggest you drop your politically correct ways and force the Muslim infestation out of your country. Use military force if you have to." Chris said.

The Prime Minister nodded, and looked away as Chris started walking around the room, "The age of political correctness has ended. The American Democratic Party that led that nonsense has been all but destroyed. The old politicians, both Republican and Democrat have been removed from office and sentenced to prison for life, and working sixteen hour shifts every day in Republic weapon's factories. The globalist elitist party will soon be taken out of the picture as well, allowing western countries to build up their strength again. Anyone who openly claims to be globalist or still tries to enforce their ideals can expect to not be in their position much longer, and will face similar fates as the rest of the globalist leaders. Or…the assassins may seek to remove you from the picture permanently. With a force like the Agroneese reawakening, we cannot allow weakness to be in positions of power. Even if we win, the Agroneese will have done enough damage to us as a species that it will take hundreds of years for us to rebuild to our former glory. The Middle East, Africa, Europe and even parts of Asia will fall within the first year. Australia will cease to exist, and even the Americas will not be untouched by this war. The Agroneese will flood your lands like a virus, forever spreading without encountering heavy resistance. If we cannot unite here and now at this very moment, we will fall. One by one until the Agroneese have taken the last infant."

The world leaders remained silent for a while, then the leader from Russia spoke up, "So, what's your plan, General? How do we fight these monsters?"

"With careful planning and the willingness to retreat when a battle cannot be won." Chris replied, "If we are to destroy this enemy once and for all, they must be fully surrounded with battle hardened soldiers and enough obstacles to slow their advance. We will never be able to push them back, but we can destroy them if we're willing to sacrifice land. Something you Russians are notorious for doing. This war will not be without enormous cost, though. At our current predictions, over 80% of the human population will be wiped out."

The world leaders broke out into muttering chatter again, but stopped at Chris spoke again, "Now is the time to decide whether you will join the final alliance to destroy this evil once and for all. But know this, if you choose to not stand with us…you will face this enemy alone with little to no support from the rest of us."

"But what of the Atlassians? Will they not come?" The leader from Japan asked.

"The Atlassians view this as a surface problem. The fact that they are about to enter into a massive election isn't helping, either. They know the Agroneese are returning, but there are many problems that stand in the way. Certain politicians have issues with the surface world, but others are not believed to possess the backbone needed to win the war. If the Atlassians join the war, it will not be in the near future. For now, the most help you'll receive will be from pre-ranking members of the Seventeen. Now, rise from your seats if you decide you'll stand in alliance with the Republic against the Agroneese. The Republic can't win this war by itself."

Silence filled the room as the world leaders thought, but they turned their attention to the English Prime Minister as he stood from his seat, England stands with the Republic."

The French followed, "France stands with the Republic."

"Spain stands with the Republic."

"Germany stands with the Republic."

"Israel stands with the Republic."

"Russia stands with the Republic."

"Japan stands with the Republic."

"South Korea stands with the Republic."

"Denmark stands with the Republic."

"Sweden stands with the Republic."

"Poland stands with the Republic."

"Egypt stands with the Republic."

"Canada stands with the Republic."

"Brazil stands with the Republic."

"Australia stands with the Republic."

"India stands with the Republic."

Chris looked at Night Hawk and nodded, and Night Hawk stood from his seat, "Very well. Go back to your countries and prepare for war. Call for drafts and get your people ready to fight."

The world leaders nodded, and proceeded to leave the room.

Night Hawk made his way to Chris and said, "Notice China didn't enter into the alliance."

"I didn't figure they would. But I have plans to deal with them in the future. We can't allow China to act independently and become the dominant super power while we're busy." Chris said.

"What do you have in mind?" Night Hawk asked.

"Leave them to me. Whether they like it or not, they will find themselves facing the Agroneese." Chris said.

Night Hawk nodded and took his leave, while Chris approached a Republic soldier who was standing guard. "Contact President Davis and have him meet with me tonight."

The soldier saluted, "Yes, General."

CHAPTER 25

One Stormy Night

Lightning strikes illuminated the room, and thunder haunted the halls as Chris stood next to a large window, looking out on the ruins of the Washington Monument. President Davis, anxious about the setting, cautiously approached his superior and spoke, "Everything is proceeding as you anticipated, General. Riots have broken out across the country, declaring the Republic is not their home, and the people aren't happy about getting into another war too much, either."

"And the military?" Chris asked.

"It remains strong, General, but our numbers have been depleted in the war. More are joining from the Midwest, South and Western regions of the country, but I fear it may not be enough to bring our military up to peak performance." President Davis said.

"Then perhaps the time has come. I do not trust the majority of these rioters would ever join the military no matter how bad things become in the future. Our military has to have more bodies before we can officially begin this war." Chris said.

"What do you propose, sir?"

Chris turned to face President Davis, just as a lightning bolt illuminated the room, "Initiate the draft. I need to know the true face of our enemy before I send in loyal soldiers who are ready and willing to do their part. I need bodies I can waste. Call for a draft starting with known members of the Westboro Baptist Church, Antifa and Black

Lives Matter. These groups are seen as scum throughout the entire country, and the people will shed no tears for those who fall against the Agroneese. It's time we ended the liberal left once and for all."

President Davis nodded, and turned away from Chris before walking toward the door. Chris watched him leave, then turned his attention back to the Washington Monument.

Printed and bound by PG in the USA